FANTASY TALES

Other books edited by Barbara Ireson
HAUNTING TALES
SHADOWS AND SPELLS
THE FABER BOOK OF NURSERY VERSE
THE FABER BOOK OF NURSERY STORIES

Retold by Barbara Ireson
THE STORY OF THE PIED PIPER
THE GINGERBREAD MAN

By Barbara Ireson
YOUR BOOK OF PARTY GAMES

FANTASY TALES

Edited by
BARBARA IRESON

FABER AND FABER
London · Boston

*First published in 1977
by Faber and Faber Limited
3 Queen Square London WC1
Reprinted 1978
Printed and bound in Great Britain by*
REDWOOD BURN LIMITED
*Trowbridge & Esher
All rights reserved*

*This collection © Faber and Faber Ltd 1977
"Obstinate Uncle Otis" © 1977 by
Robert Arthur. Reprinted by permission of
the Regents of the University of Michigan*

British Library Cataloguing in Publication Data

Fantasy tales.
 1. Fantasy fiction
 1. Ireson, Barbara
 823 '.9' 1J   PZ5
 ISBN 0-571-10922-5

Contents

Of Polymuf Stock *John Christopher*	page 11
Obstinate Uncle Otis *Robert Arthur*	27
The Tower *Marghanita Laski*	37
The Cork Elephant *Ian Serraillier*	45
The Inner Room *Robert Aickman*	49
The Never-ending Penny *Bernard Wolfe*	82
The New Sun *J. S. Fletcher*	97
The Star Beast *Nicholas Stuart Gray*	115
The Man Who Could Work Miracles *H. G. Wells*	122
The April Witch *Ray Bradbury*	140
Strange Fish *Leon Garfield*	151

Contents

The Riddle *Walter de la Mare*	167
The Tube that Stuck *Claire Creswell*	172
The Bottle Imp *R. L. Stevenson*	188

Acknowledgements

The editor is grateful for permission to use the following copyright material:
Of Polymuf Stock by John Christopher;
Obstinate Uncle Otis by Robert Arthur. Reprinted by permission of the Regents of the University of Michigan;
The Tower by Marghanita Laski;
The Cork Elephant by Ian Serraillier. © Ian Serraillier 1945, first published in *Grey Walls Stories*, chosen by Wrey Gardiner, Grey Walls Press;
The Inner Room by Robert Aickman;
The Never-ending Penny by Bernard Wolfe;
The Star Beast by Nicholas Stuart Gray. Reprinted by permission of Faber and Faber Ltd from *Mainly in Moonlight* by Nicholas Stuart Gray;
The Man Who Could Work Miracles from *The Short Stories of H. G. Wells*. Reprinted by permission of the estate of H. G. Wells;
The April Witch. from *The Golden Apples of the Sun* by Ray Bradbury, published by Rupert Hart-Davis. Copyright 1952 by Ray Bradbury. Reprinted by permission of A. D. Peters & Co., Ltd, and of Harold Matson Company Inc.;
Strange Fish by Leon Garfield;
The Riddle by Walter de la Mare. Reprinted by permission of the Literary Trustees of Walter de la Mare and the Society of Authors as their representatives;
The Tube that Stuck by Claire Creswell.

Of Polymuf Stock

JOHN CHRISTOPHER

I was born true man but of polymuf stock.

Until I was nine years old I knew nothing of this. I was the son, it seemed, of Andrew Harding, the chief of the Captains in the Prince's council. The Hardings were one of the oldest and noblest families in the city. I had an elder brother, Gregory, and two elder sisters. I lived in the great Harding house which looked at the Palace from across the square, and though smaller was not much less magnificent. I had a polymuf nurse and polymuf servants in plenty to do my bidding.

One day I found myself alone in a poor part of the city near the East Gate. I had been with a friend but we had quarrelled and separated. The quarrel was over nothing and probably came from disappointment. I had a new kite and we had meant to fly it from the grazing meadows but the day was hot and still and it would have been a waste of time to try. I suppose the sultry heat, to which we were little accustomed, tried our tempers also.

It was probably the heat which made me think of going outside the city into the country. I had never done this on my own but was in a mood to explore. The East Gate was the nearest and I made for that, but lost my way in the warren of mean streets and alleys that surrounded it. The houses looked pinched and crowded and badly in need of repair, and there were smells that made me wrinkle my nose. A dead cat which I saw in a gutter must have been there close on a week.

In one crumbling rotting street I found three boys of about my own age following me. Their tunics were of cheap cloth and could have done with mending, and both they and their clothes would have been better for washing. They jeered at me and I ignored them; then came past and planted themselves in my path. One demanded my name and I told him: Isak Harding. It made matters worse because they were Blainites.

The Hardings and the Blaines had been rivals for generations. This was for the most part hidden under a show of politeness but at a lower level, among the followers of each family, the feud was more open and more bitter. The three young Blainites were delighted, I suppose, to find a Harding in their territory and at their mercy. They would scarcely have dared touch me, since I was noble, but taunts leave no marks. They made plenty of these and in the end it was I who turned to violence. I picked on the chief of my tormentors, who also happened to be the biggest, and launched myself at him.

Had things been equal I would have been no match for him because he was stronger as well as taller and plainly used to rough fighting. But he was held back by the realization of my rank —the son of a Captain—and probably by the thought that even if he beat me retribution was likely to follow. I had no such scruples and bore him to the ground. I had him pinned and was rubbing his face in the dirt when we were pulled apart and lifted to our feet. A crowd of older people had collected.

Questions were asked and my name required again. When I gave it one man said:

"Isak! That's the one who . . ."

He dropped his voice to a whisper which I could not catch. I heard other whispers and saw glances exchanged. I saw smiles and sniggers. It meant nothing at the time except that they were Blainites. I noticed with satisfaction that my recent opponent was crying and turned from them. I had gone several paces when I heard a voice cry:

"Polymuf! The Harding polymuf brat."

That meant nothing either. It was nonsense. I knew I had no malformation of the body. I walked on, heading back towards the city's centre. Boys followed me, chanting:

"Polymuf! Polymuf!"

Of Polymuf Stock

It was some new stupidity the Blainites had thought of to insult their betters; no more than that. I came into Bird Street and there were troopers comparing notes about the finches that hung in cages outside the shops, and the boys fell back and left me.

I forgot about it the same day, or thought I did. Then a month later I heard the jeer repeated in the street. After that I noticed other things: curious looks, conversations broken off when I came within earshot. I still did not believe they could signify anything real or important, or I would not have spoken of it to David Greene, the one with whom I had quarrelled in the summer.

He knew nothing either but he asked, and was told, and told me.

Every child that was born had to be taken to the Seer in the Seance Hall, to be scrutinized for defects of the body. Those that had none were classed as true men, and the short-legged ones as dwarfs. The others, even where the deviation was no more than an extra finger or toe, or one less than was normal, were polymufs, whose destiny was to serve true men, who had no rights and could own no land or property.

If a child was born dwarf or polymuf from human stock it was taken from its mother and given to a dwarf or polymuf foster-mother to rear. The reverse was true also. And this, David said, had happened in my case. I had been brought to the Seance Hall by polymuf parents, judged true man by the Seer, and given to the Hardings.

I listened with shock and horror. It was one thing to feel unease, to suspect vaguely that there was something which needed explaining; quite another to face such as this. I saw David's eyes watching me. He was not smiling but I read the smile behind them, and more: pity and contempt. I said:

"It is a lie!"

He shrugged. "Perhaps. It is what they say."

I felt myself shivering and forced my limbs to stillness; but they would not be still. So I made an excuse to leave him and ran back to the house. It was a cold grey morning, threatening

Of Polymuf Stock

rain. The doorman rose from his stool to salute me, his right shoulder lifting from his twisted back.

My nurse Betty was seeing to my room. The housemaids had already cleaned it but she was never satisfied with their work and must always do a final tidying and setting to rights. I had meant to put the question to her—was this story true?—as soon as I found her, because as long as I could remember I had taken questions and troubles to her for answering and soothing.

But she looked at me from her single eye, just a little to the right of the nose bridge, and I could not do it. Knowing her from an infant I had grown used to her appearance: I recognized the deformity but it had meant nothing. Suddenly it meant a great deal, and I felt revulsion and a nausea that made my stomach heave. I turned quickly and ran. She called after me but I paid no heed.

I ran out of the house and across the courtyard behind. I was heading for the stables, another familiar refuge on bad days and one which unlike Betty had no connection with my present shame. I was weeping as I ran. My eyes blinded with tears, I could scarcely see where I was going. As I reached the stables a man came out and I ran into him. I was checked and held and my father's voice said:

"What haste, boy?"

I looked up and could not speak. He said:

"And tears? A Harding does not cry, when he is nine years old."

I said, gasping: "A Harding, sir? Or a polymuf's brat?"

He stared at me, his face closed and seeming hard. I thought he would strike me and almost welcomed the thought. But after a moment he said:

"We have talking to do, Isak. Come with me."

He was not a tall man and was sparely built. His face, too, was thin, with keen blue eyes and a well trimmed beard, turning white. It had never occurred to me before to look for resemblance to my own dark heavy features in him, but I did so now, hen turned my head away.

We sat in his business room, with the parchment rent rolls

Of Polymuf Stock

hanging on their sticks on the wall and logs crackling brightly and noisily in the hearth. He was a man who felt the cold and sought warmth where he could. He sat in his big chair, covered with the chestnut hide of a favourite horse that had been killed under him in battle, and I on a leather stool before him. He said:

"The tears have stopped. Good. Now tell me what you have heard."

I would have broken down again in the telling but his cold eyes forbade it. When I had finished, I said:

"Is it true, sir?"

He nodded and said: "As far as it goes."

I started to sob and he put a steadying hand on my shoulder.

"A Harding does not cry."

"But I am none!"

"You are."

"I am not your son."

"No," he said, "but of my line and blood. You are my grandson, Isak."

I stared, uncomprehending. He said:

"My first-born child was a girl. The Seer named her polymuf and she was taken from us. It is the law, and the Spirits command it. My wife grieved and died within two winters. Later I married again and my children were whole and human. These are your sisters and your brother."

He paused and I waited. He went on:

"Then the Seer came to me. A polymuf woman had given birth to a boy who was true man and must be given to true men for rearing. The woman was my daughter. My wife and I took you to rear as our own. You are my own, a Harding."

"My mother . . ."

"Has doubtless had other children."

"Who is she? Where does she live?"

He shook his head. "We do not know."

"But . . ."

"It is the law, Isak. The Seer knows these things but no other may. I was not told to whom she was given, nor she that you were given back to me. The Seer told me whose was your ancestry because it seemed fitting. And I . . ." He paused again. "I thanked him, and thanked the Spirits, and made an offering which he called generous. But it was a poor return for what they had given me."

"And my father?"

"Who knows?"

Who knew, indeed? I thought of the polymuf men I had passed unthinkingly in the streets, or in the house itself, with limbs too many or too few, with all the diversity of crookedness and ugliness which the evil Spirits were said to wreak on the unborn child. I thought of Grog, who used four arms to sweep the streets, and Petey who apart from a hunched back had a double row of teeth in his jaw, and showed them when he laughed gapingly for the troopers who bought him ale. Any one of them might have been my father.

"And it does not matter," my grandfather said. I stared at him, hot-eyed. "You are a Harding. Those who have dared to mock you will regret it."

I do not know what word went out nor what punishments were inflicted, but there were no more cries of "Polymuf" after me in the street. The Hardings, as I have said, were a powerful family, my grandfather the most respected of the Prince's companions. He told me to forget what I had learned and made sure that none reminded me of it.

But there was no need of reminder. What I had learned sank deep into my mind and lay there with the cold weight of iron. Polymufs, whom I had previously taken for granted, became monstrous to me. Even Betty, whom I had loved, turned repellent. I shivered away from her touch and the gaze of her single eye.

It was customary for a boy of noble family to leave home at eleven for his first spell of life in barracks. I begged to go when I was ten, and it was granted. When I returned it was with a different status and to a different room from the one that had been my nursery. I no longer required a nurse and Betty retired to the servants' quarters. I saw her from time to time and smiled and nodded but did not stay to talk with her. I believe she thought me changed and cruel, but I could do nothing else.

I returned from barracks with high praise from my Drill Sergeant. Although younger than the others, he said, I showed more promise; he had rarely known a boy so keen to excel.

The fact was that in drilling, working, learning the arts and crafts of soldiering, I could forget what I was in the ambition for what I might be. And I loved the barracks, a place of true men where no polymuf was permitted to enter. I grew drunk with the smell of horses and leather, the clash of swords and the sharp jingle of harness. The hardships of the life I accepted exultantly: these were trials for true men.

Among the other boys, too, I was respected. On my first day I fought a bigger boy and beat him. He had made a remark to which I took offence—not concerning my ancestry but the cut of my tunic. He tried to pass it off but I would not let him. I beat two others also and after that they fought shy of provoking me.

I had no friend and wanted none. They talked about me, I guessed, behind my back—maybe called me "Polymuf" when I was out of hearing. But none would hold his gaze against mine, and they watched their words when they spoke to me. I did not mind if they liked or disliked me. It was enough that they dropped their eyes before mine, and guarded their tongues.

So the later years of my childhood passed, during a time in which great events happened in the city. Prince Stephen was deposed by the Captains and replaced by Robert Perry. My grandfather should have been elected but the Blaines blocked it, preferring a man they thought more easily controlled and of no lineage. Intrigue and murder followed and within two years we had a new Prince, Robert's son, Peter, and his younger son Luke was taken into exile by the Seer, to live with the High Seers in Sanctuary. Later Luke returned and fought and killed his brother and became Prince in his place, our third within three years. And next spring, being thirteen, I was named as one of the Young Captains to fight in the Contest.

The Contest which was held every year was a tournament in which four sons of Captains led teams of boys against one other, each having four followers. Teams were eliminated in turn as their Captains were unhorsed until one was left as victor. The swords used were only of wood and blunt, but they could hurt. It was no sport for weaklings.

I was determined to win the Contest and the jewelled sword which was the Young Captain's prize, and spared no effort. The first concern was to find the best men for my team. My reputation helped because I myself was known as the best swordsman and one of the two best horsemen of my year; and those who fought with the winning Captain would receive gold. But I made sure of the ones I wanted by promising to double the sum, relying on my grandfather's pride in my achievement to make good the promise. Then I drilled them, day after day, relentlessly; beyond the bounds of what was seemly but I kept them to it.

Lastly I made alliances. It often happened that two Young Captains would agree to fight first against a third and eliminate him. Robin Becket, my chief rival, offered me such an arrangement. I accepted but found excuse not to seal it with a handshake. Then I went to Peter Gray, whose team was reckoned third in strength and with him made a bargain for the first round, and sealed it.

I had left no room for things to go wrong, and nothing did. Robin was confused and shaken when Peter and I rode together against him, and he put up little opposition. It took not much more than five minutes' fighting to bring his fall, and the clang of the bell for the first interval. When the fight resumed I set my men at Peter and here again I had the advantage of surprise: our agreement had been for the first round only but he had assumed we would stay allied to eliminate Ranald, whose team was the weakest of the four. Ranald, seeing the change, joined with us—to survive into the last round was more honour than he could have hoped for.

Peter fought hard and three of Ranald's men were down before my sword caught him under the ribs and lifted him out

Of Polymuf Stock

of his saddle. But all my four were mounted still. We waited calmly for the last bell, drove Ranald into a corner, and overthrew him.

It was the shortest Contest any could remember, and the first for many years in which a team had come through to victory without losing a man. I led my pony to the Prince's pavilion with cheers from the mob seeming to echo against the sky and the bushy top of Catherine's Hill. No one now was shouting "Polymuf". Luke, our Prince, only a few years older than myself, proffered me the hilt of the jewelled sword which I had won. He said:

"You fight well, Isak."

"Thank you, sire."

"And hard. The surgeon says that Peter has a rib stove in from that last thrust of yours."

"Must one not fight hard in battle, sire?"

"In battle, yes."

He looked as though he would say more but did not. I raised the jewelled sword to salute him, and the crowd howled even louder.

My victory was not popular among those of my age and class. Their resentment showed in their faces and there were mutterings. It was whispered that Robin, feeling himself to have been cheated, would challenge me to a duel, on foot with wooden swords, man to man. When I heard that, I took the trouble to seek him out. He sat with friends on the steps of the Buttercross. I stood and looked at him, but he said nothing.

I knew I was a match for any one of them in any kind of fight they chose, and it did not trouble me to be disliked. I was certain at least that they would neither despise nor pity me. I had grown used to my own company and was satisfied with it. I spent much time in the barracks still, schooling myself to be a warrior. Sometimes at night I stood on the city's walls and looked out down the Itchen valley, and thought of the future.

It was through arms that a man achieved success in life, but it was not military glory that provided the seal on success. It was wealth which did that. My grandfather had been a warrior, as all men of rank must be, but neither skill nor courage had given him the position he held in the city and the council of the Prince. It stemmed from the gold which flowed into the city from his farms.

So to triumph as a warrior was not an end but a means. In war one gained booty, and the better one fought for one's Prince the more one got. I vowed I would earn and get a lion's share, and the gold I gained I would not waste. Gregory was my father's true son and therefore his heir, but the day would come when I outranked him.

Glory meant wealth and wealth meant power. Men had believed once that no commoner could ever rise to the rank of Prince, but Luke's father, Robert Perry, had given the lie to that. They would say it was unthinkable that someone born of polymuf stock could reign. But it was not unthinkable, for I thought it.

I toughened body and mind for the task I had set myself. In the streets of the city I walked alone and others gave me room. I scarcely noticed them. The ones I did see, always with a shiver of revulsion and disgust, were the polymufs. That one, the giant nearly eight feet tall—was he my father? And the stooping woman, with a cloth pulled across to hide her face—was she my mother?

When we rode out on the campaign I went with the army. As a scout only, but it made a start. We rode against Romsey, with whose Prince our own had a score to settle.

His name was James and he too was young, but wily. He brought his army out of the city but on the far side of the river on which it stood. He edged southwards along the valley and our army followed on the opposite bank. It was a progress in fits and starts, with each side looking for an advantage but finding none sure enough. Two days passed in this way. It was something that the weather held fair; cloudy but warm and dry.

On the second night I was one of the scouts on the extreme southern flank. I was given a post on high ground some distance from the river, from which, at dawn the next day, I could be

Of Polymuf Stock

expected to see the Romsey outriders and report any change in their disposition. I took my place as evening faded into night. The sky, I noticed, had almost emptied of cloud and the air was very calm. In the valley white mist rose from the river's tumbling surface and spread out, still rising, over its banks.

It reached me in the small hours of the night, a thin cold miasma that clutched at throat and eyes. I could see nothing for the dark, but I could feel it. The only thing to do was to wait and hope it would clear with the rising of the sun.

It was a long night. The mist itself was black and unchanging, and it seemed to have stifled the strange small sounds of the night: the owl's cry, the swish of grass or crackle of thicket at an animal's passing. There were only long minutes and longer hours. At last, slowly, very slowly, the blackness turned to grey and the grey lightened to pearl. No more than that. I could make out a brightness in the east which told me the sun was up but if I stretched my hand out before me, my fingers turned shadowy and tenuous. I could scarcely see my feet.

I had been given no orders to cover this case. I could stay where I was until the mist lifted, or try to make my way back to the army. I decided on the latter, not through loneliness or even hunger—I had finished my hard rations during the night— but because it seemed the better course. I could do no good here and the mist, for all I knew, might last all day.

I could not see my way, and the first thing a scout learns is not to call for help except in extremity. The answer, I thought, was to get down to the river. If I turned right on reaching it I should eventually make contact with the others. I might, with the mist as thick as it was, find myself in the water first but that did not worry me. At any rate, I could not miss it.

Or so I thought: it was a simple matter of heading down the slope till I reached the river. But the slope, as I learned later, was not continually downwards; there was a ridge that intervened and there, unable to see anything but the ground a foot or two ahead and groping painfully forward, I must have turned south instead of west.

Time was as meaningless as distance but at last I realized that

Of Polymuf Stock

I was lost. I tried to work out where I might be and to correct my course but soom realized the futility of it. I was not just lost, but hopelessly so.

I knew now I must stay where I was, because any move I made was only likely to make matters worse. I must wait until I could see my way. And the mist did seem to be thinning and growing lighter. I saw the brighter pearl in the east tinged with fitful yellow and at last with gold. Then a pale disc, shown and lost again. And the sun and with it the mist broken and lifting all round. I peered about me, trying to get my bearings.

It was not easy. I was in rough country, with coarse rabbit-cropped grass and patches of scrub. In most directions the ground rose, and I could see nothing of the river. But close by there was a mound, grassed and thorned in places, which offered a vantage point.

As I climbed it I realized, from the bricks and the looseness underfoot, that this was a ruin from ancient days, before the Disaster. Such places were thought by simple people to be the haunts of evil Spirits, bound there by the Disaster into which they had led mankind, and therefore shunned. These were not the sort of fears that had ever troubled me and I had no apprehension. Even when the slope collapsed under my feet and I found myself falling, I did not think of Spirits. The rubble was unsafe, that was all: I cursed my foolishness in not taking more care.

And after that I was only concerned with trying to break my fall and with fending off loose bricks that flew around me. I dropped a long way and landed on one knee, so painfully that I thought I had broken my leg. The dust and rubble settled about me while I writhed in pain. After a time I could rub it and feel that there was no fracture. It hurt but I could move, even sit up. There was room to do that; I was not pinned down as I so easily might have been. High up a jagged hole framed the sky. Very little light came from it—I could see almost nothing of my surroundings. I felt in my pack, which had fortunately not been dragged from me in the fall. I found my tinder-box and a stub of candle. I lit it and could see again.

I was in a room whose ceiling I had crashed through at one corner. Rubble that had come with me lay scattered on the floor but only in this spot. The rest of the room was untouched. And furnished. I saw chairs, a long table, a sideboard against the far wall. Table and sideboard were piled with objects that were covered with dust and cobwebs, so that one could not make out the individual shapes but only a jumbled mound.

The table was nearer. I climbed painfully to my feet and approached it. One of the first things I recognized, at the table's edge, was a candle. I lit it from my own; it flickered then burnt more brightly. A drop of melted wax made a hole in the coating of spider's webs surrounding its holder. The candlestick was of metal. I rubbed the dust away and saw a soft yellow gleam. The metal was gold.

I looked at the other objects on the table. There were pots and plates, more candlesticks, salvers, jugs, vases. Some were gold and the rest, though badly tarnished, were plainly silver. I moved to the sideboard and found other treasures. Lidded pots, with handles and spouts to pour from, silver dishes whose sides were worked in a delicate pattern of leaves and fruit, the fruit something like gooseberries but weirdly clustered together, a heavy intricate chain of gold . . . The sideboard had cupboards under it. The door of one sprang open as I dropped the chain. There was still more inside: a big silver bowl was piled with smaller ones.

I was confused, and astonished. This was greater booty than a warrior, however successful in battle, could hope to gain in a score of campaigns. And it must have lain here for more than a hundred years. No one owned it unless the Spirits did, and being insubstantial they could have little use for it. It was mine and I was rich—richer, maybe, than my grandfather Harding.

Wariness followed on the thrill of triumph and delight. Even if I could carry all this with me it would be unwise to do so. In fact I must take very little: a couple of small pots, say. But I could mark the place and come to it whenever I wished and get what I needed. It was safer here than anywhere. This was mostly deserted land, lying close to the great ruins of the Disaster, and

Of Polymuf Stock

even if a shepherd came within sight of it he would not venture near: all country people believed in the Spirits, and feared them.

I took a small pot of gold and a plate of the same metal, no more than four inches across, and put them in my pack. I picked up a golden candlestick but replaced it. I was not going to be so stupid as to be greedy. When I was older . . . gold and silver would buy not only houses, farms, servants, but men also. I would have more followers than the Blaines and the Hardings together. And with men one had power. Enough, when the time was ripe, to take the city. And other cities.

Holding up my candle I saw a door beyond the table. I crossed the room and tried the handle. It opened easily, though creakingly.

Inside there were buckets. They were neither of wood nor metal but of that substance called plast which the ancients made and which countrymen, when they turn it up during digging, are careful to burn, washing their hands if they have touched it. It is often brightly coloured but is not painted because the colour goes right through. I saw a blue bucket and two yellow ones. All were full, heaped with bracelets and brooches and necklaces and other jewelry, of gold set with many precious stones. Here was not just riches, but wealth incalculable.

I looked further in the room. A wooden chest, three feet square and of the same height, more than half full of jewels; and a bowl, a couple of feet across, crammed to the brim and with a string of large pearls spilling over the edge. And a bed. A figure lay there.

I knew he was dead. I knew also that there is even less to fear from the dead than from the Spirits the Seer tells of. I went closer, expecting to see the gleam of bones picked white by time. But flesh still covered him—dried and darkened, pulled away from the grinning teeth and blackened at the eyeholes, but preserved. He had died in a dry summer, perhaps, and his flesh had withered instead of rotting. It sometimes happens.

His face looked mean and pinched. So would any man's whose skin had shrunk and turned to leather, but I wondered if in fact his features had changed so much. It was he who had brought the treasure here—I was sure of that. When the Disaster came and the huge cities tumbled like children's play bricks—the cities so vast that a score of Winchesters could be lost within the bounds of one—most of the people, thousands times a thousand, died in them. The few that survived fled into the country to grub a living.

But he had not. He had gone back into the ruins, risking earthquake and plague and starvation, to dig for gold and silver and precious stones. They were a rich people, our ancestors, and there would be much to find. He had brought it here, load after load, to his underground storeroom. A dozen or so trinkets lay on the bed beside him, like the toys a child puts by his pillow at night, and on his wrist I saw three tiny clocks, each fastened to a gold bracelet.

How long had he lived here? Years, probably—such a haul could not have been unearthed from the ruins in any short time. And how died? Of sickness or old age? Or perhaps of hunger, having no food in reach and being unwilling to leave his treasure to hunt for some.

The Disaster had happened... people had died in numbers that one could not begin to imagine... the world had been shattered into small ugly pieces... and he had stayed here, counting his wealth by candlelight. He had withered until death came, then withered further. He had changed not much more than the gold. Even the rats had shunned him.

A sudden fear struck me which had nothing to do with Spirits or the dead man lying on the bed. It was rather a chill despair striking deep inside me, a sense of hopelessness biting into my heart and bones. I had a desperate need to leave this place, not because of its ghosts but because there were none. There was nothing but emptiness and desolation, and barren treasure.

I ran back to the other room. Even standing on the table the hole in the ceiling would be out of reach, but if the table were upended... I dragged it across to the wall, sending its heap of cobwebbed metal clattering to the ground, and, ignoring the pain in my leg, scrambled up and balanced precariously on top.

Of Polymuf Stock

I would have to leap to reach the jagged hole above me: would the broken laths take my weight or collapse? There was no point in hesitation. I leapt, felt the edge give, then clawed my way up until I reached a beam.

I straddled it for a moment. The way was open to the sky and the world outside. I had started the last few feet when I remembered something. I felt in my pack and found the golden pot and plate. I pitched them down and heard them crash in the darkness.

The day was bright now, with only a thin white steam rising from the ground and the sky clear apart from wispy cloud. I soon found the river and followed it northwards. Ten minutes later I came to a village. It would be the one, I guessed, built round the river's southernmost ford, which meant that the army was no more than two or three miles away.

But the village itself was enough. I hurried, limping, towards it, filled with joy at the sound of a dog's barking, the sight of smoking chimneys. At the outskirts a man drew water from a well. He wore a servant's clothes and as he turned to me I saw that one eye was lower in his face than the other, with a cast in it, and that his right arm was stiff and crooked.

He bowed his head, saying: "Greetings, master."

I looked at him, not shrinking away.

I said: "Greetings, brother."

Obstinate Uncle Otis

ROBERT ARTHUR

My Uncle Otis was the most obstinate man in Vermont. If you know Vermonters, you know that means he was the most obstinate man in the world. It is nothing but the solemn truth to say that Uncle Otis was so obstinate he was more dangerous than the hydrogen bomb.

You find that hard to believe. Naturally. So I shall tell you just why Uncle Otis was dangerous—dangerous not only to all of mankind but to the solar system as well. Yes, and quite possibly to the entire universe.

His name was Morks, like mine—Otis Morks. He lived in Vermont and I had not seen him for some time. Then one morning I received an urgent telegram from my Aunt Edith, his sister. It said: OTIS STRUCK BY LIGHTNING. SITUATION SERIOUS. COME AT ONCE.

I left on the next train. Not only was I concerned about Uncle Otis, but there was an undertone of unexplained urgency in those ten commonplace words that compelled me to haste.

Late that afternoon I descended in Hillport, Vermont. The only taxi, an ancient saloon car, was driven by a village character named Jud Perkins. Jud was also constable, and as I climbed into his decrepit vehicle I saw that he had a revolver strapped to his waist.

I also noticed, across the square, a knot of towns-people standing staring at something. Then I realized they were staring at an empty pedestal that had formerly held a large bronze statue to a local statesman named Ogilby—an individual Uncle Otis had always held in the utmost contempt.

Obstinate Uncle Otis

Obstinately, Uncle Otis would never believe that anybody would erect a statue to Ogilby, and had always refused to admit that there actually was such a statue in the village square. But there had been, and now it was gone.

The old car lurched into motion. I leaned forward and asked Jud Perkins where the statue had gone. He turned to squint at me sideways.

"Stole," he informed me. "Yestidday afternoon, about five. In plain view. Yessir, took between two winks of an eye. We was all in Simpkins' store—me 'n' Simpkins 'n' your Uncle Otis Morks 'n' your Aunt Edith 'n' some other. Somebody said as how the town ought to clean Ogilby's statue—become plumb pigeonfied last few years. Your Uncle Otis stuck out his chin.

" 'What statue?' he wanted to know, his eyebrows bristlin'. 'There ain't no such thing as a statue to a blubbery-mouthed nincompoop like Ogilby in this town!'

"So, though I knowed it wasn't any use, he wouldn't believe in th' statue if he walked into it an' broke his leg—never met as obstinate a man as Otis Morks for not believing in a thing he don't like—anyway, I turned round to point at it. And it was gone. Minute before it had been there. Now it wasn't. Stole between one look an' th' next."

Jud Perkins spat out the window and turned to look at me in an authoritative manner.

"If you want to know who done it," he said, "these here Fifth Columnists, that's who." (I should add that this occurred during World War II.) "They took Ogilby 'cause he's bronze, see? Over there, they need copper an' bronze for making shells. So they're stealin' it an' shippin' it over by submarine. But I got my eyes skinned for 'em if they come round here again. I got me my pistol an' I'm on th' watch."

We bumped and banged out towards Uncle Otis's farm, and Jud Perkins continued bringing me up to date on local affairs. He told me how Uncle Otis had come to be struck by lightning—out of his own obstinacy, as I had suspected.

"Day before yestidday," Jud told me, between expectorations of tobacco juice, "your Uncle Otis was out in th' fields when it

Obstinate Uncle Otis

blowed up a thunderstorm. He got in under a big oak tree. Told him myself a thousand times trees draw lightning, but he's too obstinate to listen.

"Maybe he thought he c'd ignore that lightning, like he ignores Willoughby's barn across the road, or Marble Hill, that his cousin Seth lawed away from him so that now he won't admit there is any such hill. Or th' new dam th' state put in to make a reservoir, and flooded some grazin' land he always used, so that now your Uncle Otis acts 's if you're crazy when you talk about there bein' a dam there.

"Well, maybe he thought he c'd ignore that lightning, but lightning's hard to ignore. It hit that oak, splintered it an' knocked Otis twenty feet. Only reason it didn't kill him, I guess, is because he's always had such prime good health. Ain't been sick a day in his life except that week twenty years ago when he fell off a horse an' had his amnesia an' thought he was a farm machinery salesman named Eustace Lingham, from Cleveland, Ohio.

"Your Aunt Edith seen it happen and run out and drag him in. She put him to bed an' called Doc Perkins. Doc said it was just a shock, he'd come to pretty soon, but keep him in bed two, three days.

"Sure enough, your Uncle Otis came to, 'bout supper, but he wouldn't stay in bed. Said he felt fine, and by dad, yestidday in Simpkins' store I never seen him lookin' more fit. Acted ten years younger. Walked like he was on springs an' seemed to give out electricity from every pore."

I asked if increasing age had softened Uncle Otis's natural obstinacy any. Jud spat with extra copiousness.

"Made it worse," he said flatly. "Most obstinate man in Vermont, your Uncle Otis. Dad blast it, when he says a thing ain't, even though it's right there in front of him, blamed if he don't say it so positive you almost believe him.

"Sat on his front stoop myself, only last week, with that old barn of Willoughby's spang in th' way of th' view, and your Uncle Otis lookin' at it 's if it weren't there.

" 'Fine view,' I said, 'iffi'n only that barn warn't there,' an' your Uncle Otis looked at me like I was crazy.

Obstinate Uncle Otis

" 'Barn?' he said. 'What barn? No barn there an' never has been. Finest view in Vermont. See for twenty miles.' "

Jud Perkins chuckled and just missed running down a yellow dog and a boy on a bicycle.

"There's people got so much faith they can believe what ain't," he said. "But your Uncle Otis is th' only man I ever met so obstinate he c'n disbelieve in things that is."

I was in a thoughtful mood when Jud Perkins dropped me at Uncle Otis's gate. Uncle Otis wasn't in sight, but I headed round to the rear of the house and Aunt Edith came hurrying out of the kitchen, her apron, skirts, hair and hands all fluttering.

"Oh, Murchison!" she cried. "I'm so glad you're here. I don't know what to do, I simply don't. The most dreadful thing happened to Otis, and—"

Then I saw Otis himself, going down the walk to get the evening paper from a tin receptacle at the gate. His small, spare figure upright and a stubborn jaw out-thrust, his bushy white eyebrows bristling, he looked unaltered to me. But Aunt Edith only wrung her hands when I said so.

"I know," she sighed. "If you didn't know the truth, you'd think it actually did him good to be hit by lightning. But here he comes. I can't tell you any more now. After supper! He mustn't be allowed to guess—Oh, I do hope nothing dreadful happens before we can stop it."

And then, as Uncle Otis approached with his paper, she fled back into the kitchen.

Uncle Otis certainly did not seem changed, unless for the better. As Jud Perkins had remarked, he seemed younger. He shook my hand heartily and my arm tingled, as if from an electric shock. His eyes sparkled. His whole being seemed keyed up and buoyant with mysterious energy.

We strolled towards the front porch and stood facing the rotting old barn across the road that had spoiled the view. Grasping for a conversational topic as I studied Uncle Otis to discover what Aunt Edith meant, I suggested it was too bad the storm two days before hadn't blown the barn down and finished it.

Obstinate Uncle Otis

"Barn?" Uncle Otis scowled at me. "What barn? No barn there, boy! Nothing but th' view—finest view in Vermont. If you c'n see a barn there you'd better get to a doctor fast as you can hike."

As Jud had said, he spoke so convincingly that in spite of myself I had to turn for another look at the structure. I remained staring quite some time, I expect, and probably I blinked.

Because Uncle Otis was telling the truth.

There wasn't any barn—now.

All through supper a suspicion of the incredible truth grew on me. And after supper, while Uncle Otis read his paper in the parlour, I followed Aunt Edith into the kitchen.

She only sighed when I told her about the barn, and looked at me with haunted eyes.

"Yes," she whispered, "it's Otis. I knew when the statue . . . went—yesterday when we were in Simpkins' store. I was looking right at it when Otis said what he did and it—it was just gone, right from under my eyes. That's when I sent you the telegram."

"You mean," I asked, "that since Uncle Otis was struck by lightning, his obstinacy has taken a new turn? He used to think things he didn't like didn't exist, and that was all. But now, when he thinks it, due to some peculiar heightening of his tremendously obstinate will power, the things *don't* exist? He just disbelieves them right out of existence?"

Aunt Edith nodded. "They just *go*!" she cried, almost wildly. "When he says a thing's not, now it's *not*."

I confess the idea made me uneasy. There were a number of unpleasant possibilities that occurred to me. The list of things— and people—Uncle Otis didn't believe in was long and varied.

"What," I asked, "do you suppose the limit is? A statue, a barn —where do you suppose it stops?"

"I don't know," she told me. "Maybe there isn't any limit to it. Otis is an *awfully* obstinate man and—well, suppose something reminds him about the dam? Suppose he says there isn't any dam? It's a hundred feet high and all that water behind it—"

She did not have to finish. If Uncle Otis suddenly disbelieved the Hillport dam out of existence, the impounded water that would be set free would wipe away the village, and might kill the whole five hundred inhabitants.

"And then, of course, there are all those far-off countries with the funny names he's never believed were real," Aunt Edith whispered. "Like Zanzibar and Martinique."

"And Guatemala and Polynesia," I agreed, frowning. "If he were reminded of one of those by something, and took it into his head to declare it didn't exist, there's no telling what might happen. The sudden disappearance of any one of them—why, tidal waves and earthquakes would be the least we could expect."

"But what can we do to stop him?" Aunt Edith wanted to know, desperately. "We can't tell him that he mustn't—"

She was interrupted by a snort as Uncle Otis marched into the kitchen with the evening paper.

"Listen to this!" he commanded, and read us a short item, the gist of which was that Seth Youngman, the second cousin who had lawsuited his hill away from him, was planning to sell Marble Hill to a New York company that would quarry it. Then Uncle Otis threw the paper down on the kitchen table in disgust.

"What they talking about?" he barked, his eyebrows bristling. "Marble Hill? No hill around here by that name, and never has been. And Seth Youngman never owned a hill in his life. What kind of idiots get this paper out, I want to know?"

He glowered at us. And in the silence, a faint distant rumbling, as of displaced stones, could be heard. Aunt Edith and I turned as one. It was still light, and from the kitchen window we could see to the northwest, where Marble Hill stood up against the horizon like a battered felt hat—or where it *had* stood.

The ancient prophets may have had faith strong enough to move mountains. But Uncle Otis was possessed of something far more remarkable, it seemed—a lack of faith which could unmove them.

Uncle Otis himself, unaware of anything unusual, picked up the paper again, grumbling.

Obstinate Uncle Otis

"Everybody's crazy these days," he declared. "Piece here about President Roosevelt. Not Teddy Roosevelt, but somebody called Franklin. Can't even get a man's name straight. Everybody ought to know there's no such president as Franklin Roo—"

"Uncle Otis!" I shouted. "Look, there's a mouse!"

Uncle Otis stopped and turned. There *was* a mouse, crouched under the stove, and it was the only thing I could think of to distract Uncle Otis's attention before he expressed his disbelief in Franklin D. Roosevelt. I was barely in time. I dabbed at my brow. Uncle Otis scowled.

"Where?" he demanded. "No mouse there I can see."

"Th—" I started to point. Then I checked myself. As soon as he had spoken, of course, the mouse was gone. I said instead that I must have been mistaken. Uncle Otis snorted and strode back towards the parlour. Aunt Edith and I looked at each other.

"If he'd said—" she began, "—if he'd finished saying there isn't any President Roose—"

She never completed the sentence. Uncle Otis, going through the doorway, caught his foot in a hole worn through the linoleum and fell full length into the hall. As he went down, his head struck a table, and he was unconscious when we reached him.

I carried Uncle Otis into the parlour and laid him on the old horsehair sofa. Aunt Edith brought a cold compress and spirits of ammonia. Together we worked over Uncle Otis's limp form, and presently he opened his eyes, blinking at us without recognition.

"Who're you?" he demanded. "What happened to me?"

"Otis!" Aunt Edith cried. "I'm your sister. You fell and hit your head. You've been unconscious."

Uncle Otis glowered at us with deep suspicion. "Otis?" he repeated. "My name's not Otis. Who you think I am, anyway?"

"But it *is* Otis!" Aunt Edith wailed. "You're Otis Morks, my brother, and you live in Hillport, Vermont. You've lived here all your life."

Uncle Otis's lower lip stuck out obstinately.

"My name's *not* Otis Morks," he declared, rising. "I'm

Obstinate Uncle Otis

Eustace Lingham, of Cleveland, Ohio. I sell farm machinery. I'm not your brother. I've never seen you before, either of you. I've got a headache and I'm tired of talking. I'm going out to get some fresh air. Maybe it'll make my head feel better."

Dumbly Aunt Edith stood to one side. Uncle Otis marched out into the hall and through the front door. Aunt Edith, peering out of the window, reported that he was standing on the front steps, looking up at the stars.

"It's happened again," she said despairingly. "His amnesia's come back. Just like the time twenty years ago when he fell off a horse and thought he was this Eustace Lingham from Cleveland for a whole week.

"Oh, Murchison, now we've got to call the doctor. But if the doctor finds out about the other, he'll want to shut him up. Only if anybody tries to shut Otis up, he'll just disbelieve in them and the place they want to shut him up in, too. Then they—they—"

"But if something isn't done," I pointed out, "there's no telling what may happen. He's bound to read about President Roosevelt again. You can't miss his name in the papers these days, even in Vermont. Or else he'll come across a mention of Madagascar or Guatemala."

"Or get into a fuss with the income tax people," Aunt Edith put in. "He keeps getting letters from them about why he's never paid any income tax. The last letter, they said they were going to send somebody to call on him in person. But he says there isn't any such thing as an income tax, so there can't be any income tax collectors. So if a man comes here saying he's an income tax collector, Uncle Otis will just not believe in him. Then..."

Helplessly we looked at each other. Aunt Edith grabbed my arm.

"Murchison!" she gasped. "Quick! Go out with him. We mustn't leave him alone. Only last week he decided that there aren't any such things as stars!"

I did not hesitate an instant. A moment later I was on the porch beside Uncle Otis, who was breathing in the cool evening

Obstinate Uncle Otis

air and staring upwards at the spangled heavens, a look of deepest disbelief on his face.

"Stars!" he barked, stabbing a skinny forefinger towards the star-dotted sky. "A hundred million billion trillion dillion miles away, every last one of 'em! And every one of 'em a hundred times bigger 'n the sun! That's what the book said. You know what *I* say? I say bah! Nothing's that big, or that far off. You know what those things they look at through telescopes and call stars are? They're not stars at all. Fact is, there's no such thing as st—"

"Uncle Otis!" I cried loudly. "A mosquito!"

And I brought my hand down on the top of his head with solid force.

I had to distract him. I had to keep him from saying it. The universe is a big thing, of course, probably too big even for Uncle Otis to disbelieve out of existence. But I didn't dare take a chance. So I yelled and slapped him.

But I'd forgotten about the return of his ancient amnesia and his belief that he was Eustace Lingham of Cleveland. When he had recovered from my blow he stared at me coldly.

"I'm not your Uncle Otis!" he snapped. "I'm nobody's Uncle Otis. I'm nobody's brother, either. I'm Eustace Lingham and I've got a headache. I'm going to have my cigar and I'm going to bed, and in the morning I'm going back to Cleveland."

He turned, stamped inside, and went up the stairs.

I trailed after him, unable to think of a helpful plan, and Aunt Edith followed us both up the stairs. She and I came to a stop at the top. Together we watched Uncle Otis stride into his room and close the door.

After that we heard the bedsprings squeak as he sat down. This was followed by the scratching of a match and in a moment we smelled cigar smoke. Uncle Otis always allowed himself one cigar, just before going to bed.

"Otis Morks!" we heard him mutter to himself, and one shoe dropped to the floor. "Nobody's got such a name. It's a trick of some kind. Don't believe there is any such person."

Then he was silent. The silence continued. We waited for him to drop the other shoe . . . and when a full minute had passed, we gave each other one horrified look, rushed to the door and threw it open.

Aunt Edith and I stared in. The window was closed and locked. A cigar in an ash tray on a table by the bed was sending a feather of smoke upwards. There was a hollow in the bed covers, slowly smoothing out, where someone might have been sitting a moment before. A single one of Uncle Otis's shoes lay on the floor beside the bed.

But Uncle Otis, of course, was gone. He had disbelieved himself out of existence . . .

The Tower

MARGHANITA LASKI

The road begins to rise in a series of gentle curves, passing through pleasing groves of olives and vines. Five kilometres on the left is the fork for Florence. To the right may be seen the Tower of Sacrifice (470 steps) built in 1535 by Niccolo di Ferramano; superstitious fear left the tower intact when, in 1549, the surrounding village was completely destroyed . . .

Triumphantly Caroline lifted her finger from the fine italic type. There was nothing to mar the success of this afternoon. Not only had she taken the car out alone for the first time, driving unerringly on the right-hand side of the road, but what she had achieved was not a simple drive but a cultural excursion. She had taken the Italian guide-book Neville was always urging on her, and hesitantly, haltingly, she had managed to piece out enough of the language to choose a route that took in four well-thought-of frescoes, two universally-admired campaniles, and one wooden crucifix in a village church quite a long way from the main road. It was not, after all, such a bad thing that a British Council meeting had kept Neville in Florence. True, he was certain to know all about the campaniles and the frescoes, but there was just a chance that he hadn't discovered the crucifix, and how gratifying if she could, at last, have something of her own to contribute to his constantly accumulating hoard of culture.

But could she add still more? There was at least another hour of daylight, and it wouldn't take more than thirty-five minutes to get back to the flat in Florence. Perhaps there would just be

The Tower

time to add this tower to her dutiful collection? What was it called? She bent to the guide-book again, carefully tracing the text with her finger to be sure she was translating it correctly, word by word.

But this time her moving finger stopped abruptly at the name of Niccolo di Ferramano. There had risen in her mind a picture—no, not a picture, a portrait—of a thin white face with deepset black eyes that stared intently into hers. Why a portrait? she asked, and then she remembered.

It had been about three months ago, just after they were married, when Neville had first brought her to Florence. He himself had already lived there for two years, and during that time had been at least as concerned to accumulate Tuscan culture for himself as to disseminate English culture to the Italians. What more natural than that he should wish to share—perhaps even show off—his discoveries to his young wife?

Caroline had come out to Italy with the idea when she had worked through one or two galleries and made a few trips—say to Assisi and Siena—she would have done her duty as a British Council wife, and could then settle down to examining the Florentine shops, which everyone had told her were too marvellous for words. But Neville had been contemptuous of her programme. "You can see the stuff in the galleries at any time," he had said, "but I'd like you to start with the pieces that the ordinary tourist doesn't see," and of course Caroline couldn't possibly let herself be classed as an ordinary tourist. She had been proud to accompany Neville to castles and palaces privately owned to which his work gave him entry, and there to gaze with what she hoped was pleasure on the undiscovered Raphael, the Titian that had hung on the same wall ever since it was painted, the Giotto fresco under which the family that had originally commissioned it still said their prayers.

It had been on one of these pilgrimages that she had seen the face of the young man with the black eyes. They had made a long slow drive over narrowly ill-made roads and at last had come to a castle on the top of a hill. The family was, to Neville's disappointment, away, but the housekeeper remembered him and led them to a long gallery lined with five centuries of family portraits.

Though she could not have admitted it even to herself, Caroline had become almost anaesthetized to Italian art. Dutifully she had followed Neville along the gallery, listening politely while in his light well-bred voice he had told her intimate anecdotes of history, and involuntarily she had let her eyes wander round the room, glancing anywhere but at the particular portrait of Neville's immediate dissertation.

It was thus that her eye was caught by a face on the other side of the room, and forgetting what was due to politeness she caught her husband's arm and demanded, "Neville, who's that girl over there?"

But he was pleased with her. He said, "Ah, I'm glad you picked that one out. It's generally thought to be the best thing in the collection—a Bronzino, of course," and they went over to look at it.

The picture was painted in rich pale colours, a green curtain, a blue dress, a young face with calm brown eyes under plaits of honey-gold hair. Caroline read out the name under the picture—*Giovanna di Ferramano, 1531–1549*. That was the year the village was destroyed, she remembered now, sitting in the car by the roadside, but then she had exclaimed, "Neville, she was only eighteen when she died."

"They married young in those days," Neville commented, and Caroline said in surprise, "Oh, was she married?" It had been the radiantly virginal character of the face that had caught at her inattention.

"Yes, she was married," Neville answered, and added, "Look at the portrait beside her. It's Bronzino again. What do you think of it?"

And this was when Caroline had seen the pale young man. There were no clear light colours in this picture. There was only the whiteness of the face, the blackness of the eyes, the hair, the clothes, and the glint of gold letters on the pile of books on which the young man rested his hand. Underneath this picture was written *Portrait of an Unknown Gentleman*.

The Tower

"Do you mean he's her husband?" Caroline asked. "Surely they'd know if he was, instead of calling him an Unknown Gentleman?"

"He's Niccolo di Ferramano all right," said Neville. "I've seen another portrait of him somewhere, and it's not a face one would forget, but," he added reluctantly, because he hated to admit ignorance, "there's apparently some queer scandal about him, and though they don't turn his picture out, they won't even mention his name. Last time I was here, the old Count himself took me through the gallery. I asked him about little Giovanna and her husband." He laughed uneasily. "Mind you, my Italian was far from perfect at that time, but it was horribly clear that I shouldn't have asked." "But what did he *say*?" Caroline demanded. "I've tried to remember," said Neville. "For some reason it stuck in my mind. He said either 'She was lost' or 'She was damned', but which word it was I can never be sure. The portrait of Niccolo he just ignored altogether."

"What was wrong with Niccolo, I wonder?" mused Caroline, and Neville answered, "I don't know but I can guess. Do you notice the lettering on those books up there, under his hand? It's all in Hebrew or Arabic. Undoubtedly the unmentionable Niccolo dabbled in Black Magic."

Caroline shivered. "I don't like him," she said. "Let's look at Giovanna again," and they had moved back to the first portrait, and Neville had said casually, "Do you know, she's rather like you."

"I've just got time to look at the tower," Caroline now said aloud, and she put the guide-book back in the pigeon-hole under the dashboard, and drove carefully along the gentle curves until she came to the fork for Florence on the left.

On the top of a little hill to the right stood a tall round tower. There was no other building in sight. In a land where every available piece of ground is cultivated, there was no cultivated ground around this tower. On the left was the fork for Florence: on the right a rough track led up to the top of the hill.

Caroline knew that she wanted to take the fork to the left, to Florence and home and Neville and—said an urgent voice inside her—for safety. This voice so much shocked her that she got out of the car and began to trudge up the dusty track towards the tower.

After all, I may not come this way again, she argued; it seems silly to miss the chance of seeing it when I've already got a reason for being interested. I'm only just going to have a quick look—and she glanced at the setting sun, telling herself that she would indeed have to be quick if she were to get back to Florence before dark.

And now she had climbed the hill and was standing in front of the tower. It was built of narrow red bricks, and only thin slits pierced its surface right up to the top where Caroline could see some kind of narrow platform encircling it. Before her was an arched doorway. I'm just going to have a quick look, she assured herself again, and then she walked in.

She was in an empty room with a low arched ceiling. A narrow stone staircase clung to the wall and circled round the room to disappear through a hole in the ceiling.

"There ought to be a wonderful view at the top," said Caroline firmly to herself, and she laid her hand on the rusty rail and started to climb, and as she climbed, she counted.

"—thirty-nine, forty, forty-one," she said and with the forty-first step she came through the ceiling and saw over her head, far far above, the deep blue evening sky, a small circle of blue framed in a narrowing shaft round which the narrow staircase spiralled. There was no inner wall; only the rusty railing protected the climber on the inside.

"—eighty-three, eighty-four—" counted Caroline. The sky above her was losing its colour and she wondered why the narrow slit windows in the wall had all been so placed that they spiralled round the staircase too high for anyone climbing it to see through them.

"It's getting dark very quickly," said Caroline at the hundred-and-fiftieth step. "I know what the tower is like now. It would be much more sensible to give up and go home."

At the two-hundred-and-sixty-ninth step, her hand, moving forward on the railing, met only empty space. For an interminable second she shivered, pressing back to the hard brick on the other side. Then hesitantly she groped forwards, upwards, and at last her fingers met the rusty rail again, and again she climbed.

But now the breaks in the rail became more and more frequent. Sometimes she had to climb several steps with her left shoulder pressed tightly to the brick wall before her searching hand could find the tenuous rusty comfort again.

At the three-hundred-and-seventy-fifth step, the rail, as her moving hand clutched it, crumpled away under her fingers. "I'd better just go by the wall," she told herself, and now her left hand traced the rough brick as she climbed up and up.

"Four-hundred-and-twenty-two, four-hundred-and-twenty-three," counted Caroline with part of her brain. "I really ought to go down now," said another part, "I wish—oh, I want to go down now—" but she could not. "It would be so silly to give up," she told herself, desperately trying to rationalize what drove her on. "Just because one's afraid—" and then she had to stifle that thought too and there was nothing left in her brain but the steadily mounting tally of the steps.

"—four-hundred-and-seventy!" said Caroline aloud with explosive relief, and then she stopped abruptly because the steps had stopped too. There was nothing ahead but a piece of broken railing barring her way, and the sky, drained now of all its colour, was still some twenty feet above her head.

"But how idiotic," she said to the air. "The whole thing's absolutely pointless," and then the fingers of her left hand, exploring the wall beside her, met not brick but wood.

She turned to see what it was, and then in the wall, level with the top step, was a small wooden door. "So it does go somewhere after all," she said, and she fumbled with the rusty handle. The door pushed open and she stepped through.

She was on a narrow stone platform about a yard wide. It seemed to encircle the tower. The platform sloped downwards away from the tower and its stones were smooth and very shiny —and this was all she noticed before she looked beyond the stones and down.

The Tower

She was immeasurably, unbelievably high and alone and the ground below was a world away. It was not credible, not possible that she should be so far from the ground. All her being was suddenly absorbed in the single impulse to hurl herself from the sloping platform. "I cannot go down any other way," she said, and then she heard what she said and stepped back, frenziedly clutching the soft rotten wood of the doorway with hands sodden with sweat. There is no other way, said the voice in her brain, there is no other way.

"This is vertigo," said Caroline. "I've only got to close my eyes and keep still for a minute and it will pass off. It's bound to pass off. I've never had it before but I know what it is and it's vertigo." She closed her eyes and kept very still and felt the cold sweat running down her body.

"I should be all right now," she said at last, and carefully she stepped back through the doorway on to the four-hundred-and-seventieth step and pulled the door shut before her. She looked up at the sky, swiftly darkening with night. Then, for the first time, she looked down into the shaft of the tower, down to the narrow unprotected staircase spiralling round and round and round, and disappearing into the dark. She said—she screamed—"I can't go down."

She stood still on the top step, staring downwards, and slowly the last light faded from the tower. She could not move. It was not possible that she should dare to go down, step by step down the unprotected stairs into the dark below. It would be much easier to fall, said the voice in her head, to take one step to the left and fall and it would all be over. You cannot climb down.

She began to cry, shuddering with the pain of her sobs. It could not be true that she had brought herself to this peril, that there could be no safety for her unless she could climb down the menacing stairs. The reality *must* be that she was safe at home with Neville—but this was the reality and here were the stairs; at last she stopped crying and said "Now I shall go down."

"One!" she counted and, her right hand tearing at the brick wall, she moved first one and then the other foot down to the second step. "Two!" she counted, and then she thought of the

The Tower

depth below her and stood still, stupefied with terror. The stone beneath her feet, the brick against her hand were too frail protections for her exposed body. They could not save her from the voice that repeated that it would be easier to fall. Abruptly she sat down on the step.

"Two," she counted again, and spreading both her hands tightly against the step on each side of her, she swung her body off the second step, down on the third. "Three," she counted, then "four" then "five", pressing closer and closer into the wall, away from the empty drop on the other side.

At the twenty-first step she said, "I think I can do it now." She slid her right hand up the rough wall and slowly stood upright. Then with the other hand she reached for the railing it was now too dark to see, but it was not there.

For timeless time she stood there, knowing nothing but fear. "Twenty-one," she said, "twenty-one," over and over again, but she could not step on to the twenty-second stair.

Something brushed her face. She knew it was a bat, not a hand, that touched her but still it was horror beyond conceivable horror, and it was this horror, without any sense of moving from dread to safety, that at last impelled her down the stairs.

"Twenty-three, twenty-four, twenty-five—" she counted, and around her the air was full of whispering skin-stretched wings. If one of them should touch her again, she must fall. "Twenty-six, twenty-seven, twenty-eight—" The skin of her right hand was torn and hot with blood, for she would never lift it from the wall, only press it slowly down and force her rigid legs to move from the knowledge of each step to the peril of the next.

So Caroline came down the dark tower. She could not think. She could know nothing but fear. Only her brain remorselessly recorded the tally. "Five-hundred-and-one," it counted, "five-hundred-and-two—and three—and four—"

The Cork Elephant

IAN SERRAILLIER

But listen to this. I spent the day on Hey Tor, wandering about and exploring the rock battlements. I never noticed the storm coming up till the rain dropped suddenly upon me. As you know, it's pretty bleak up there, no shelter at all, and I just had to run for it—over the stony turf to the Newton road, then downhill as hard as I could pelt.

I stopped at the first cottage and knocked three times. My hat was dripping like a gutterless roof and I was wet to the skin. Was nobody in? I was just going when the door squeaked open and I saw a face I vaguely remembered.

"Come in," said the man. "We're old friends, aren't we?"

He took my hat from me, and my raincoat.

"Poor fellow, you're soaked. Wait, I'll put these in the kitchen to dry." When he returned he said, "You remember me, don't you? Graham Polterson."

Scraping at memory I turned up the image of a weedy, pimpled youth reading an interminable lecture to a school zoology society.

He fastened on my thoughts and smiled.

"Elephants, wasn't it?" I said.

He nodded. "That's all that anyone remembers about me."

"Ten years is a long time," I said.

He treated me well, lit a fire, lent me shirt and flannels, gave me tea. Over toast and crumpets we talked of our schooldays, of mists on Exmoor, and then of—I forget now just what it was. He was a bit hard to talk to, distant and self-absorbed.

The Cork Elephant

After a long silence of fire-gazing he startled me with, "I've something here might take your fancy. Care to see it?"

Opening a cupboard he brought out a canary cage. He unlocked it and took out a lump of cork, which he held up eagerly for my inspection. I looked at it. What was I meant to say? I looked more closely and saw that it had been roughly hacked—probably with a blunt pocket-knife—into the shape of an elephant. So rough was it I took it for a child's work. Cork isn't much of a medium for a sculptor. It's too shrivelled, like a dried sponge, and it crumbles so easily. I don't think the sculptor had found his job easy; the legs were stubby and uneven, the eyes two holes that might have been scoured out with the point of a screwdriver. The tail—a piece of wire hooked on with a tin-tack—was an admission of defeat.

My bewilderment pleased Graham. He grinned as he placed the elephant on the floor and asked me to kneel beside it. "Now then," he said when I was on all fours, "stroke it."

No, it wasn't a musical box. Too light to carry any weight. I was afraid of knocking it over, so I put out one hand to steady it, intending to stroke it with the other. But he grabbed at the hand as if it were thieving and drew it behind my back. "Use one hand," he said.

I touched the creature, and at once withdrew my hand, shocked.

"Don't be scared. It can't hurt you."

My hand was tingling.

"It's a strange feeling when you're not used to it," he encouraged. "Stroke it gently, like velvet."

Carefully I began to stroke: long, easy strokes. Yes, I could feel it as velvet. Cork was gentler to the touch than it looked. The animal seemed to stand squarely, to brace itself to receive my strokes, even to enjoy them: as a dog enjoys having his back scratched.

"Now touch the ears."

As I felt them, the thick, crumbled roughcast was lost. They became thin and silky as leaves, moved ever so slightly in my fingers and warmed with life. In some mysterious way the

The Cork Elephant

animal had changed. From the awkward legs (shapeless as a workman's corduroys) the back rose to a lovely curved ridge. The tail was tufted, no wire but a continuation of the spine, and it hung weightily, straight as a line. The skin was tight over the frame, loose and baggy in the groin, creased with the numberless creases that make the youngest elephant old. And I remember the smooth, noble brow, the humorous wisdom of the eyes, the huge haunches, and, most wonderful of all, the trunk, with its delicate fernlike curl, sensitive as a man's little finger.

Graham picked a crumb from his plate and offered it. The trunk floated to it, received it, and with a fragile, delicious rhythm curled it into the mouth.

I heard music, dreamy and oriental. (A gramophone? I was too fascinated to notice.) The gentle mastication ceased gradually; there was a swaying and a drifting, and the elephant began to dance. Yes, to dance. The toes lifted, the forefoot nails shone, and the clumsy tree-legs moved heavily to music, with a dragging, underwater movement. And when at last the music and the enchanted motions ended, the whole body slackened, and the elephant, kneeling ponderously, lapsed on to his side and rested.

Graham lifted him back into the cage and covered it with a cloth.

I asked a hundred questions. He answered them with, "I made him myself." And he told me of a cork tree that used to grow in a cottage garden by an estuary, not far away. He had stolen a piece from it to make the elephant. "It was a sight, that tree, and a proper trap for the visitors—they'd pay twopence to see it. But the cottage is empty now. Nobody goes that way. The tree's dead." Then he told me how to go there.

I didn't stay much longer. But before I left I took a final peep at the elephant. When Graham removed the cloth I saw what I had seen at first, no being, but a crude, shrivelled thing of cork. Quite extinct.

The next day was the last of my holiday. I went to the estuary and found the cottage, half-battered and glassless, in a wilderness of nettles. I broke a way through cordons of wild flowers, leaves with prickle teeth, lance thistles, bur marigold waist-high, and

The Cork Elephant

waving hosts of curled dock with helmets bright red. In the middle of all this tangled loveliness was the tree, wasted, horribly scarred, a mockery of death. Just two sprouting leaves I saw, a feeble pretence of life.

I knelt down among the trampled flowers and dug my knife into the bark. It crumbled badly, but I managed to get a fair piece, which I wrapped carefully in my handkerchief.

I took the cork home with me and with a brand new knife carved out a passable copy of the elephant. Then I stroked it.

I have stroked it many times since, but always it topples over unless I steady it with one hand. I've tried all kinds of wire tails, all kinds of tin-tacks. I've given bead eyes to the sockets to find it life. Yes, I've written to Graham, but he doesn't answer.

This morning I cleared my room out, and on my way to meet you I chucked the wretched thing into the wood. You'd have a job to find it.

The Inner Room

ROBERT AICKMAN

It was never less than half an hour after the engine stopped running that my father deigned to signal for succour. If in the process of breaking down, we had climbed, or descended, a bank, then first we must all exhaust ourselves pushing. If we had collided, there was, of course, a row. If, as had happened that day, it was simply that, while we coasted along, the machinery had ceased to churn and rattle, then my father tried his hand as a mechanic. That was the worst contingency of all: at least, it was the worst one connected with motoring.

I had learned by experience that neither rain nor snow made much difference, and certainly not fog; but that afternoon it was hotter than any day I could remember. I realized later that it was the famous long summer of 1921, when the water at the bottom of cottage wells turned salt, and when eels were found baked and edible in their mud. But to know this at the time, I should have had to read the papers, and though, through my mother's devotion, I had the trick of reading before my third birthday, I mostly left the practice to my younger brother, Constantin. He was reading now from a pudgy volume, as thick as it was broad, and resembling his own head in size and proportion. As always, he had resumed his studies immediately the bumping of our almost springless car permitted, and even before motion had ceased. My mother sat in the front seat inevitably correcting pupils' exercises. By teaching her native German in five schools at once, three of them distant, one of them fashionable, she surprisingly managed to maintain the four of us, and even our car. The front offside door of the car leaned dangerously open into the seething highway.

"I say," cried my father.

The young man in the big yellow racer shook his head as he tore by. My father had addressed the least appropriate car on the road.

"I say."

I cannot recall what the next car looked like, but it did not stop.

My father was facing the direction from which we had come, and sawing the air with his left arm, like a very inexperienced policeman. Perhaps no one stopped because all thought him eccentric. Then a car going in the opposite direction came to a standstill behind my father's back. My father perceived nothing. The motorist sounded his horn. In those days horns squealed, and I covered my ears with my hands. Between my hands and my head my long fair hair was like brittle flax in the sun.

My father darted through the traffic. I think it was the Portsmouth Road. The man in the other car got out and came to us. I noticed his companion, much younger and in a cherry-coloured cloche, begin to deal with her nails.

"Broken down?" asked the man. To me it seemed obvious, as the road was strewn with bits of the engine and oozy blobs of oil. Moreover, surely my father had explained?

"I can't quite locate the seat of the trouble," said my father.

The man took off one of his driving gauntlets, big and dirty.

"Catch hold for a moment." My father caught hold.

The man put his hand into the engine and made a casual movement. Something snapped loudly.

"Done right in. If you ask me, I'm not sure she'll ever go again."

"Then I don't think I'll ask you," said my father affably. "Hot, isn't it?" My father began to mop his tall corrugated brow, and front-to-back ridges of grey hair.

"Want a tow?"

"Just to the nearest garage." My father always spoke the word in perfect French.

"Where to?"

The Inner Room

"To the nearest car repair workshop. If it would not be troubling you too much."

"Can't help myself now, can I?"

From under the back seat in the other car, the owner got out a thick, frayed rope, black and greasy as the hangman's. The owner's friend simply said "Pleased to meet you," and began to replace her scalpels and enamels in their cabinet. We jolted towards the town we had traversed an hour or two before; and were then untied outside a garage on the outskirts.

"Surely it is closed for the holiday?" said my mother. Hers is a voice I can always recall upon an instant: guttural of course, but beautiful, truly golden.

"'Spect he'll be back," said our benefactor, drawing in his rope like a fisherman. "Give him a bang." He kicked three times very loudly on the dropped iron shutter. Then without another word he drove away.

It was my birthday, I had been promised the sea, and I began to weep. Constantin, with a fretful little wriggle, closed further into himself and his books; but my mother leaned over the front seat of the car and opened her arms to me. I went to her and sobbed on the shoulder of her bright red dress.

"Kleine Lene, wir stecken schön in der Tinte."

My father, who could pronounce six languages perfectly but speak only one of them, never liked my mother to use her native tongue within the family. He rapped more sharply on the shutter. My mother knew his ways, but, where our welfare was at stake, ignored them.

"Edgar," said my mother, "let us give the children presents. Especially my little Lene." My tears though childish, and less viscous than those shed in later life, had turned the scarlet shoulder of her dress to purple. She squinted smilingly sideways at the damage.

My father was delighted to defer the decision about what next to do with the car. But, as pillage was possible, my mother took with her the exercises, and Constantin his fat little book.

We straggled along the main road, torrid, raucous, adequate

only for a gentler period of history. The grit and dust stung my face and arms and knees, like granulated glass. My mother and I went first, she holding my hand. My father struggled to walk at her other side, but for most of the way, the path was too narrow. Constantin mused along in the rear, abstracted as usual.

"It is true what the papers say," exclaimed my father. "British roads were never built for motor traffic. Beyond the odd car, of course."

My mother nodded and slightly smiled. Even in the lineless hopsacks of the twenties, she could not ever but look magnificent, with her rolling, turbulent honey hair, and Hellenic proportions. Ultimately we reached the High Street. The very first shop had one of its windows stuffed with toys; the other being stacked with groceries and draperies and coal-hods, all dingy. The name "Popular Bazaar", in wooden relief as if glued on in building blocks, stretched across the whole front, not quite centre.

It was not merely an out of fashion shop, but a shop that at the best sold too much of what no one wanted. My father comprehended the contents of the toy department window with a single, anxious glance, and said "Choose whatever you like. Both of you. But look very carefully first. Don't hurry." Then he turned away and began to hum a fragment from *The Lady of the Rose*.

But Constantin spoke at once. "I choose those telegraph wires." They ranged beside a line of tin railway that stretched right across the window, long undusted and tending to buckle. There were seven or eight posts, with six wires on each side of the post. Though I could not think why Constantin wanted them, and though in the event he did not get them, the appearance of them, and of the rusty track beneath them, is all that remains clear in my memory of that window.

"I doubt whether they're for sale," said my father. "Look again. There's a good boy. No hurry."

"They're all I want," said Constantin, and turned his back on the uninspiring display.

"Well, we'll see," said my father. "I'll make a special point of it with the man . . ." He turned to me. "And what about you? Very few dolls, I'm afraid."

The Inner Room

"I don't like dolls any more." As a matter of fact, I had never owned a proper one, although I suffered from this fact only when competing with other girls, which meant very seldom, for our friends were few and occasional. The dolls in the window were flyblown and detestable.

"I think we could find a better shop from which to give Lene a birthday present," said my mother, in her correct, dignified English.

"We must not be unjust," said my father, "when we have not even looked inside."

The inferiority of the goods implied cheapness, which unfortunately always mattered; although, as it happened, none of the articles seemed actually to be priced.

"I do not like this shop," said my mother. "It is a shop that has died."

Her regal manner when she said such things was, I think, too Germanic for my father's Englishness. That, and the prospect of unexpected economy, perhaps led him to be firm.

"We have Constantin's present to consider as well as Lene's. Let us go in."

By contrast with the blazing highway, the main impression of the interior was darkness. After a few moments, I also became aware of a smell. Everything in the shop smelt of that smell, and, one felt, always would do so; the mixed odour of any general store, but at once enhanced and passé. I can smell it now.

"We do not necessarily want to buy anything," said my father, "but, if we may, should like to look round?"

Since the days of Mr Selfridge the proposition is supposed to be taken for granted, but at that time the message had yet to spread. The bazaar-keeper seemed hardly to welcome it. He was younger than I had expected (an unusual thing for a child, but I had probably been awaiting a white-bearded gnome); though pale, nearly bald, and perceptibly grimy. He wore an untidy grey suit and bedroom slippers.

"Look about you, children," said my father. "Take your time. We can't buy presents every day."

I noticed that my mother still stood in the doorway.

"I want those wires," said Constantin.

"Make quite sure by looking at the other things first."

Constantin turned aside bored, his book held behind his back. He began to scrape his feet. It was up to me to uphold my father's position. Rather timidly, I began to peer about, not going far from him. The bazaar-keeper silently watched me with eyes colourless in the twilight.

"Those toy telegraph poles in your window," said my father after a pause, fraught for me with anxiety and responsibility. "How much would you take for them?"

"They are not for sale," said the bazaar-keeper, and said no more.

"Then why do you display them in the window?"

"They are a kind of decoration, I suppose." Did he not know?, I wondered.

"Even if they're not normally for sale, perhaps you'll sell them to me," said my vagabond father, smiling like Rothschild. "My son, you see, has taken a special fancy to them."

"Sorry," said the man in the shop.

"Are you the principal here?"

"I am."

"Then surely as a reasonable man," said my father, switching from superiority to ingratiation——

"They are to dress the window," said the bazaar man. "They are not for sale."

This dialogue entered through the back of my head as, diligently and unobtrudingly, I conned the musty stock. At the back of the shop was a window, curtained all over in grey lace: to judge by the weak light it offered, it gave on to the living quarters. Through this much filtered illumination glimmered the façade of an enormous dolls' house. I wanted it at once. Dolls had never been central to my happiness, but this abode of theirs was the most grown-up thing in the shop.

It had battlements, and long straight walls, and a variety of pointed windows. A gothic revival house, no doubt; or even mansion. It was painted the colour of stone; a grey stone darker than the grey light, which flickered round it. There was a two-leaved front door, with a small classical portico. It was impossible to see the whole house at once, as it stood grimed and neglected on the corner of the wide trestle-shelf. Very slowly I walked along two of the sides; the other two being dark against the walls of the shop. From a first-floor window in the side not immediately visible as one approached, leaned a doll, droopy and unkempt. It was unlike any real house I had seen, and, as for dolls' houses, they were always after the style of the villa near Gerrard's Cross belonging to my father's successful brother. My uncle's house itself looked much more like a toy than this austere structure before me.

"Wake up," said my mother's voice. She was standing just behind me.

"What about some light on the subject?" enquired my father.

A switch clicked.

The house really was magnificent. Obviously, beyond all financial reach.

"Looks like a model for Pentonville Gaol," observed my father.

"It is beautiful," I said. "It's what I want."

"It's the most depressing-looking plaything I ever saw."

"I want to pretend I live in it," I said, "and give masked balls." My social history was eager but indiscriminate.

"How much is it?" asked my mother. The bazaar-keeper stood resentfully in the background, sliding each hand between the thumb and fingers of the other.

"It's only second-hand," he said. "Tenth-hand, more like. A lady brought it in and said she needed to get rid of it. I don't want to sell you something you don't want."

"But suppose we *do* want it?" said my father truculently. "Is nothing in this shop for sale?"

"You can take it away for a quid," said the bazaar-keeper. "And glad to have the space."

"There's someone looking out," said Constantin. He seemed to be assessing the house, like a surveyor or valuer.

"It's full of dolls," said the bazaar-keeper. "They're thrown in. Sure you can transport it?"

The Inner Room

"Not at the moment," said my father, "but I'll send someone down." This, I knew would be Moon the seedman, who owned a large canvas-topped lorry, and with whom my father used to fraternize on the putting green.

"Are you quite sure?" my mother asked me.

"Will it take up too much room?"

My mother shook her head. Indeed, our home, though out of date and out at elbows, was considerably too large for us.

"Then, please."

Poor Constantin got nothing.

Mercifully, all our rooms had wide doors; so that Moon's driver, assisted by the youth out of the shop, lent specially for the purpose, could ease my birthday present to its new resting place, without tilting it or inflicting a wound upon my mother's new and self-applied paint. I noticed that the doll at the first-floor side window had prudently withdrawn. For my house, my parents had allotted me the principal spare room, because in the centre of it stood a very large dinner table, once to be found in the servants' hall of my father's childhood home in Lincolnshire, but now the sole furniture our principal spare room contained. (The two lesser spare rooms were filled with cardboard boxes, which every now and then toppled in heart-arresting avalanches on still summer nights.) On the big table the driver and the shop boy set my house. It reached almost to the sides, so that those passing along the narrow walks would be in peril of tumbling into a gulf; but, the table being much longer than it was wide, the house was provided at front and back with splendid parterres of deal, embrocated with caustic until they glinted like fluorspar.

When I had settled upon the exact site for the house, so that the garden front would receive the sun from the two windows, and a longer parterre stretched at the front than at the back, where the columned entry faced the door of the room, I withdrew to a distant corner while the two males eased the edifice into exact alignment.

"Snug as a bug in a rug," said Moon's driver when the perilous walks at the sides of the house had been made straight and equal.

The Inner Room

"Snugger," said Moon's boy.

I waited for their boots, mailed with crescent slivers of steel, to reach the bottom of our creaking, coconut-matted stair, then I tiptoed to the landing, looked, and listened. The sun had gone in just before the lorry arrived, and down the passage the motes had ceased to dance. It was three o'clock, my mother was still at one of her schools, my father was at the rifle range. I heard the men shut the back door. The principal spare room had never before been occupied, so that the key was outside. In a second, I transferred it to the inside, and shut and locked myself in.

As before in the shop, I walked slowly round my house, but this time round all four sides of it. Then, with the knuckles of my thin white forefinger, I tapped gently at the front door. It seemed not to have been secured, because it opened, both leaves of it, as I touched it. I pried in, first with one eye, then with the other. The lights from various of the pointed windows blotched the walls and floor of the miniature entrance hall. None of the dolls was visible.

It was not one of those dolls' houses of commerce from which sides can be lifted in their entirety. To learn about my house, it would be necessary, albeit impolite, to stare through the windows, one at a time. I decided first to take the ground floor. I started in a clockwise direction from the front portico. The front door was still open, but I could not see how to shut it from the outside.

There was a room to the right of the hall, leading into two other rooms along the right side of the house, of which, again, one led into the other. All the rooms were decorated and furnished in a Mrs Fitzherbert-ish style; with handsomely striped wallpapers, botanical carpets, and chairs with legs like sticks of brittle golden sweetmeat. There were a number of pictures. I knew just what they were: family portraits. I named the room next the hall, the occasional room, and the room beyond it, the morning room. The third room was very small: striking out confidently, I named it the Canton Cabinet, although it contained neither porcelain nor fans. I knew what the rooms in a great house should be called, because my mother used to show

The Inner Room

me the pictures in large, once fashionable volumes on the subject which my father had bought for their bulk at junk shops.

Then came the long drawing room, which stretched across the entire garden front of the house, and contained the principal concourse of dolls. It had four pointed French windows, all made to open, though now sealed with dust and rust; above which were bulbous triangles of coloured glass, in tiny snowflake panes. The apartment itself played at being a cloister in a Horace Walpole convent; lierne vaulting ramified across the arched ceiling, and the spidery Gothic pilasters were tricked out in medieval patchwork, as in a Puseyite church. On the stout golden wallpaper were decent Swiss pastels of indeterminate subjects. There was a grand piano, very black, scrolly, and, no doubt, resounding; four shapely chandeliers; a baronial fireplace with a mythical blazon above the mantel; and eight dolls, all of them female, dotted about on chairs and ottomans with their backs to me. I hardly dared to breathe as I regarded their woolly heads, and noted the colours of their hair: two black, two nondescript, one grey, one a discoloured silver beneath the dust, one blonde, and one a dyed-looking red. They wore woollen Victorian clothes, of a period later, I should say, than that when the house was built, and certainly too warm for the present season; in varied colours, all of them dull. Happy people, I felt even then, would not wear these variants of rust, indigo, and greenwood.

I crept onwards; to the dining-room. It occupied half its side of the house, and was dark and oppressive. Perhaps it might look more inviting when the chandelier blazed, and the table candles, each with a tiny purple shade, were lighted. There was no cloth on the table, and no food or drink. Over the fireplace was a big portrait of a furious old man: his white hair was a spiky aureole round his distorted face, beetroot-red with rage; the mouth was open, and even the heavy lips were drawn back to show the savage, strong teeth; he was brandishing a very thick walking stick which seemed to leap from the picture and stun the beholder. He was dressed neutrally, and the painter had not provided him with a background: there was only the aggressive figure menacing the room. I was frightened.

The Inner Room

Two rooms on the ground floor remained before I once more reached the front door. In the first of them a lady was writing with her back to the light and therefore to me. She frightened me also; because her grey hair was disordered and of uneven length, and descended in matted plaits, like snakes escaping from a basket, to the shoulders of her coarse grey dress. Of course, being a doll, she did not move, but the back of her head looked mad. Her presence prevented me from regarding at all closely the furnishings of the writing room.

Back at the north front as I resolved to call it, perhaps superseding the compass rather than leading it, there was a cold-looking room, with a carpetless stone floor and white walls, upon which were the mounted heads and horns of many animals. They were all the room contained, but they covered the walls from floor to ceiling. I felt sure that the ferocious old man in the dining-room had killed all these creatures, and I hated him for it. But I knew what the room would be called: it would be the trophy room.

Then I realized that there was no kitchen. It could hardly be upstairs. I had never heard of such a thing. But I looked.

It wasn't there. All the rooms on the first floor were bedrooms. There were six of them, and they so resembled one another, all with dark ochreous wallpaper and narrow brass bedsteads corroded with neglect, that I found it impracticable to distinguish them other than by numbers, at least for the present. Ultimately I might know the house better. Bedrooms 2, 3 and 6 contained two beds each. I recalled that at least nine people lived in the house. In one room the dark walls, the dark floor, the bed linen, and even the glass in the window were splashed, smeared, and further darkened with ink: it seemed apparent who slept there.

I sat on an orange box and looked. My house needed painting and dusting and scrubbing and polishing and renewing; but on the whole I was relieved that things were not worse. I had felt that the house had stood in the dark corner of the shop for no one knew how long, but this, I now saw, could hardly have been true. I wondered about the lady who had needed to get rid of it.

The Inner Room

Despite that need, she must have kept things up pretty thoroughly. How did she do it? How did she get in? I resolved to ask my mother's advice. I determined to be a good landlord, although, like most who so resolve, my resources were nil. We simply lacked the money to regild my long drawing room in proper gold leaf. But I would bring life to the nine dolls now drooping with boredom and neglect . . .

Then I recalled something. What had become of the doll who had been sagging from the window? I thought she must have been jolted out, and felt myself a murderess. But none of the windows was open. The sash might easily have descended with the shaking; but more probably the poor doll lay inside on the floor of her room. I again went round from room to room, this time on tiptoe, but it was impossible to see the areas of floor just below the dark windows. . . . It was not merely sunless outside, but heavily overcast. I unlocked the door of our principal spare room, and descended pensively to await my mother's return and tea.

Wormwood Grange, my father called my house, with penological associations still on his mind. (After he was run over, I realized for the first time that there might be a reason for this, and for his inability to find work worthy of him.) My mother had made the most careful inspection on my behalf, but had been unable to suggest any way of making an entry, or at least of passing beyond the hall, to which the front doors still lay open. There seemed no question of whole walls lifting off, of the roof being removable, or even of a window being opened, including, mysteriously, on the first floor.

"I don't think it's meant for children, Liebchen," said my mother, smiling her lovely smile. "We shall have to consult the Victoria and Albert Museum."

"Of course it's not meant for children," I replied. "That's why I wanted it. I'm going to receive, like La Belle Otero."

Next morning, after my mother had gone to work, my father came up, and wrenched and prodded with his unskilful hands.

"I'll get a chisel," he said. "We'll prise it open at each corner, and when we've got the fronts off, I'll go over to Woolworth's and buy some hinges and screws. I expect they'll have some."

At that I struck my father in the chest with my fist. He seized my wrists, and I screamed that he was not to lay a finger on my beautiful house, that he would be sure to spoil it, that force never got anyone anywhere. I knew my father: when he took an idea for using tools into his head, the only hope for one's property lay in a scene, and in the implication of tears without end in the future, if the idea were not dropped.

While I was screaming and raving, Constantin appeared from the room below, where he worked at his books.

"Give us a chance, Sis," he said. "How can I keep it all in my head about the Thirty Years' War when you haven't learnt to control your tantrums?"

Although two years younger than I, Constantin should have known that I was past the age for screaming except of set purpose.

"You wait until he tries to rebind all your books, you silly sneak," I yelled at him.

My father released my wrists.

"Wormwood Grange can keep," he said. "I'll think of something else to go over to Woolworth's for." He sauntered off.

Constantin nodded gravely. "I understand," he said. "I understand what you mean. I'll go back to my work. Here, try this." He gave me a small, chipped nail file.

I spent most of the morning fiddling very cautiously with the imperfect jemmy, and trying to make up my mind about the doll at the window.

I failed to get into my house and I refused to let my parents give me any effective aid. Perhaps by now I did not really want to get in, although the dirt and disrepair, and the apathy of the dolls, who so badly needed plumping up and dispersing, continued to cause me distress. Certainly I spent as long trying to shut the front door as trying to open a window or find a concealed spring (that idea was Constantin's). In the end I wedged the two halves of the front door with two halves of match; but I felt that the arrangement was make-shift and undignified. I refused everyone access to the principal spare room until something more appropriate could be evolved. My plans for routs and orgies had to be deferred: one could hardly riot among dust and cobwebs.

Then I began to have dreams about my house, and about its occupants.

One of the oddest dreams was the first. It was three or four days after I entered into possession. During that time it had remained cloudy and oppressive, so that my father took to leaving off his knitted waistcoat; then suddenly it thundered. It was long, slow, distant, intermittent thunder; and it continued all the evening, until, when it was quite dark, my bedtime and Constantin's could no longer be deferred.

"Your ears will get accustomed to the noise," said my father. "Just try to take no notice of it."

Constantin looked dubious; but I was tired of the slow, rumbling hours, and ready for the different dimensions of dreams.

I slept almost immediately, although the thunder was rolling round my big, rather empty bedroom, round the four walls, across the floor, and under the ceiling, weighting the black air as with a smoky vapour. Occasionally, the lightning glinted, pink and green. It was still the long-drawn-out preliminary to a storm; the tedious, imperfect dispersal of the accumulated energy of the summer. The rollings and rumblings entered my dreams, which flickered, changed, were gone as soon as come, failed, like the lightning, to concentrate or strike home, were as difficult to profit by as the events of an average day.

After exhausting hours of phantasmagoria, anticipating so many later nights in my life, I found myself in a black wood with huge, dense trees. I was following a path, but reeled from tree to tree, bruising and cutting myself on their hardness and roughness. There seemed no end to the wood or to the night; but suddenly, in the thick of both, I came upon my house. It stood solid, immense, hemmed in, with a single light, little more, it seemed, than a night-light, burning in every upstairs window (as often in dreams, I could see all four sides of the house at once), and illuminating two wooden wedges, jagged and swollen, which held tight the front doors. The vast trees dipped and swayed their elephantine boughs over the roof; the wind peeked and creaked through the black battlements. Then there was a blaze of whitest lightning, proclaiming the storm itself. In the second it endured, I saw my two wedges fly through the air, and the double front door burst open.

For the hundredth time, the scene changed, and now I was back in my room, though still asleep or half asleep, still dragged from vision to vision. Now the thunder was coming in immense, calculated bombardments; the lightning ceaseless and searing the face of the earth. From being a weariness the storm had become an ecstasy. It seemed as if the whole world would be in dissolution before the thunder had spent its impersonal, unregarding strength. But, as I say, I must still have been at least half asleep, because between the fortissimi and the lustre I still from time to time saw scenes, meaningless or nightmarish, which could not be found in the wakeful world; still, between and through the volleys, heard impossible sounds.

I do not know whether I was asleep or awake when the storm rippled into tranquillity. I certainly did not feel that the air had been cleared; but this may have been because, surprisingly, I heard a quick soft step passing along the passage outside my room, a passage uncarpeted through our poverty. I well knew all the footsteps in the house, and this was none of them.

Always one to meet trouble half-way, I dashed in my nightgown to open the door. I looked out. The dawn was seeping, without effort or momentum, through every cranny, and showed shadowy the back of a retreating figure, the size of my mother but with woolly red hair and long rust-coloured dress. The padding feet seemed actually to start soft echoes amid all that naked woodwork. I had no need to consider who she was or whither she was bound. I burst into the purposeless tears I so despised.

In the morning, and before deciding upon what to impart, I took Constantin with me to look at the house. I more than half expected big changes; but none was to be seen. The sections of match-sticks were still in position, and the dolls as inactive and diminutive as ever, sitting with their backs to me on chairs and sofas in the long drawing room; their hair dusty, possibly even mothy. Constantin looked at me curiously, but I imparted nothing.

Other dreams followed; though at considerable intervals. Many children have recurring nightmares of oppressive realism and terrifying content; and I realized from past experience that I must outgrow the habit or lose my house—my house at least. It is true that my house now frightened me, but I felt that I must not be foolish and should strive to take a grown-up view of painted woodwork and nine understuffed dolls. Still it was bad when I began to hear them in the darkness; some tapping, some stumping, some creeping, and therefore not one, but many, or all; and worse when I began not to sleep for fear of the mad doll (as I was sure she was) doing something mad, although I refused to think what. I never dared again to look; but when something happened, which, as I say, was only at intervals (and to me, being young, they seemed long intervals), I lay taut and straining among the forgotten sheets. Moreover, the steps themselves were never quite constant, certainly too inconstant to report to others; and I am not sure that I should have heard anything significant if I had not once seen. But now I locked the door of our principal spare room on the outside, and altogether ceased to visit my beautiful, impregnable mansion.

I noticed that my mother made no comment. But one day my father complained of my ingratitude in never playing with my handsome birthday present. I said I was occupied with my holiday task: *Moby Dick*. This was an approved answer, and even, as far as it went, a true one, though I found the book pointless in the extreme, and horribly cruel.

"I told you the Grange was the wrong thing to buy," said my father. "Morbid sort of object for a toy."

"None of us can learn except by experience," said my mother.

My father said "Not at all," and bristled.

All this, naturally, was in the holidays. I was going at the time to one of my mother's schools, where I should stay until I could begin to train as a dancer, upon which I was conventionally but entirely resolved. Constantin went to another, a highly cerebral co-educational place, where he would remain until, inevitably, he won a scholarship to a university, perhaps a foreign one. Despite our years, we went our different ways dangerously on small dingy bicycles. We reached home at assorted hours, mine being the longer journey.

One day I returned to find our dining-room table littered with peculiarly uninteresting printed drawings. I could make nothing of them whatever (they did not seem even to belong to the kind of geometry I was—regretfully—used to); and they curled up on themselves when one tried to examine them, and bit one's finger. My father had a week or two before taken one of his infrequent jobs; night work of some kind a long way off, to which he had now departed in our car. Obviously the drawings were connected with Constantin, but he was not there.

I went upstairs, and saw that the principal spare room door was open. Constantin was inside. There had of course been no question of the key to the room being removed. It was only necessary to turn it.

"Hallo, Lene," Constantin said in his matter-of-fact way. "We've been doing axonometric projection, and I'm projecting your house." He was making one of the drawings; on a sheet of thick white paper. "It's for home-work. It'll knock out all the others. They've got to do their real houses."

It must not be supposed that I did not like Constantin, although often he annoyed me with his placidity and precision. It was weeks since I had seen my house, and it looked unexpectedly interesting. A curious thing happened: nor was it the last time in my life that I experienced it. Temporarily I became a different person; confident, practical, simple. The clear evening sun of autumn may have contributed.

"I'll help," I said. "Tell me what to do."

"It's a bore I can't get in to take measurements. Although we haven't *got* to. In fact, the Clot told us not. Just a general impression, he said. It's to give us the *concept* of axonometry. But, golly, it would be simpler with feet and inches."

To judge by the amount of white paper he had covered in what could only have been a short time, Constantin seemed to me to be doing very well, but he was one never to be content with less than perfection.

"Tell me," I said, "what to do, and I'll do it."

"Thanks," he replied, sharpening his pencil with a special instrument. "But it's a one-man job this. In the nature of the case. Later, I'll show you how to do it, and you can do some other building if you like."

I remained, looking at my house and fingering it, until Constantin made it clearer that I was a distraction. I went away, changed my shoes, and put on the kettle against my mother's arrival, and our high tea.

When Constantin came down (my mother had called for him three times, but that was not unusual), he said, "I say Sis, here's a rum thing."

My mother said: "Don't use slang, and don't call your sister Sis."

He said, as he always did when reproved by her, "I'm sorry, Mother." Then he thrust the drawing paper at me. "Look, there's a bit missing. See what I mean?" He was showing me with his stub of emerald pencil, pocked with toothmarks.

Of course, I didn't see. I didn't understand a thing about it.

"After tea," said my mother. She gave to such familiar words not a maternal but an imperial decisiveness.

"But Mum——" pleaded Constantin.

"Mother," said my mother.

Constantin started dipping for sauerkraut.

Silently we ate ourselves into tranquillity; or, for me, into the appearance of it. My alternative personality, though it had survived Constantin's refusal of my assistance, was now beginning to ebb.

"What is all this that you are doing?" enquired my mother in the end. "It resembles the Stone of Rosetta."

"I'm taking an axonometric cast of Lene's birthday house."

"And so?"

But Constantin was not now going to expound immediately.

The Inner Room

He put in his mouth a finger of rye bread smeared with homemade cheese. Then he said quietly: "I got down a rough idea of the house, but the rooms don't fit. At least, they don't on the bottom floor. It's all right, I think, on the top floor. In fact that's the rummest thing of all. Sorry Mother." He had been speaking with his mouth full, and now filled it fuller.

"What nonsense is this?" To me it seemed that my mother was glaring at him in a way most unlike her.

"It's not nonsense, Mother. Of course I haven't measured the place, because you can't. But I haven't done axonometry for nothing. There's a part of the bottom floor I can't get at. A secret room or something."

"Show me."

"Very well, Mother." Constantin put down his remnant of bread and cheese. He rose, looking a little pale. He took the drawing round the table to my mother.

"Not that thing. I can't understand it, and I don't believe you can understand it either." Only sometimes to my father did my mother speak like that. "Show me in the house."

I rose too.

"You stay here, Lene. Put some more water in the kettle and boil it."

"But it's my house. I have a right to know."

My mother's expression changed to one more familiar. "Yes, Lene," she said, "you have a right. But please not now. I ask you."

I smiled at her and picked up the kettle.

"Come, Constantin."

I lingered by the kettle in the kitchen, not wishing to give an impression of eavesdropping or even undue eagerness, which I knew would distress my mother. I never wished to learn things that my mother wished to keep from me; and I never questioned her implication of "All in good time."

But they were not gone long, for well before the kettle had begun even to grunt, my mother's beautiful voice was summoning me back.

"Constantin is quite right," she said, when I had presented

myself at the dining-room table, "and it was wrong of me to doubt it. The house is built in a funny sort of way. But what does it matter?"

Constantin was not eating.

"I am glad that you are studying well, and learning such useful things," said my mother.

She wished the subject to be dropped, and we dropped it.

Indeed, it was difficult to think what more could be said. But I waited for a moment in which I was alone with Constantin. My father's unhabitual absence made this difficult and it was completely dark before the moment came.

And when, as was only to be expected, Constantin had nothing to add, I felt, most unreasonably, that he was joined with my mother in keeping something from me.

"But what *happened*?" I pressed him. "What happened when you were in the room with her?"

"What do you think happened?" replied Constantin, wishing, I thought, that my mother would re-enter. "Mother realized that I was right. Nothing more. What does it matter anyway?"

That final query confirmed my doubts.

"Constantin," I said. "Is there anything I ought to do?"

"Better hack the place open," he answered, almost irritably.

But a most unexpected thing happened, that, had I even considered adopting Constantin's idea, would have saved me the trouble. When next day I returned from school, my house was gone.

Constantin was sitting in his usual corner, this time absorbing Greek paradigms. Without speaking to him (nothing unusual in that when he was working), I went straight to the principal spare room. The vast deal table, less scrubbed than once, was bare. The place where my house had stood was very visible, as if indeed a palace had been swept off by a djinn. But I could see no other sign of its passing: no scratched woodwork, or marks of boots, or disjointed fragments.

Constantin seemed genuinely astonished at the news. But I doubted him.

"You knew," I said.
"Of course I didn't know."
Still, he understood what I was thinking.
He said again: "I didn't know."
Unlike me on occasion he always spoke the truth.
I gathered myself together and blurted out: "Have they done it themselves?" Inevitably I was frightened, but in a way I was also relieved.
"Who do you mean?"
"They."
I was inviting ridicule, but Constantin was kind.
He said: "I know who I think has done it, but you mustn't let on. I think Mother's done it."
I did not enquire uselessly into how much more he knew than I. I said: "But *how*?"
Constantin shrugged. It was a habit he had assimilated with so much else.
"Mother left the house with us this morning and she isn't back yet."
"She must have put Father up to it."
"But there are no marks."
"Father might have got help." There was a pause. Then Constantin said: "Are you sorry?"
"In a way," I replied. Constantin with precocious wisdom left it at that.
When my mother returned, she simply said that my father had already lost his new job, so that we had had to sell things.
"I hope you will forgive your father and me," she said. "We've had to sell one of my watches also. Father will soon be back to tea."
She too was one I had never known to lie; but now I began to perceive how relative and instrumental truth could be.

I need not say: not in those terms. Such clear concepts, with all they offer of gain and loss, come later, if they come at all. In fact, I need not say that the whole of what goes before is so heavily filtered through later experience as to be of little evidential value.

The Inner Room

But I am scarcely putting forward evidence. There is so little. All I can do is to tell something of what happened, as it now seems to me to have been.

I remember sulking at my mother's news, and her explaining to me that really I no longer liked the house and that something better would be bought for me in replacement when our funds permitted.

I did ask my father when he returned to our evening meal, whistling and falsely jaunty about the lost job, how much he had been paid for my house.

"A trifle more than I gave for it. That's only business."

"Where is it now?"

"Never you mind."

"Tell her," said Constantin. "She wants to know."

"Eat your herring," said my father very sharply. "And mind your own business."

And, thus, before long my house was forgotten, my occasional nightmares returned to earlier themes.

It was, as I say, for two or three months in 1921 that I owned the house and from time to time dreamed that creatures I supposed to be its occupants, had somehow invaded my home. The next thirty years, more or less, can be disposed of quickly: it was the period when I tried conclusions with the outer world.

I really became a dancer; and, although the upper reaches alike of the art and of the profession notably eluded me, yet I managed to maintain myself for several years, no small achievement. I retired, as they say, upon marriage. My husband aroused physical passion in me for the first time, but diminished and deadened much else. He was reported missing in the late misguided war. Certainly he did not return to me. I at least still miss him, though I often despise myself for doing so.

My father died in a street accident when I was fifteen: it happened on the day I received a special commendation from the sallow Frenchman who taught me to dance. After his death my beloved mother always wanted to return to Germany.

The Inner Room

Before long I was spiritually self-sufficient enough, or said I was to make that possible. Unfailingly, she wrote to me twice a week, although to find words in which to reply was often difficult for me. Sometimes I visited her, while the conditions in her country became more and more uncongenial to me. She had a fair position teaching English language and literature at a small university; and she seemed increasingly to be infected by the new notions and emotions raging around her. I must acknowledge that sometimes their tumult and intoxication unsteadied my own mental gait, although I was a foreigner and by no means of sanguine temperament. It is a mistake to think that all professional dancers are gay.

Despite what appeared to be increasing sympathies with the new régime, my mother disappeared. She was the first of the two people who mattered to me in such very different ways, and who so unreasonably vanished. For a time I was ill, and of course I love her still more than anybody. If she had remained with me, I am sure I should never have married. Without involving myself in psychology, which I detest, I shall simply say that the thought and recollection of my mother, lay, I believe, behind the self-absorption my husband complained of so bitterly and so justly. It was not really myself in which I was absorbed but the memory of perfection. It is the plain truth that such beauty, and goodness, and depth, and capacity for love were my mother's alone.

Constantin abandoned all his versatile reading and became a priest, in fact a member of the Society of Jesus. He seems exalted (possibly too much so for his colleagues and superiors), but I can no longer speak to him or bear his presence. He frightens me. Poor Constantin!

On the other hand, I, always dubious, have become a complete unbeliever. I cannot see that Constantin is doing anything but listen to his own inner voice (which has changed its tone since we were children); and mine speaks a different language. In the long run, I doubt whether there is much to be desired but death; or whether there is endurance in anything but suffering. I no longer see myself feasting crowned heads on quails.

The Inner Room

So much for biographical intermission. I proceed to the circumstances of my second and recent experience of landlordism.

In the first place, I did something thoroughly stupid. Instead of following the road marked on the map, I took a short cut. It is true that the short cut was shown on the map also, but the region was much too unfrequented for a wandering footpath to be in any way dependable, especially in this generation which has ceased to walk beyond the garage or the bus stop. It was one of the least populated districts in the whole country and, moreover, the slow autumn dusk was already perceptible when I pushed at the first, dilapidated gate.

To begin with, the path trickled and flickered across a sequence of small damp meadows, bearing neither cattle nor crop. When it came to the third or fourth of these meadows, the way had all but vanished in the increasing sogginess, and could be continued only by looking for the stile or gate in the unkempt hedge ahead. This was not especially difficult as long as the fields remained small; but after a time I reached a depressing expanse which could hardly be termed a field at all, but was rather a large marsh. It was at this point that I should have returned and set about tramping the winding road.

But a path of some kind again continued before me, and I perceived that the escapade had already consumed twenty minutes. So I risked it, although soon I was striding laboriously from tussock to brown tussock in order not to sink above my shoes into the surrounding quagmire. It is quite extraordinary how far one can stray from a straight or determined course when thus preoccupied with elementary comfort. The hedge on the far side of the marsh was still a long way ahead, and the tussocks themselves were becoming both less frequent and less dense, so that too often I was sinking through them into the mire. I realized that the marsh sloped slightly downwards in the direction I was following, so that before I reached the hedge, I might have to cross a river. In the event, it was not so much a river, as an indeterminately bounded augmentation of the softness, and moistness, and ooziness: I struggled across, jerking from false foothold to palpable pitfall, and before long despairing even of the attempt to step securely. Both my feet were now soaked to well above the ankles, and the visibility had become less than was entirely convenient.

When I reached what I had taken for a hedge, it proved to be the boundary of an extensive thicket. Autumn had infected much of the greenery with blotched and dropping senility; so that bare brown briars arched and tousled, and purple thorns tilted at all possible angles for blood. To go farther would demand an axe. Either I must retraverse the dreary bog in the perceptibly waning light, or I must skirt the edge and seek an opening in the thicket. Undecided, I looked back. I realized that I had lost the gate through which I had entered upon the marsh on the other side. There was nothing to do but creep as best I could upon the still treacherous ground along the barrier of dead dog-roses, mildewed blackberries, and rampant nettles.

But it was not long before I reached a considerable gap, from which through the tangled vegetation seemed to lead a substantial track, although by no means a straight one. The track wound on unimpeded for a considerable distance, even becoming firmer underfoot; until I realized that the thicket had become an entirely indisputable wood. The brambles clutching maliciously from the sides had become watching branches above my head. I could not recall that the map had showed a wood. If, indeed, it had done so, I should not have entered upon the footpath, because the only previous occasion in my life when I had been truly lost, in the sense of being unable to find the way back as well as being unable to go on, had been when my father had once so effectively lost us in a wood that I have never again felt the same about woods. The fear I had felt for perhaps an hour and a half on that occasion, though told to no one, and swiftly evaporating from consciousness upon our emergence, had been the veritable fear of death. Now I drew the map from where it lay against my thigh in the big pocket of my dress. It was not until I tried to read it that I realized how near I was to night. Until it came to print, the problems of the route had given me cat's eyes.

The Inner Room

I peered, and there was no wood, no green patch on the map, but only the wavering line of dots advancing across contoured whiteness to the neck of yellow road where the short cut ended. But I did not reach any foolish conclusion. I simply guessed that I had strayed very badly: the map was spattered with green marks in places where I had no wish to be; and the only question was in which of these many thickets I now was. I could think of no way to find out. I was nearly lost, and this time I could not blame my father.

The track I had been following still stretched ahead, as yet not too indistinct; and I continued to follow it. As the trees around me became yet bigger and thicker, fear came upon me; though not the death fear of that previous occasion, I felt now that I knew what was going to happen next; or, rather, I felt I knew one thing that was going to happen next, a thing which was but a small and far from central part of an obscure, inapprehensible totality. As one does on such occasions, I felt more than half outside my body. If I continued much farther, I might change into somebody else.

But what happened was not what I expected. Suddenly I saw a flicker of light. It seemed to emerge from the left, to weave momentarily among the trees, and to disappear to the right. It was not what I expected, but it was scarcely reassuring. I wondered if it could be a will o' the wisp, a thing I had never seen, but which I understood to be connected with marshes. Next a still more prosaic possibility occurred to me, one positively hopeful: the headlight of a motor-car turning a corner. It seemed the likely answer, but my uneasiness did not perceptibly diminish.

I struggled on, and the light came again: a little stronger, and twisting through the trees around me. Of course another car at the same corner of the road was not an impossibility, even though it was an unpeopled area. Then, after a period of soft but not comforting dusk, it came a third time; and, soon, a fourth. There was no sound of an engine: and it seemed to me that the transit of the light was too swift and fleeting for any car.

And then what I had been awaiting, happened. I came suddenly upon a huge square house. I had known it was coming, but still it struck at my heart.

It is not every day that one finds a dream come true; and, scared though I was, I noticed details: for example, that there did not seem to be those single lights burning in every upstairs window. Doubtless dreams, like poems, demand a certain licence; and, for the matter of that, I could not see all four sides of the house at once, as I had dreamed I had. But that perhaps was the worst of it: I was plainly not dreaming now.

A sudden greeny-pink radiance illuminated around me a morass of weed and neglect; and then seemed to hide itself among the trees on my right. The explanation of the darting lights was that a storm approached. But it was unlike other lightning I had encountered: being slower, more silent, more regular.

There seemed nothing to do but run away, though even then it seemed sensible not to run back into the wood. In the last memories of daylight, I began to wade through the dead knee-high grass of the lost lawn. It was still possible to see that the wood continued, opaque as ever, in a long line to my left; I felt my way along it, in order to keep as far as possible from the house. I noticed, as I passed, the great portico, facing the direction from which I had emerged. Then, keeping my distance, I crept along the grey east front with its two tiers of pointed windows, all shut and one or two broken; and reached the southern parterre, visibly vaster, even in the storm-charged gloom, than the northern, but no less ravaged. Ahead, and at the side of the parterre far off to my right, ranged the encircling woodland. If no path manifested, my state would be hazardous indeed; and there seemed little reason for a path, as the approach to the house was provided by that along which I had come from the marsh.

As I struggled onwards, the whole scene was transformed: in a moment the sky became charged with roaring thunder, the earth with tumultuous rain. I tried to shelter in the adjacent wood, but instantly found myself enmeshed in vines and suckers, lacerated by invisible spears. In a minute I should be drenched.

The Inner Room

I plunged through the wet weeds towards the spreading portico. Before the big doors I waited for several minutes, watching the lightning, and listening. The rain leapt up where it fell, as if the earth hurt it. A rising chill made the old grass shiver. It seemed unlikely that anyone could live in a house so dark; but suddenly I heard one of the doors behind me scrape open. I turned. A dark head protruded between the portals, like Punch from the side of his booth.

"Oh." The shrill voice was of course surprised.

I turned. "May I please wait until the rain stops?"

"You can't come inside."

I drew back; so far back that a heavy drip fell on the back of my neck from the edge of the portico. With absurd melodrama, there was a loud roll of thunder.

"I shouldn't think of it," I said. "I must be on my way the moment the rain lets me." I could still see only the round head sticking out between the leaves of the door.

"In the old days we often had visitors." This statement was made in the tone of a Cheltenham lady remarking that when a child she often spoke to gypsies. "I only peeped out to see the thunder."

Now, within the house, I heard another, lower voice, although I could not hear what it said. Through the long crack between the doors, a light slid out across the flagstones of the porch and down the darkening steps.

"She's waiting for the rain to stop," said the shrill voice.

"Tell her to come in," said the deep voice. "Really, Emerald, you forget your manners after all this time."

"I *have* told her," said Emerald very petulantly, and withdrawing her head. "She won't do it."

"Nonsense," said the other. "You're always telling lies." I got the idea that thus she always spoke to Emerald.

Then the doors opened, and I could see the two of them silhouetted in the light of a lamp which stood on a table behind them; one much the taller, but both with round heads, and both wearing long, unshapely garments. I wanted very much to escape, and failed to do so only because there seemed nowhere to go.

The Inner Room

"Please come in at once," said the taller figure, "and let us take off your wet clothes."

"Yes, yes," squeaked Emerald, unreasonably jubilant.

"Thank you. But my clothes are not at all wet."

"None the less, please come in. We shall take it as a discourtesy if you refuse."

Another roar of thunder emphasized the impracticability of continuing to refuse much longer. If this was a dream, doubtless, and to judge by experience, I should awake.

And a dream it must be, because there at the front door were two big wooden wedges; and there to the right of the hall, shadowed in the lamplight, was the trophy room; although now the animal heads on the walls were shoddy, fungoid ruins, their sawdust spilled and clotted on the cracked and uneven flagstones of the floor.

"You must forgive us," said my tall hostess. "Our landlord neglects us sadly, and we are far gone in wrack and ruin. In fact I do not know what we should do were it not for our own resources." At this Emerald cackled. Then she came up to me, and began fingering my clothes.

The tall one shut the door.

"Don't touch," she shouted at Emerald, in her deep, rather grinding voice. "Keep your fingers off."

She picked up the large oil lamp. Her hair was a discoloured white in its beams.

"I apologize for my sister," she said. "We have all been so neglected that some of us have quite forgotten how to behave. Come, Emerald."

Pushing Emerald before her, she led the way.

In the occasional room and the morning room, the gilt had flaked from the gingerbread furniture, the family portraits started from their heavy frames, and the striped wallpaper drooped in the lamplight like an assembly of sodden, half-inflated balloons.

At the door of the Canton Cabinet, my hostess turned. "I am taking you to meet my sisters," she said.

"I look forward to doing so," I replied, regardless of truth, as in childhood.

The Inner Room

She nodded slightly, and proceeded. "Take care," she said. "The floor has weak places."

In the little Canton Cabinet, the floor had, in fact, largely given way, and been plainly converted into a hospice for rats. And then, there they all were, the remaining six of them, thinly illumined by what must surely be rushlights in the four shapely chandeliers. But now, of course, I could see their faces.

"We are all named after our birthstones," said my hostess. "Emerald you know. I am Opal. Here are Diamond and Garnet, Cornelian and Chrysolite. The one with the grey hair is Sardonyx, and the beautiful one is Turquoise."

They all stood up. During the ceremony of introduction, they made odd little noises.

"Emerald and I are the eldest, and Turquoise of course is the youngest."

Emerald stood in the corner before me, rolling her dyed red head. The long drawing room was raddled with decay. The cobwebs gleamed like steel filigree in the beam of the lamp, and the sisters seemed to have been seated in cocoons of them, like cushions of gossamer.

"There is one other sister, Topaz. But she is busy writing."

"Writing all our diaries," said Emerald.

"Keeping the record," said my hostess.

A silence followed.

"Let us sit down," said my hostess. "Let us make our visitor welcome."

The six of them gently creaked and subsided into their former places. Emerald and my hostess remained standing.

"Sit down, Emerald. Our visitor shall have *my* chair as it is the best." I realized that inevitably there was no extra seat.

"Of course not," I said. "I can only stay for a minute. I am waiting for the rain to stop," I explained feebly to the rest of them.

"I insist," said my hostess.

I looked at the chair to which she was pointing. The padding was burst and rotten, the woodwork bleached and crumbling to collapse. All of them were watching me with round, vague eyes in their flat faces.

The Inner Room

"Really," I said, "no, thank you. It's kind of you, but I must go." All the same, the surrounding wood, and the dark marsh beyond it loomed scarcely less appalling than the house itself and its inmates.

"We should have more to offer, more and better in every way, were it not for our landlord." She spoke with bitterness, and it seemed to me that on all the faces the expression changed. Emerald came towards me out of her corner, and again began to finger my clothes. But this time her sister did not correct her; and when I stepped away, she stepped after me and went on as before.

"She has failed in the barest duty of sustenation."

I could not prevent myself starting at the pronoun. At once, Emerald caught hold of my dress, and held it tightly.

"But there is one place she cannot spoil for us. One place where we can entertain in our own way."

"Please," I cried. "Nothing more. I am going now."

Emerald's pygmy grip tautened.

"It is the room where we eat."

All the watching eyes lighted up, and became something they had not been before.

"I may almost say where we feast."

The six of them began again to rise from their spidery bowers.

"Because *she* cannot go there."

The sisters clapped their hands, like a rustle of leaves.

"There we can be what we really are."

The eight of them were now grouped round me. I noticed that the one pointed out as the youngest was passing her dry, pointed tongue over her lower lip.

"Nothing unladylike, of course."

"Of course not," I agreed.

"But firm," broke in Emerald, dragging at my dress as she spoke. "Father said that must always come first."

"Our father was a man of measureless wrath against a slight," said my hostess. "It is his continuing presence about the house which largely upholds us."

"Shall I show her?" said Emerald.

"Since you wish to," said her sister disdainfully.

From somewhere in her musty garments Emerald produced a scrap of card, which she held out to me.

"Take it in your hand. I'll allow you to hold it."

It was a photograph, obscurely damaged.

"Hold up the lamp," squealed Emerald. With an aloof gesture her sister raised it.

It was a photograph of myself when a child, bobbed and waistless. And through my heart was a tiny brown needle.

"We've all got things like it," said Emerald jubilantly. "Wouldn't you think her heart would have rusted away by now?"

"She never had a heart," said the elder sister scornfully, putting down the light.

"She might not have been able to help what she did," I cried.

I could hear the sisters catch their fragile breath.

"It's what you do that counts," said my hostess regarding the discoloured floor, "not what you feel about it afterwards. Our father always insisted on that. It's obvious."

"Give it back to me," said Emerald staring into my eyes. For a moment I hesitated.

"Give it back to her," said my hostess in her contemptuous way. "It makes no difference now. Everyone but Emerald can see that the work is done."

I returned the card, and Emerald let go of me as she stuffed it away.

"And now will you join us?" asked my hostess. "In the inner room?" As far as was possible, her manner was almost casual.

"I am sure the rain has stopped," I replied. "I must be on my way."

"Our father would never have let you go so easily, but I think we have done what we can with you."

I inclined my head.

"Do not trouble with adieux," she said. "My sisters no longer expect them." She picked up the lamp. "Follow me. And take care. The floor has weak places."

"Good-bye," squealed Emerald.

The Inner Room

"Take no notice, unless you wish," said my hostess.

I followed her through the mouldering rooms and across the rotten floors in silence. She opened both the outer doors and stood waiting for me to pass through. Beyond, the moon was shining, and she stood dark and shapeless in the silver flood.

On the threshold, or somewhere on the far side of it, I spoke. "I did nothing," I said. "Nothing."

So far from replying, she dissolved into the darkness and silently shut the door.

I took up my painful, lost, and forgotten way through the wood, across the dreary marsh, and back to the little yellow road.

The Never-ending Penny

BERNARD WOLFE

To a poverty-stricken Mexican-Californian peach-picker with a large family, money was an everlasting problem.

So it went, peaches all day, complaints all night. "If not too big a work, could you make the voice somewhat softer?" he said to his wife. "I pick the peaches ten large hours today and even my ears fall down from tiredness."

He refrained from observing that her tongue might soon fall down from its labours.

"Pick the peaches ten years and the house will still be small like no house," she said. "We are seven, we shall soon be eight, and we continue to live in a house with one room, not a house, a species of shed, and therefore we live like pigs and what do peaches have to do with it?"

He studied their own well-fatted pig that was down at the corner of the property snouting some superior mud from here to there. He refrained from pointing out that this shoat of theirs lived fantastically better than they did, having as many rooms as he had muds, no peaches to pick, no woman to make loud noises in his ears.

"We need at the minimum two rooms more," she said. "Then our neighbours will see that we are people and not some animals in a barn or a sty."

He did not draw her attention to the fact that she was making noises better suited to the barn or the sty. He liked Herminia, though she had a tendency to overtalk.

The Never-ending Penny

He adjusted his back to a more comfortable position against the adobe wall, wiggled his dusty toes, and considered the sun, which was dropping away behind the mountain like a darkening boil.

"I have explained before and I will explain again," he said. "To build even two small rooms requires many hundreds of adobe bricks. To mix the adobe, shape the bricks, dry the bricks, then further to place the bricks, is an immense labour. I pick the peaches ten hours a day for Mr Johannsen and this is enough immense labour."

These words were said with a first-grade teacher's kind and crisis-easing voice.

"And when you do not pick the peaches for Mr Johannsen?"

"Then I pick the beef tomatoes for Mr Predieu and the iceberg lettuces for Mr Scarpio. When I am not picking other people's various things it is my taste to sit against the wall and pick my teeth."

"For that," she said, "it is the first necessary to chew on something."

"I agree with a whole heart. I will ask only why you bother to make this very true and intelligent observation?"

"Because if you do not build the two needed rooms you will very soon be without the things to chew on. Do I make this plain? Your cook will be home in Durango, where human beings do not live like animals. You can write me a long letter about how you do not pick the teeth any more."

She went in the house with both hands made into fists, her rounded belly leading the way. Five children's voices came up in a soprano thunder, asking mama dear and nice mamacita, for some pieces of crisped tortilla.

Life could be hard in this California. Troubles here had the tendency to grow like peaches and lettuces, in bunches. Though it was to be understood that even the much accepting Herminia would not wish to bring out still another child in one cramped room. Yet adobe bricks would not grow in bunches, like peaches, lettuces and troubles.

He got to his feet and walked down close by the pig, to the

The Never-ending Penny

well, to get himself some water. Standing there in his envelope of constant trouble, the tin dipper at his mouth, he said more or less to the pig, "I wish I had the miraculous penny."

This was what people like him sometimes said when they felt their troubles forming into a sealed envelope, themselves inside.

The pig manoeuvred over on his back and flopped his happy feet in the air, perhaps trying to kick the sun.

From the bottom of the well a voice said, "What?"

When spoken to, Diosdado liked to give straight and full answers. So he explained:

"I was speaking of the penny that never ends, that when it is spent is replaced in the pocket with another penny. It is the poor man's idea of great wealth, of all the riches of the world to have a penny in his pocket that always gives birth to another penny—"

The voice said, "If you have to empty out your head every time you're asked a question, write a book or hire a hall."

Then Diosdado realized that he was leaning into the well, talking to somebody at the bottom of his well.

A man with a one-room house guards what is his with more spirit than a man who owns international strings of castles.

He leaned over some more and said, "What do you think you're doing there in my well?"

"I do this without thinking," the voice said, "because it's my job and the thing I'm trained to do. These days we all specialize."

"What is that, your job?"

"Listening. You think it's easy when you mumble?"

"Then you listen to this," Diosdado said. "This is my well and I want you to get out of it and off my property."

"This well," the voice said, "is as much Mr Bixby's as it is yours."

"Who owns a hole is who did the digging. You go back to this liar of a Mr Bixby of yours and you—"

"Man, will you use your damned head for once? For more than to keep your ears in place? You dug this hole, yes, what belongs to you is the hole. You did not make the water that comes into the hole. I stress this, the water comes down from those San Berdoo mountains, from certain forest lands owned

The Never-ending Penny

by a certain Mr George Carol Bixby. Now, will you stop wasting my time and answer one simple question? Did I understand you to say you would like the miraculous penny, the never-ending penny?"

"These were my words. It is only an expression—"

"All right."

"What did you say?"

"I said, all right."

"All right what?"

"All right, you can have the never-ending penny. You've got it. Spend it in good health."

Diosdado turned a sympathy-seeking face to the lurching, wallowing pig. "Mister," he said, "you get down in my well where you have no right to be, a person I have never been introduced to, and you tell me bad jokes. It is impossible to have such an article as the never-ending penny. This is only an article people wish for. It is an express—"

"I know what it is without speeches from you," the voice said. "The self-perpetuating penny, you might say, is my business. If you don't want it, fine, just say so. If you do, it's yours. What coins do you have in your pocket?"

Diosdado made another face at the pig, one pleading for the two sane parties left in the world to join against a general madness, and pulled all the coins from his pocket.

"Four pennies, two dimes and a quarter. This is what I have in my pocket and in the world."

"Fine. Now, put them in your shirt pocket, all but one penny. Put this single penny back in your pants."

"If it gives you pleasure."

"Now take the penny out, then feel in the pocket again."

Diosdado withdrew the penny, placed it in his right hand, reached inside again with his left.

There was another penny in his pocket.

He pulled this one out and explored once more.

There was a third penny.

There was a fourth. There was a fifth.

The Never-ending Penny

When there were fifteen or more pennies in the sweaty hand he looked for explanations to the pig, with beggar's eyes. The pig was busy juggling the sun with his paws. Diosdado began to shiver.

He thought he understood, partly, anyway, the excitement of this moment. Once, when a boy in Durango, while walking down a country road, he had seen a shine in the dust. His foot explored the mystery. The shining objects were bright new centavo pieces. At the sight of these unexpected riches he had felt precisely this kind of throat-tightening and eye-widening heat in a flash flood through his body. For one ballooning, scooping moment Diosdado had thought, what a glory if this place of miracles should turn out to be a well, a cornucopia, a production line of pennies. Can there be too much of a good thing?

Maybe this, the centavo with a big fertility, has always been a general dream of seven-year-olds. Maybe this is why it finally became a saying, an expression. But even a *six*-year-old, even one not very bright, knows that the nice idea is finally in the head and not in the world. Some young sense of the true nature of things tells him that the perpetual penny is a pleasant wish, not a reasonable expectation. Dreams, he somehow knows, circle around the impossible.

Now here he was, he Diosdado, with the dream of dreams in his pocket. He was a small boy again, kicking at the Durango road and finding the road fully co-operative, sensitive to his balloons and scoops of moods, jumping to his large orders.

"If you have the power to give this thing," he said shakenly into the well, "why do you give it to me, a nobody?"

"For one thing," the voice said, "you asked for it."

"It is enough only to ask?"

"Oh, no, oh, no, we can't go around giving these things out just for the asking. A lot of our countrymen come up north here, you know, many of them have troubles and ask for the repeating penny. We follow them and we listen to them. In my territory, for example, Southern California, I give out two or three of these pennies in a year, an average year. There's no set quota."

The Never-ending Penny

"People around here call for the miraculous penny all the time, why am I the one to get it, sir?"

"One, you're a steady worker. Two, you don't spend all your earnings in the nearby bars. Three, you're reasonably good to your wife, though you make silent comments at her. Four, you have another child coming and could use the penny, or think you could. Don't ask for more reasons. Let's just say I like your curly hair."

Diosdado scratched his head. Absent-mindedly he pulled two more pennies from the production line in his pocket.

"But, listen, if two or three people around here get the penny each year, how have I never heard about this?"

"News like this doesn't get around, fellow. The owners of these family-bearing pennies develop a very strong urge not to tell anybody about it. You'll see."

Diosdado pulled three more coins from his penny garden of a pocket.

"I've got to run now," the voice said. "Somebody over at the Bixby place is making a racket about wanting the penny. It's probably nothing, just a false alarm. Most of my calls come from drunken bums in roadside bars who have just run out of tequila and pulque money, but I've got to go and see. O, one more thing. I have the power to grant you two wishes. Now you have the first."

"And the second, what is that?"

"You make the wishes, I grant them. Do you expect me to do all the work around here?"

That night Diosdado did not eat his supper. The kids hooted and threw frijoles at each other and he sat there over his food seeing and hearing nothing. The newly acquired pennies in his pocket were a ton of hotness against his thigh, several times he was on the verge of blurting out to Herminia the incredible thing that had happened but each time his tongue got stiff.

Herminia wanted to know why he did not eat his frijoles. He said he had eaten many peaches this afternoon at Mr Johannsen's and was not hungry. With embroidered casualness he announced he was going to cut some kindling and went out.

The Never-ending Penny

As soon as he was inside his wood and tool shed he bolted the door and went to work.

Diosdado soon discovered that he could pull pennies from his pocket at the rate of one a second, sixty a minute, three thousand six hundred an hour. This meant he was making thirty-six dollars an hour, roughly what he got for a full week's work in Mr Johannsen's orchard. It was good pay for a job that could be done with one hand, without climbing a ladder.

For one hour he stood drawing out the coppers and dropping them on the dirt floor. His arm was tired, a cylinder of hurt. He thought he might sit down for a time but it was too hard to reach into his pocket from a sitting position. Next he tried taking his pants off and lying down, but it was a strange thing, the penny would not reproduce itself when the pants were not actually on his body. He had to become a rich man standing up. At the end of the second hour he had almost seven thousand pennies on the floor, almost seventy dollars, and his arm was full of fever and gassy beer, there were shooting pains from the wrist to the shoulders. He was getting rich and he was getting lumbago.

He considered how much faster the harvesting of this penny crop would go if he could call in Herminia and the kids to help with the picking. With his whole family working they could go through the night in shifts. But it did not seem right to bring others into the secret, not even his near and dear.

Herminia called to him to bring some wood and he answered that he would be right there.

Now there was a problem. He could not leave a small fortune in pennies lying around in plain sight on the shed floor. He felt it was better if his family did not know about the pennies that grew like toadstools that wish to make headlines.

In the corner there were some coarse burlap bags, left over from last year's flood season when he had prepared sandbags to build up the banks of the nearby stream. His seven thousand pennies almost filled one bag, which he hid under some odds and ends of lumber.

He went toward the house wondering why it was that he kept looking back. He was about to be the richest man in the world

The Never-ending Penny

and he looked over his shoulder as though he had something to hide.

During the next days, whenever he had a minute, he went to the shed to pull pennies and fill burlap bags. Before the week was up he had to buy a new supply of bags at the general store, and his arm was so sore that he was not able to pick many peaches for Mr Johannsen.

Finally he had so many full bags that there was no way to hide them in the shed. Some new thing had to be done with them to keep them out of sight.

He began to discuss the matter with himself:

"What are pennies for, exactly? For spending, this is certain, yet I do not consider the possibility. Why not? Well, the first thing is, there is no way to spend ten thousand pennies, then ten times ten thousand, and so on. If I ordered adobe bricks from the brickyard and offered the man bags of pennies for them he would say, where did you get all these pennies, Diosdado? He would get suspicious and tell the chief of police about it, or the tax collector, or both. Pennies can be deposited in the bank of course, just like dollars. Yet peach pickers do not usually have money of any type to place in the bank. The president of the bank would think the matter over and report it to the tax collector, or the chief of police or both. There is but one way. I must hide these bags from all eyes. From my wife and my children, them especially. I did not know what a trouble it can be to have money. Surely it is not robbery if I take pennies from my own left pocket, so why do I feel like a robber and keep looking over my shoulder?"

So he did not spend the pennies. Neither did he tell his wife about them. He hit on a way to hide the bags. He ordered a quantity of planks from the lumberyard and these he placed firmly in the ground in upright pairs, exactly along the lines where the walls for the extra rooms would eventually have to go. Between each pair of planks, using them for supports, he piled a vertical row of his plump bags, exactly as he had piled them to make a new bank for the flooding stream. Each bag contained

The Never-ending Penny

ten thousand pennies, one hundred dollar's worth of pennies. The piles formed continuous walls, they looked exactly like walls.

Herminia watched with narrowing eyes.

"You wanted more rooms?" he said to her. "How can I make rooms if I do not first make walls?"

"I tell all the neighbours you are a good husband," she said, "but now I see you want to kill your whole family. What way is this to build walls without adobe? Make walls of sand and when the bags rot away in the weather the walls will fall down on our heads and we will be killed and buried in the same time. True, this way we save burial expenses. We have to cut down somewhere."

"This is a new procedure of making the bricks," he said, hating himself. "First, a special sand is put in the bags, second, they are permitted to shape and harden in the sun. It is a totally new process, woman. It was invented by the authorities on such things in the U.S.A. Department of Agriculture, Adobe Brick Division. Those of the government know the wall business better than you."

He wanted to kick and punch himself when he saw the full trust and respect in her eyes. But at least the pennies would be safe in his home-made bank. Because of the protecting planks the children could not feel around with their fingers to find out that these walls were filled with a sunshiny sand of dreams and sayings.

But the chief of police did take notice. He saw the walls going up and he drove in to have a look.

"Pretty big house you're putting up there," he said. "Where'd you get the money for the materials? Come on, Diosdado, come clean, you rob a bank some place?"

Diosdado said he seldom had the occasion, let alone the constitution, even to go in a bank, let alone rob it, the funds came from picking the good peach crop.

But the chief's words were a worry.

The tax collector came by too.

"You're turning the place into a regular mansion," he said with too much arithmetic in his eyes. "A four-star palace. You must have had a peachy year, ha, ha, to afford improvements like

The Never-ending Penny

these." There were dollar signs in his eyes as he drove away. This was another worry.

By now the walls, the deceitful walls, were up ten feet or more. Diosdado took a pencil and paper and did some figuring. According to his count he had piled up two thousand bags, which came to twenty thousand dollars' worth of pennies. He was a man worth twenty thousand dollars and he did not have the cash to go in the store to buy a side of bacon or a new kitchen table, let alone more burlap bags. Added to this, the chief of police and the tax collector had their mathematical eyes on him.

If no more bags would fit into the walls, any he filled from now on would have to be hidden in another way. There was no other way. Besides, Diosdado was beginning to wonder if there was any sense to piling up more pennies in secret. To collect bigger and bigger moneys and be further and further away from the possibility of spending them, to do all this heavy work and have no pay from it, nothing but some false walls put up with backbreaking labour, more labour by far than it would have taken to make true and useful adobe walls, that is, walls about which a man would not have to tell rotten lies to his trusting wife, this did not seem reasonable. His arm was very tired. It hung limp at his side, a tube of misery. He was now the slowest picker in Mr Johannsen's orchards.

He decided that, for the time being, he would not collect any more pennies.

Easier said than done. How do you go about throwing away a breeding penny like this? A damned rabbit of a penny? Several times, in disgust, he tried to fling it from him. Each time, its twin brother turned up cosily in his pocket.

He began truly to hate this penny. He had not had a good night's sleep for weeks, even before the visits from the township officials. He had the stronger and stronger feeling that, ever since he had begun to collect the pennies, he had been involved in something criminal, something absolutely against the law. He was looking over his shoulder all the time now. His neck was getting as stiff as his arm.

He consulted with himself once more:

The Never-ending Penny

"I see why I have broken no law, yet feel like the Number One on the wished-for list of the FBI. I begin to see. This is not my money, though it happens to be in my pocket. It is not money at all, though it looks and feels like true money. The difficulty is that if you are given the magic of the seven-year-old you must begin to think and act like a seven-year-old in order to enjoy the gift. Why do I not speak to my wife any more? Because my pennies are the only thing I can speak of and they are the one thing I must not speak of. Why can't I tell Herminia about the pennies? Not because of the danger she might talk. Not that so much, though she is a champion talker. Chiefly because if I spoke of this magic she would see the seven-year-old in my eyes again, and this is not for a woman to see in a more so than not grown man. Why do I feel I am breaking the law? Because the first law is to act your age, which in my case is thirty-nine and not seven. This calamity of a penny cuts many inches off my height and how tall is a man to begin with? Besides, my arm hurts all the time. I must get rid of this affliction and plague of a penny."

But how lose a penny that won't get lost?

Standing by the well, speaking more or less to the up-side-down pig as it pranced pointlessly, he said, "I certainly wish I'd never heard of this miserable penny."

From deep in the well there was a sound like the rush of wind. After a few seconds the voice said as though from far off, "I'll be right there."

Diosdado waited. Pretty soon the voice came through stronger, though panting a little, saying, "Sorry to keep you waiting but those drunken bums over at the Bixby place keep running out of drinking money and yelling for the penny. Well. You were saying?"

"I have a worry," Diosdado said. "It seems to me there is something illegal about this magic penny."

There was silence for a while. Then the voice said with some irritation, "Look, up there you make laws, down here we make pennies. It's a division of labour. Don't tell me your troubles, I've got enough of my own."

The Never-ending Penny

"But I have to live with the law," Diosdado said, "and this penny is clearly against the law. I will tell you my thinking. There are only so many pennies in the country, an amount fixed by the government people. Therefore, if you put a large number of them in my pocket you must be taking them out of somebody else's pocket. If you are a true magician why do you have to be a thief? More, you must be robbing the poor, because it is chiefly the poor who save pennies. I have no use for the whole system."

"Didn't you hear what I said?" the voice came back. "We don't steal the pennies, we make them."

"Then you are counterfeiters. Isn't this a violation of the law, to counterfeit?"

"I don't have to sit here and take your insults," the voice said. "These pennies are most emphatically not counterfeits. We follow the specifications of the mint people of the U.S. Treasury in making these pennies, so-and-so much copper, such-and-such percentages of other metals, everything down to the last decimal point. We use no inferior materials, each penny we give you is a perfect coin of the realm. There's not a bad penny in the lot."

"All the same, all the same. There are supposed to be a certain number of pennies and no more. It's not right for me to have the power to add a million or a billion billion billion, this could upset all figures and banks. It must be against the law for a peach picker to have the strength to overthrow the whole money system and also the government."

"You didn't call me over here to discuss the monetary system. What's really on your mind, man?"

"I don't want this penny."

"All right."

"What?"

"I said all right. Throw it down here."

Diosdado drew the coin from his pocket, breathed deeply, and dropped it down the well. Time passed. There was a sound, not of splashing, rather of a big and drawn-out yawn, accompanied by a flatted whistling. He thought he heard the ringing of a cash register from far away.

The Never-ending Penny

He reached into his left pocket. It was filled with a glorious emptiness. He felt a weight of some long tons of lifting from his shoulders.

"This is the second wish?" he said.

"Precisely," the voice said.

"Those who make the first, they always make the second?"

"Most always. As soon as they find out they can't spend these pennies, keep watching over their shoulders, stop talking to their wives, get funny looks from the tax collector, and so on."

"Nobody ever keeps the penny?"

"How it is in other territories I don't know, but since I've been on the job here there was only one man who didn't try to give it back. He was a gardener and tree pruner over to La Jolla. Know what happened to him? Interesting case, I wrote it up for our records. He went around telling everybody in town he had a nice mamma penny that kept making little baby pennies. This is not the kind of talk people wish to hear from a grown man, an experienced gardener and tree pruner. They did not wait to see the breeding penny demonstrated, they quickly locked him up in a hospital for people who make wild talk. Naturally, I had to step in. We couldn't sit back and let this man build big piles of pennies all over the hospital just to show off, this sort of thing has a tendency to make people gossip and turn their attention from business. We don't have the authority to take the penny back unless its owner so requests, but in emergencies we can change the never-ending penny into a never-ending something else. What I changed this penny into was a Life Saver, wild cherry flavour. Now this man was going around the hospital telling all the doctors what he had in his pocket was not a mamma penny but a mamma Life Saver, wild cherry flavour. You can understand that this just made the doctors more sure they had done right in locking him up. What did this man begin to do with his self-replenishing Life Saver? Nobody would look at it. For lack of anything better, he began to eat the Life Savers. He ate and ate, and always had one more. So far as I know he's still eating away, all day long and far into the night, and I can tell you he's getting pretty damn sick of wild cherry.

The Never-ending Penny

He was originally a bitsy fellow, one hundred twenty in his stocking feet, and they tell me he just passed two hundred and is still going strong. Good-bye, friend. Maybe you've learned something from this. You *can* get too much of a good thing. But don't write the experience off as a total loss. You've got something to show for it. Just take a good look around. Good-bye now, and don't take any wooden—sorry. Got to rush. Those drunks over at Bixby's are making a racket again. Bye, bye."

Diosdado looked around his property. He saw a well, a shed, a hut, a mud hollow, a self-inebriated pig, in that order—nothing new. What did that voice mean, he, Diosdado, had something to show for it? All he had for it was an arm that was a hose made from end to end of major ache, and this was not to be shown.

But then he saw something that had not been there before the trouble-making penny. Attached to the original hut were two unusually large, very luxurious rooms, or almost rooms. Add ceiling and finish the walls properly and nobody could take them for anything but rooms. They were most emphatically not banks, because though moneys had been deposited in them these moneys were not for withdrawing. The walls could certainly be finished in the right manner. There could be no withdrawals from this gone-out-of-business bank.

Herminia came over to him from the hut and he put his arm around her, saying:

"Woman, you talk too much, but from time to time you say something. It is true, without adobe those walls do not work. Whatever the Agriculture Department says, those bags of sand will rot in the weather and make troubles. I will put plenty of adobe over the walls, on both sides; also, I will add ceilings, and you will have the two largest rooms on this side of the San Berdoos. Then my cook will not go back to Durango and I will always have something to chew on before I pick my teeth, yes?"

"Agreed," Herminia said. "This is a business deal not to be turned down," and she put one arm round his waist, then the other.

For over a week Diosdado picked no peaches. He worked around the clock, placing boards to make a roof, mixing adobe

The Never-ending Penny

and plastering it over the bags and their wooden supports. Finally the walls, and also the roof, were covered with solid, substantial, homey-looking adobe. No rains could get in here, and no tax collectors.

The afternoon Diosdado finished his labours he walked over to the well with Herminia and turned to take a good look at the finished structure. It was a real house, a good house, the best-looking house in the valley.

"This is a house that could not be paid for in pennies," he said, half into the well, half toward the wallowing pig, very little for Herminia's ear.

With her tendency to comment on everything, Herminia said, "There is not enough money in all the world, pennies or dollars, to pay for this house," and put her arm around his waist.

He patted her promise-leavened belly and looked down into the valley toward the other huts and cabins nestled here and there. He thought about a hundred-twenty-pound man getting to be two hundred on one Life Saver, wild cherry flavour, and shivered. He wondered how many other homes in this valley had twenty-thousand-dollar walls, but he was afraid to speculate about this too much.

Down in the mud hollow the pig rolled on his back like a vacationing millionaire, trying, for lack of anything better to do, to punt away the molten centavo of a sun.

The New Sun

J. S. FLETCHER

From the time that he had taken up the study of astronomy as a pleasant means of spending his newly acquired leisure, and had built himself a small but well-equipped observatory as an adjunct to his house, which stood on one of the highest slopes of Leith Hill, Mequillen had formed the habit of rising from his bed every two or three hours of a cloudy night to see if the sky had cleared. To some men such a habit would have been highly inconvenient, for many obvious reasons. But Mequillen was in a lucky position. He was unmarried; he possessed much more than ample means; he had therefore no business or profession to attend to, and accordingly no train to catch of a morning in order to keep office hours. He could sleep at any time of the day he chose; and if he did jump out of bed at two o'clock in the morning, to find that the sky was still cloudy, he could jump back and go to sleep again on the instant. And he was, moreover, an enthusiast of the first order.

On a certain night in the February of 19—, Mequillen, who had gone to bed at ten o'clock, suddenly awoke, switched on the electric light at the side of his bed, and, seeing that it was then ten minutes past twelve, sprang out, shuffled himself into his thickly padded dressing-gown, and hurried up the winding stair which led to the observatory. One glance into the night showed him a perfectly clear sky. From the vast dome of heaven, wondrously blue, the stars shone out like points of fire. And Mequillen, with a sigh of satisfaction, began his work at the telescope, comparing the sky, field by field, with his star chart, on the chance of finding new variable stars. After his usual fashion, he was immediately absorbed, and the sky remaining clear, he went on working, unconscious of time, until a deep-toned clock in the room beneath struck the hour of three. Then Mequillen started, and realized that he had been so absorbed that he had not noticed the striking of one or two, and he leaned back from the telescope in a suddenly assumed attitude of relaxation, stretching his arms, and casting up his eyes to the still clear vault above him. The next instant he became rigid; the next he began to tremble with excitement; the next he could have shouted for joy. For there, in the constellation which astronomers have named Andromeda, Mequillen detected a new star!

He knew as he gazed and gazed, intoxicated with the delight and wonder of his discovery, that the burning and glittering object at which he was looking had never shown its light to man before. There was no need to turn to his star charts. Mequillen, being a rich man, was always equipped with the latest information from all the great observatories of the world. That star, burning with such magnificence, was on no chart. Nay, he himself had taken a photograph of that particular field in the heavens only twenty-four hours previously, wherein were stars to the twelfth magnitude; but the star at which he gazed was not amongst them. It had suddenly blazed up and as he watched he saw it visibly, plainly, increase in brightness and magnitude.

"A new star!" he murmured mechanically. "A new star! I wonder who else has seen it?"

Mequillen continued to watch until, as the February dawn drew near, the clouds spread great curtains between him and the heavens, and sky and stars were blotted out. Then he went to his bed, and, in spite of his excitement, he slept soundly until ten o'clock in the morning.

When Mequillen woke and looked out across the Surrey hills and vales, the entire landscape was being rapidly blotted out by a curious mist, or fog, which seemed to come from nowhere. A vast, mighty blanket of yellow seemed to be dropped between him and everything as he looked. At one moment he saw the

The New Sun

summit of a hill many miles away; the next he could not even see his own garden beneath his windows. And when he went downstairs, half an hour later, the fog had become of the colour of grey ash, and the house was full of it, and the electric light was turned on everywhere, and to little effect.

Mequillen's sister, Adela, who kept house for him—with the assistance of a housekeeper and several female servants—came to him in his study, looking scared.

"Dan," she said, "isn't there something queer about this fog? It's—it's getting worse."

Mequillen laid down a bundle of letters which he had just taken up, and walked out to the front door and into the garden. He looked all around him, and he sniffed.

"H'm! It certainly does seem queer, Addie," he said. "We've certainly never had a fog like this in these parts since we knew them."

The girl sniffed too.

"Dan," she said, "it's like as if it were the very finest dust. And—look there!"

She had been wiping her hand with a tiny wisp of a handkerchief as she spoke, and now she held the handkerchief out to Mequillen.

"Look!" she repeated.

Mequillen looked down, and saw a curious stain—a species of smudge or smear of a faint grey colour. Without making any remark he ran the tip of his finger along the nearest object, an espalier. The same smudge or smear appeared on his finger.

"It's on everything," whispered the girl. "See, it's on my cheek! It is some sort of dust, Dan. What's the matter?"

But Mequillen made no answer. He asked for breakfast, and they went in together. By that time the interior of the house was as full of the fog as the exterior was hidden by it, and everything that they touched—plate, china, linen—gave off the grey smear. And by noon everything was wrapped in an ashen-grey atmosphere, and the electrical lights had no power beyond a very limited compass.

"This is vexatious," said Mequillen. "I was going to have the motor out and take you across to Greenwich. I wanted to make an inquiry at the Observatory. Do you know, Addie, I found a new star last night!"

"A new star!" she said wonderingly. "But you won't go, Dan?"

"Won't go?" he said, laughing. "I should like to see anybody go anywhere in this, though it may be only local. By George! Weren't the Cockerlynes coming out to dine and sleep tonight?"

Addie nodded.

"Well, I hope they won't run into this," continued Mequillen. "Ah! I'll ring Dick Cockerlyne up, and ask him what the weather's like in town. And then I'll ring up the Observatory."

He went off to the small room in which the telephone was placed. His sister followed him, and as they passed close beneath the cluster of lights in the hall Mequillen saw that the girl's face was drawn and pallid. He stopped sharply.

"Why, Addie," he said; "frightened?"

She laid her hand on his arm, and he felt it trembling.

"Dan," she whispered. "I'm—I'm horribly frightened! What —what is this? You know, there's never been anything like this before—in our time. What's happened?"

Mequillen laughed, and patted the hand that lay on his arm.

"Come, come, Addie!" he said soothingly. "This isn't like you. I think this fog is uncommon, and I can't account for it, but I've no doubt it can be accounted for. Now, let me ring up Cockerlyne. I've a notion we shall hear they've got a bright morning there in London."

The girl shook her head, made as if she would follow him to the telephone, and then suddenly turned away. In the silence a woman's shrill scream rang out.

"That's cook—in hysterics," said Addie. "I shall have to be brave for the sake of the servants, Dan. They're all as frightened as—as I am."

Nearly an hour later Mequillen came out of the little room, and called his sister into the study. He closed the door, and beckoned her into the arc of the electric light.

"This is queer!" he said, in a whisper. "I've been talking to Cockerlyne and to the Observatory. Dick says this fog struck

The New Sun

London at ten o'clock. It's just there as it is here, and everything's at a standstill. Dick hasn't the remotest notion how he's going to get away from the city. But—that's nothing. Addie, it's all over Europe."

The girl made a little inarticulate sound of horror in her throat, and her face whitened.

"All over Europe, so they say at Greenwich," continued Mequillen. "From Lisbon to Moscow, and from Inverness to Constantinople! Land and sea—it's everywhere. It—well, it's something unexplainable. Such a thing has never been known before. But it's no use getting frightened, Addie; you must be brave. It's no doubt some natural phenomenon that will be accounted for. And—phew, how very hot this room is!"

The girl went close to her brother, and laid her hand on his arm.

"Dan," she said, "it isn't the room. See the fire's very low, and the ventilating fan's working. It's the same everywhere. Come into the garden."

Mequillen followed her out of the house, knitting his brows, and snapping his fingers, after his wont when he was puzzled. For several days the weather had been unusually cold for the time of year. Released now from the preoccupation of the last few hours, he suddenly realized that the day was as hot as a July day should be under normal conditions. He turned to an outdoor thermometer.

"Why—why," he exclaimed, "it's over seventy now! Seventy in February! Addie, something's happened to this old world of ours. That's certain. Look there!"

As they watched the mercury rose one, two, three figures. The brother and sister stared at each other. And Mequillen suddenly dropped his hand with a gesture of helplessness.

"Well," he said, "there's nothing to be done but to wait. I—I don't understand it."

They went back into the house together, and into Mequillen's study, only to stand and stare at each other in silence. Then Addie made a sudden effort at conversation.

"Tell me about the new star, Dan," she said.

Mequillen started.

"The new star!" he exclaimed. "The new star! My God, I wonder if that has anything to do with this? If——"

The parlourmaid, white and scared, came noiselessly into the circle of electric light within which the brother and sister were standing.

"You are wanted at the telephone, sir," she said.

Mequillen went off. In a few minutes he came back, shaking his head.

"That was the Observatory," he said quietly. "This fog, or whatever it is, is all over the world—over South Africa, North and South America, India, Australia, anyway. And the heat's increasing."

"And—the reason?" whispered Addie.

Mequillen sat down, and dropped his head in his hands.

"There's no man can tell the reason," he answered. "He can't even make a guess at it. Something's happened, that's all. We must wait—wait."

And he took up the letters which had remained unopened on his desk and began to sort them out and to read them.

"Let us go on with our ordinary routine," he said. "That will be best."

The girl left the room, jangling a bunch of keys. But within half an hour she was back, accompanied by the housekeeper.

"Dan," she said quietly, "the servants want to go. They think the end of the world's come, and they want to get to their own homes."

"How do they propose to reach them?" asked Mequillen. "They can't see a yard before them."

"I told them that, Mr Mequillen," said the housekeeper, "but it was of no use. You see, sir, they all live pretty close to here, and they say they can find their way blindfolded. They'd better go, sir, or we shall have more hysterics."

"Give me some money for them, Dan," said Addie.

Mequillen rose, and, unlocking a drawer, handed a cashbox to his sister.

"I don't see what good money can do them if the world's coming to an end," he said with a laugh. "Well, let them do what they like."

The New Sun

When the two women had left him, Mequillen went outside again, and looked at the thermometer hanging on the wall.

"My God," he said, "eighty already! What can it mean?"

And then, standing there in the strange all-wrapping fog in his quiet garden on the slope of the peaceful Surrey hills, Mequillen's thoughts turned to the great city lying only a few miles away. What was happening in London? He saw, with small exercise of imagination, the congested traffic, the discomfort, the inconvenience, the upsetting of all arrangement and order in an ordinary fog. What, then, must be the effect of this extraordinary one? For Mequillen was sufficiently versed in science to know that the world had never—never, at any rate, since historical records of it began—known such a day as this. And supposing it lasted, supposing——

And then he interrupted his train of thought to glance once more at the thermometer.

"Yes, yes!" he muttered to himself. "Yes, but supposing the heat goes on increasing, increasing as it's increased during the last few hours? My God, it's awful to contemplate!"

The house was very quiet when the frightened servants had left it. Mequillen and his sister made some attempt to eat the lunch which the housekeeper prepared; but the attempt was a farce, and presently they found themselves pacing up and down, from room to room, from house to garden, waiting for they knew not what. There was no change in the atmosphere, so far as the fog was concerned, but the thermometer rose steadily, until at six o'clock at night it was at ninety, and they were feeling as if they must soon gasp for breath. And, unknown to Addie, Mequillen went to the telephone, and eventually got into communication with Dick Cockerlyne, who was still at his city office.

"Dick!" he said as steadily as he could. "Are you still there?"

"I am," came back the answer, in tones that Mequillen could scarcely recognize.

"How is it with you there?"

One word came along. Mequillen felt it to be the only word that could come.

"Hell!"

Mequillen shivered, and again spoke.

"Dick, what is happening? What——"

And then he was sharply rung off. From that moment he had no further communication with the outer world. Once—twice—thrice he tried the telephone again before midnight; no response was given. And all around the house a silence reigned which was like the silence of a deserted ocean. Nothing but the fog was there—not a voice, even of fear or terror, came up from the valley. And the heat went on steadily increasing.

There was no sleep for Mequillen or his sister or the housekeeper that night. They had all changed into the lightest summer garments they could find, by the middle of the night the two women were lying prostrate with exhaustion, and the thermometer was a long way over one hundred degrees. Mequillen did all that knowledge could suggest to him to obtain relief and coolness for them, but there was no air—the atmosphere was still, lifeless, leaden. And when the morning came the all-enveloping fog was still there, and the heat was still increasing.

How they got through that second day Mequillen never knew. He had visions of what might be going on in places where the water supply was bad. He, fortunately, was in command of a splendid and probably inexhaustible supply; he had, too, a well-stocked larder and a well-provided cellar of good wine. Only just able to crawl about, he looked to the two women—the housekeeper, a woman of full habit, was more than once on the verge of collapse; Addie's wiriness and excellent physique kept her going. But as it grew to the second midnight they were all gasping for breath, and Mequillen, making brave efforts to keep the women alive, knew that before many hours were over all would be over with them too. And then, as he lay stretched out in a lounging-chair, anxiously watching his sister who lay on a sofa close by, the door was pushed open, and Dick Cockerlyne, reeling like a drunken man, staggered in, and dropped headlong at Mequillen's side.

Mequillen summoned up what strength remained in him, and set himself with clenched teeth and fierce resolution to bring

Cockerlyne round. Cockerlyne was a big man, a fellow of brawn and muscle, that in ordinary times would have thought nothing of walking fifty miles on end, if need arose; now, looking at his great limbs, scarcely hidden by the thin silk shirt and flannel trousers which clothed them, Mequillen saw that he was wasted as if he had undergone starvation. His face had aged by ten years, and there was a look of horror in its lines and in his half-open eyes which told of human fear and terror. And once more Mequillen wondered what was going on in London.

As he poured liquid—a weak mixture of brandy-and-seltzer —down the fallen man's throat, Mequillen glanced at his sister. She had paid no attention whatever to Cockerlyne's entrance; she lay motionless, her hands clasped across her bosom, slowly and regularly gasping for breath. But Mequillen knew what would rouse her, for she and Cockerlyne had been engaged for the past six months, and were about to be married, and one great source of her anxiety during the past two days had been in her fears for his safety. And as he saw Cockerlyne returning to consciousness, he turned to her.

"Addie!" he whispered. "Here is Dick!"

The girl slowly opened her eyes and turned her head, and a faint flush came into her white cheeks. Mequillen reached across, and handed her a glass out of which he had been giving her liquid food at intervals during the past hour.

"Drink that, and then get up and help me with him," he said.

Cockerlyne opened his eyes to the full at last, and saw the brother and sister, and he struggled up from the floor.

"I got through, anyway," he said. "I thought that if we— are all going to—to die, eh?—I'd see Addie first. I—have I been fainting, Dan?"

"Lie down again, Addie, this instant!" commanded Mequillen sharply. "Now then, Dick, drink the rest of that brandy-and-seltzer, and then you shall have some of this concentrated meat extract. No nonsense, now. What we've all got to do is to keep up strength till this—passes. I'm off to our housekeeper. I forbid you two to move or to speak until I come back."

When he returned Mequillen found his sister staring at

Cockerlyne, and Cockerlyne staring at her, as if they were looking their last at each other.

"Come, come!" he said, with the best imitation of a laugh that he could raise. "We're not at that stage yet. Now, then, obey your doctor."

And he fed them both as if they were children, and presently had the gratification of seeing the colour come back to Cockerlyne's face, and a new light into his eyes. The big man suddenly rose, and shook his limbs, and smiled grimly. There were sandwiches on the table, and he reached over and took one in each hand, and began to eat voraciously.

"Chuck the nursing, Dan," he growled. "I'm all right. I said I'd get it done, and I've done it. I'm here!"

Mequillen saw with thankfulness that Cockerlyne was going to be something to stand by. He nodded with assumed coolness.

"All right, old chap," he said. "And—how did you get here?"

Cockerlyne moistened his tongue.

"Fought through it," he said grimly. "I've been thirty hours at it—thirty hours!"

"Yes?" said Mequillen.

"You know," continued Cockerlyne, "you know when you telephoned to me at six last night? After that I think I went mad for a while. Then I got out of the office, and somehow got to the Bank station of the South London—the Tube trains ran now and then. I don't know how I did it, but I travelled that way as far as the train ran—Clapham, or somewhere. And then—well, I just made along this way. Of course, I knew every bit of the road. It was like sleep-walking."

Mequillen nodded, and, picking up a fan, resumed his occupation of trying to agitate the air about his sister's face.

"Well, you're here, Dick," he said. "But—London?"

Cockerlyne shivered.

"London is—oh, I don't know what London is!" he answered. "I think half the people are dead, and the other half mad. Once or twice I went out into the streets. One man you met was on his knees, praying aloud; the next was—oh, I don't know! It seemed that hell was let loose; and yet the churches were

The New Sun

crammed to the doors. And people were fighting for the liquor in the dram-shops and the public-houses. I—I don't seem to remember much; perhaps I'm mad myself now. How long will it be, Dan?"

"How long will what be?" asked Mequillen.

"The—the end? I expect this is the end, isn't it?" said Cockerlyne. "What else can it be?"

"Don't talk rot!" said Mequillen sharply. "I thought you'd come round again. Here, pour some of the stuff out of that bottle into that glass, and carry it to the housekeeper in the next room. Pull yourself together, man!"

"Sorry," said Cockerlyne, and rose to carry out Mequillen's commands. "I—I'm light-headed, perhaps. Don't ask me any more about what I saw. It sends me off."

He went away to the housekeeper, and Mequillen heard him speaking to her in the dry, croaking tones in which they all spoke. And presently Cockerlyne came hurriedly back, and, standing at the open door, beckoned to him with a shaking hand. Mequillen rose, and shambled across to him, looking an interrogation.

"Come out to the garden!" whispered Cockerlyne, and led the way to the front door. "Listen!" he said. "I caught the sound in there! Listen!"

Mequillen grasped one of the pillars of the porch and strained his ears. And somewhere, so far off that it might have been thousands of miles away, he heard what he knew to be the coming of a mighty wind, and instinctively he tightened his grip on the pillar.

"It's a cyclone coming, Cockerlyne!" he shouted, though all around them was still and quiet. "It'll sweep all before it—house, everything! Quick—the two women!"

But before either man could turn to the open door the great fog was swept away before their eyes as if it had been literally snatched from them by some gigantic hand from heaven, and where it had been was a burning and a dazzling light of such power that in an instant they were grovelling on the ground before it with their eyes pressed instinctively into the crooks of their quivering elbows.

The New Sun

Of the two men, Mequillen was the first to comprehend what had happened, and with his comprehension came coolness and resource. Never had he thought so quickly in his life.

"Dick," he whispered, "keep your eyes shut tightly, and turn and creep back into the hall. I'm doing the same thing. You know the little room on the left? Don't open your eyes until you get in there. Now, then," he continued, with a gasp, as the two men reached the room and stood upright, "you can open them here, for the shutters are up. Ah! And yet, you see, although this room should be quite dark, it's almost as light as a normal winter morning."

Cockerlyne stared stupidly about him.

"For God's sake, Dan, what's happened?" he exclaimed.

Mequillen was fumbling in a drawer. He brought out two silk mufflers, and passed one to his friend.

"I have a very good idea as to what's happened," he answered gravely. "And I'll tell you in a few minutes. But first muffle your eyes—there, you'll see through two thicknesses of the silk. Now for the women. Fortunately, the curtains are closely drawn in both rooms, or I should have feared for their eyesight in that sudden rush of light—light, Dick, such as this globe has never seen before! Dick, we've got to blindfold them, and then get them into the darkest place in this house. There's an underground room—not a cellar—which I've sometimes used for experiments. We must get them downstairs."

It was easy to see, in spite of the mufflers, that the light in the hall was blinding, and in the curtained study as bright as on an open sea on a cloudless day in summer. And Addie was lying on her sofa with her arms crossed over her forehead and eyes, obviously surprised and distressed by the sudden glare.

"Don't move your arms!" exclaimed Mequillen sharply. "Keep your eyes shut as tight as you can."

"What is it?" she asked. "Has the fog gone, and the sun come?"

"The fog has gone, and a sun has come," replied Mequillen. "And its light is unbearable—just yet. Now, Addie, I am going to blindfold you and take you and Mrs Jepson down to the underground room. We shall all have to get used to the light by degrees. Do just what I tell you, and Dick and I will make you comfortable."

But when the two women were safely disposed of in a room into which scarcely any light ever penetrated in an ordinary way, but which was then as light as noontide, Mequillen drew Cockerlyne into the study, and, groping his way to the windows, closed the shutters and drew the curtains over them.

"Now you can take off your muffler," he said quietly. "There, you see it's light enough even now, to read print and to see the time. And—you perceive the time? Half-past twelve, midnight!"

Cockerlyne's face blanched. He swallowed something, and straightened himself.

"What is this, Mequillen?" he asked quietly. "Do you *know*?"

Mequillen shook his head.

"Not with certainty," he answered. "But I think I know. Forty-eight hours ago I discovered a new star, which increased in magnitude at a surprising rate even while I watched it. Now I think that it is a new sun."

"A—new—sun!" exclaimed Cockerlyne. "Impossible!"

"Call it what you will," said Mequillen. "It is, I am certain, at any rate, a vast heavenly body of fire, which was travelling towards this part of space at an inconceivable rate when I first saw it, and is probably at this moment nearer to us than our sun is. Do you feel that the heat is increasing?"

"Yes," replied Cockerlyne; "but it is different in character."

"It is different in character because the wrapping of infinitely fine dust which has been round us has been drawn away," said Mequillen. "But it will increase in intensity."

Cockerlyne gripped the table.

"And?" he whispered.

"In an hour or two we shall be shrivelled up, consumed, like shreds of wool thrown into a furnace!" answered Mequillen.

Cockerlyne straightened himself.

"All right, Dan," he said quietly. "I'm glad I came here. What's to be done now?"

The New Sun

Mequillen had turned to a nest of drawers in one of the recesses of his study. He brought out some spectacles fitted with lenses of very dark glass, and handed one to Cockerlyne.

"We will make an attempt to see this new sun," he said. "Put these spectacles on, and for the present fold that muffler about your eyes again once. You'll see through both muffler and spectacles. And now come up to the observatory."

In the observatory, Cockerlyne understood little or nothing of the preparations which Mequillen made. Conscious only of the terrible heat, he stood waiting and thinking of the fate which was about to befall them; and suddenly a terrible impatience seized upon him. If there was but an hour or so to live, his place was with the woman he loved.

"Look here, Dan!" he exclaimed. "I'm going down! If the end's coming, then——"

But Mequillen laid a hand on his arm and drew him forward, at the same time removing the muffler from his head.

"We will go down soon, Cockerlyne," he said. "We must for we shall have to tell them. But first—look! You can look with safety now."

And then Cockerlyne, following his friend's instructions, looked, and saw widespread above him the dome of the heavens. But never had he so seen it in all his life. From north to south, from east to west, it glowed with the effulgence of shining brass; and in the north-east hung a great globe of fiery red, vaster in dimension than the sun which the world had known till then, and even when seen through the protections which Mequillen had prepared, coruscating and glittering with darting and leaping flame.

"My God!" said Cockerlyne, in a hushed voice. "My God! Dan, is that—It?"

"That is It," answered Mequillen quietly. "It is now nearly twice the magnitude of our sun, and it is coming nearer. This is no time to make calculations, or even speculations; but I believe it is, at any rate, as near to us as our sun is. Come away, Cockerlyne; I want to look out on the world. Hold my hand and follow me."

And he dragged Cockerlyne away through a trap-door and into a dark passage, and then into a darker room.

"Keep your hands over your spectacles for a while, and get accustomed to the light by degrees," he said. "I am going to open an observation shutter here, through which we can see a vast stretch of country to the north. It will be a surprise to me if much of it is not already in flames. Now, if you are ready."

Cockerlyne covered his eyes as he heard the click of the observation shutter. Even then, and through the thick black glasses which he was wearing, he felt the extraordinary glare of the light which entered. Presently Mequillen touched his arm.

"You can look now," he said. "See, it's just as I thought! The land's on fire!"

Cockerlyne looked out upon the great sweep of hill and valley, wood and common which stretches across the fairest part of Surrey from the heights above Shere and Albury to those beyond Reigate. He saw the little villages, with their spires and towers and red roofs and tall grey gables; he saw the isolated farms, the stretches of wood, the hillside coppices, the patches of heath and the expanses of green which indicated land untouched by spade or plough.

It was a scene with which he had been familiar from boyhood. Of late he had explored every nook and corner of it with Addie and Mequillen, and at all times of the year it had seemed beautiful to him. But under the glare and brilliance of this extraordinary light everything seemed changed. All over that vast prospect great pillars of smoke and flame were rising to the sky. From the valley beneath them came the shrieks and cries of men and women, and as the two men watched they saw the evergreens in Mequillen's garden suddenly turn to the whiteness of paper, and shrivel and disappear in fine ashes.

"Look there!" whispered Mequillen, pointing a shaking finger. "There—Dorking's on fire! And yonder, Reigate, too!"

Cockerlyne tried to speak, but his tongue rattled in his mouth like a dry pea, in a drier pod. He touched Mequillen's arm and pointed downward, and Mequillen nodded.

The New Sun

"Yes," he said. "We had better go down to them; they've got to know."

He took Cockerlyne by the hand and led him back to the observatory, which, in spite of the fact that all its shutters were drawn, was full of light. And as they stepped into it a spark of white flame suddenly appeared in the woodwork, and ran like lightning round the rim of the dome.

"On fire!" said Mequillen quietly. "It's no good, Cockerlyne; we can't do anything. The end's come! We—oh, my God, what's this? What *is* this? Cockerlyne—Cockerlyne, where *are* you?"

For just as suddenly as they had seen the greyness of the great fog snatched away from the earth, so now they saw the extraordinary light which had succeeded it snatched away. It was gone in the flash of an eye, with the speed of lightning, and as it went they felt the earth move and shudder, and all around them fell a blackness such as they had never known. And as the two men gripped each other in their terror there suddenly burst upon the dome of the observatory a storm of what seemed to be bullets—fierce, insistent, incessant. The serpent-like trail of fire in the woodwork quivered once and died out. And Mequillen, trembling in every limb, released his hold on Cockerlyne, and staggered against the nearest wall.

"Rain!" he said. "Rain!"

In the darkness, Mequillen heard Cockerlyne first stumble about, and then fall heavily. Then he knew that Cockerlyne had fainted, and he made his way to a switch and turned on the electric light, and got water to bring him round. But when he came round, Cockerlyne for some minutes croaked and gabbled incessantly, and it was not until Mequillen had hurried down to the dining-room for brandy for him that he regained his senses and was able to sit up, gasping and staring about him. He pointed a shaking finger to the aperture in the dome, through which the rain was pouring, unheeded by Mequillen, in a ceaseless cascade.

"Where is—It?" he gasped. "What—what's come of It?"

Mequillen shook him to his feet, and made him swallow more brandy.

The New Sun

"Pull yourself together, Cockerlyne!" he said. "This is no time to talk science; this is a time to act. Come down, man; we must see to the women! We've just escaped from fire; now we're likely to meet our deaths by water. Listen to that rain. Here, help me to close that shutter. Now, downstairs! It's lucky we're on a hillside, Cockerlyne! But the people in the valleys! Come on!"

And, leaving Cockerlyne to follow him, Mequillen ran down through the house, to find his sister and the housekeeper in the hall. As he saw them, he knew that they had realized what he now had time to realize—that the terrible heat was dying away, and that it was becoming easier and easier to breathe. As he passed it he glanced at a hanging thermometer, and saw the mercury falling in a steady, swift descent.

Mequillen caught his sister in his arms and pressed her to him. She looked anxiously into his face.

"Dick?" she said.

"He's safe—he's coming," said Mequillen.

Addie suddenly collapsed, and hid her face in her hands. The housekeeper was already in a heap in the nearest chair, sobbing and moaning. And as Cockerlyne came slowly down the stairs, Mequillen saw that, strong man as he was, his nerves had been shaken so much that he was trembling like a leaf. Once more Mequillen had to summon all his energies together in the task of bringing his companions round, and as he moved about from one to the other his quick ear heard the never-ceasing rattle of the rain, which was heavier than any tropical rain that ever fell. And presently he caught the sound of newly forming cascades and waterfalls, cutting new ways from the hill-tops to the level lands of the valleys. Now the normal coolness of middle winter was coming back. The women picked up the wraps they had thrown aside; the men hurried into greatcoats. And as the February dawn came grey and slow across the hills, Mequillen and Cockerlyne went up to the observatory, and into the little look-out turret from which they had seen the spirals of smoke and flame rising from the land only a few hours before.

The New Sun

The rain was still falling, but with no more violence than that of a tropical rainstorm. But the air was throbbing, pulsating, humming with the noise of falling waters. A hundred yards away from the house a churning and seething mass of yellow foam was tearing a path, wide and deep, through a copse of young pine; down in the valley immediately beneath them lay a newly formed lake. In the valleys on every side, as far as the eye could reach, lay patches of silvery hue, which they knew to be great sheets of water; and now the air was cool, and the hitherto tortured lungs could breathe it in comfort.

"Mequillen," said Cockerlyne, after a long silence, "what happened?"

But Mequillen shook his head.

"I am as a child standing at the edge of a great ocean," he answered. "I cannot say definitely. I think that the great star which we saw rushing upon us, was suddenly arrested, split into fragments, when that darkness fell, and that we were saved. Once more, Cockerlyne, the old world, a speck in space, will move on. For look there!"

And Cockerlyne turned as Mequillen pointed, and saw, slowly rising over the Surrey hills, the kindly sun of a grey February morning.

The Star Beast

NICHOLAS STUART GRAY

Soon upon a time, and not so far ahead, there was a long streak of light down the night sky, a flicker of fire, and a terrible bang that startled all who heard it, even those who were normally inured to noise. When day came, the matter was discussed, argued, and finally dismissed. For no one could discover any cause at all for the disturbance.

Shortly afterwards, at a farm, there was heard a scrabbling at the door, and a crying. When the people went to see what was there, they found a creature. It was not easy to tell what sort of creature, but far too easy to tell that it was hurt and hungry and afraid. Only its pain and hunger had brought it to the door for help.

Being used to beasts, the farmer and his wife tended the thing. They put it in a loose-box and tended it. They brought water in a big basin and it drank thirstily, but with some difficulty—for it seemed to want to lift it to its mouth instead of lapping, and the basin was too big, and it was too weak. So it lapped. The farmer dressed the great burn that seared its thigh and shoulder and arm. He was kind enough, in a rough way, but the creature moaned, and set its teeth, and muttered strange sounds, and clenched its front paws. . . .

Those front paws . . . ! They were so like human hands that it was quite startling to see them. Even with their soft covering of grey fur they were slender, long-fingered, with the fine nails of a girl. And its body was like that of a boy—a half-grown lad—though it was as tall as a man. Its head was man-shaped. The long and slanting eyes were as yellow as topaz, and shone from inside with their own light. And the lashes were thick and silvery.

"It's a monkey of some kind," decided the farmer.

"But so beautiful," said his wife. "I've never heard of a monkey like this. They're charming—pretty—amusing—all in their own way. But not beautiful, as a real person might be."

They were concerned when the creature refused to eat. It turned away its furry face, with those wonderful eyes, the straight nose, and curving fine lips, and would not touch the best of the season's hay. It would not touch the dog biscuits or the bones. Even the boiled cod-head that was meant for the cats' supper, it refused. In the end, it settled for milk. It lapped it delicately out of the big basin, making small movements of its hands—its forepaws—as though it would have preferred some smaller utensil that it could lift to its mouth.

Word went round. People came to look at the strange and injured creature in the barn. Many people came. From the village, the town, and the city. They prodded it, and examined it, turning it this way and that. But no one could decide just what it was. A beast for sure. A monkey, most likely. Escaped from a circus or menagerie. Yet whoever had lost it made no attempt to retrieve it, made no offer of reward for its return.

Its injuries healed. The soft fur grew again over the bare grey skin. Experts from the city came and took it away for more detailed examination. The wife of the farmer was sad to see it go. She had grown quite attached to it.

"It was getting to know me," said she. "And it talked to me—in its fashion."

The farmer nodded slowly and thoughtfully.

"It was odd," he said, "the way it would imitate what one said. You know, like a parrot does. Not real talking, of course, just imitation."

"Of course," said his wife. "I never thought it was real talk. I'm not so silly."

It was good at imitating speech, the creature. Very soon, it had learned many words and phrases, and began to string

The Star Beast

them together quite quickly, and with surprising sense. One might have thought it knew what it meant—if one was silly.

The professors and elders and priests who now took the creature in hand were far from silly. They were puzzled, and amused, and interested—at first. They looked at it, in the disused monkey-cage at the city's menagerie, where it was kept. And it stood upright, on finely-furred feet as arched and perfect as the feet of an ancient statue.

"It is oddly human," said the learned men.

They amused themselves by bringing it a chair and watching it sit down gracefully, though not very comfortably, as if it was used to furniture of better shape and construction. They gave it a plate and a cup, and it ate with its hands most daintily, looking round as though for some sort of cutlery. But it was not thought safe to trust it with a knife.

"It is only a beast," said everyone. "However clever at imitation."

"It's so quick to learn," said some.

"But not in any way human."

"No," said the creature, "I am not human. But, in my own place, I am a man."

"Parrot-talk!" laughed the elders, uneasily.

The professors of living and dead languages taught it simple speech.

After a week, it said to them:

"I understand all the words you use. They are very easy. And you cannot quite express what you mean, in any of your tongues. A child of my race——" It stopped, for it had no wish to seem impolite, and then it said, "There is a language that is spoken throughout the universe. If you will allow me——"

And softly and musically it began to utter a babble of meaningless nonsense at which all the professors laughed loudly.

"Parrot-talk!" they jeered. "Pretty Polly! Pretty Polly!"

For they were much annoyed. And they mocked the creature into cowering silence.

The professors of logic came to the same conclusions as the others.

The Star Beast

"Your logic is at fault," the creature had told them, despairingly. "I have disproved your conclusions again and again. You will not listen or try to understand."

"Who could understand parrot-talk?"

"I am no parrot, but a man in my own place. Define a man. I walk upright. I think. I collate facts. I imagine. I anticipate. I learn. I speak. What is a man by your definition?"

"Pretty Polly!" said the professors.

They were very angry. One of them hit the creature with his walking-cane. No one likes to be set on a level with a beast. And the beast covered its face with its hands, and was silent.

It was warier when the mathematicians came. It added two and two together for them. They were amazed. It subtracted eight from ten. They wondered at it. It divided twenty by five. They marvelled. It took courage. It said:

"But you have reached a point where your formulae and calculuses fail. There is a simple law—one by which you reached the earth long ago—one by which you can leave it at will——"

The professors were furious.

"Parrot! Parrot!" they shouted.

"No! In my own place——"

The beast fell silent.

Then came the priests, smiling kindly—except to one another. For with each other they argued furiously and loathingly regarding their own views on rule and theory.

"Oh, stop!" said the creature, pleadingly.

It lifted its hands towards them and its golden eyes were full of pity.

"You make everything petty and meaningless," it said. "Let me tell you of the Master-Plan of the Universe. It is so simple and nothing to do with gods or rules, myths or superstition. Nothing to do with fear."

The priests were so outraged that they forgot to hate one another. They screamed wildly with one voice:

"Wicked!"

They fled from the creature, jamming in the cage door in their haste to escape and forget the soul-less, evil thing. And the

The Star Beast

beast sighed and hid its sorrowful face, and took refuge in increasing silence.

The elders grew to hate it. They disliked the imitating and the parrot-talk, the golden eyes, the sorrow, the pity. They took away its chair, its table, its plate and cup. They ordered it to walk properly—on all fours, like any other beast.

"But in my own place——"

It broke off there. Yet some sort of pride, or stubbornness, or courage, made it refuse to crawl, no matter what they threatened or did.

They sold it to a circus.

A small sum was sent to the farmer who had first found the thing, and the rest of its price went into the state coffers for making weapons for a pending war.

The man who owned the circus was not especially brutal, as such men go. He was used to training beasts, for he was himself the chief attraction of the show, with his lions and tigers, half-drugged and toothless as they were. He said it was no use being too easy on animals.

"They don't understand over-kindness," said he. "They get to despising you. You have to show who's master."

He showed the creature who was master.

He made it jump through hoops and do simple sums on a blackboard. At first it also tried to speak to the people who came to look at it. It would say, in its soft and bell-clear tones:

"Oh, listen—I can tell you things——"

Everyone was amazed at its cleverness and most entertained by the eager way it spoke. And such parrot-nonsense it talked!

"Hark at it!" they cried. "It wants to tell us things, bless it!"

"About the other side of the moon!"

"The far side of Saturn!"

"Who taught it to say all this stuff?"

"It's saying something about the block in mathematics now!"

"And the language of infinity!"

"Logic!"

"And the Master-Plan!"

They rolled about, helpless with laughter in their ringside seats.

The Star Beast

It was even more entertaining to watch the creature doing its sums on the big blackboard, which two attendants would turn so that everyone could admire the cleverness: 2 and 2, and the beautifully-formed 4 that it wrote beneath. $10 - 8 = 2$. Five into 20. 11 from 12.

"How clever it is," said a small girl, admiringly.

Her father smiled.

"It's the trainer who's clever," he said. "The animal knows nothing of what it does. Only what it has been taught. By kindness, of course," he added quickly, as the child looked sad.

"Oh, good," said she, brightening. "I wouldn't like it hurt. It's so sweet."

But even she had to laugh when it came to the hoop-jumping. For the creature hated doing it. And, although the long whip of the trainer never actually touched its grey fur, yet it cowered at the cracking sound. Surprising, if anyone had wondered why. And it ran, upright on its fine furred feet, and graceful in spite of the red and yellow clothes it was wearing, and it jumped through the hoops. And then more hoops were brought. And these were surrounded by inflammable material and set on fire. The audience was enthralled. For the beast was terrified of fire, for some reason. It would shrink back and clutch at its shoulder, its arm, its thigh. It would stare up wildly into the roof of the great circus canopy—as if it could see through it and out to the sky beyond—as though it sought desperately for help that would not come. And it shook and trembled. And the whip cracked. And it cried aloud as it came to each flaming hoop. But it jumped.

And it stopped talking to the people. Sometimes it would almost speak, but then it would give a hunted glance towards the ring-master, and lapse into silence. Yet always it walked and ran and jumped as a man would do these things—upright. Not on all fours, like a proper beast.

And soon a particularly dangerous tightrope dance took the fancy of the people. The beast was sold to a small touring animal-show. It was getting very poor in entertainment value, anyway. It moved sluggishly. Its fur was draggled and dull. It

The Star Beast

had even stopped screaming at the fiery hoops. And—it was such an eerie, man-like thing to have around. Everyone was glad to see it go.

In the dreary little show where it went, no one even pretended to understand animals. They just showed them in their cages. Their small, fetid cages. To begin with, the keeper would bring the strange creature out to perform for the onlookers. But it was a boring performance. Whip or no whip, hunger or less hunger, the beast could no longer run or jump properly. It shambled round and round, dull-eyed and silent. People merely wondered what sort of animal it was, but not with any great interest. It could hardly even be made to flinch at fire, not even when sparks touched its fur. It was sold to a collector of rare beasts. And he took it to his little menagerie on the edge of his estate near a forest.

He was not really very interested in his creatures. It was a passing hobby for a very rich man. Something to talk about among his friends. Only once he came to inspect his new acquisition. He prodded it with a stick. He thought it rather an ugly, dreary animal.

"I heard that you used to talk, parrot-fashion," said he. "Go on, then, say something."

It only cowered. He prodded it some more.

"I read about you when they had you in the city," said the man, prodding harder. "You used to talk, I know you did. So talk now. You used to say all sorts of clever things. That you were a man in your own place. Go on, tell me you're a man."

"Pretty Polly," mumbled the creature, almost inaudibly.

Nothing would make it speak again.

It was so boring that no one took much notice or care of it. And one night it escaped from its cage.

The last glimpse that anyone saw of it was by a hunter in the deeps of the forest.

It was going slowly looking in terror at rabbits and squirrels. It was weeping aloud and trying desperately to walk on all fours.

The Man Who Could Work Miracles

H. G. WELLS

It is doubtful whether the gift was innate. For my own part, I think it came to him suddenly. Indeed, until he was thirty he was a sceptic, and did not believe in miraculous powers. And here, since it is the most convenient place, I must mention that he was a little man, and had eyes of a hot brown, very erect red hair, a moustache with ends that he twisted up, and freckles. His name was George McWhirter Fotheringay—not the sort of name by any means to lead to any expectation of miracles—and he was clerk at Gomshott's. He was greatly addicted to assertive argument. It was while he was asserting the impossibility of miracles that he had his first intimation of his extraordinary powers. This particular argument was being held in the bar of the Long Dragon, and Toddy Beamish was conducting the opposition by a monotonous but effective "So *you* say," that drove Mr Fotheringay to the very limit of his patience.

There were present, besides these two, a very dusty cyclist, landlord Cox, and Miss Maybridge, the perfectly respectable and rather portly barmaid of the Dragon. Miss Maybridge was standing with her back to Mr Fotheringay, washing glasses; the others were watching him, more or less amused by the present ineffectiveness of the assertive method. Goaded by the Torres Vedras tactics of Mr Beamish, Mr Fotheringay determined to make an unusual rhetorical effort. "Looky here, Mr Beamish," said Mr Fotheringay. "Let us clearly understand what a miracle is. It's something contrariwise to the course of

The Man Who Could Work Miracles

nature done by power of Will, something what couldn't happen without being specially willed."

"So *you* say," said Mr Beamish, repulsing him.

Mr Fotheringay appealed to the cyclist, who had hitherto been a silent auditor, and received his assent—given with a hesitating cough and a glance at Mr Beamish. The landlord would express no opinion, and Mr Fotheringay, returning to Mr Beamish, received the unexpected concession of a qualified assent to his definition of a miracle.

"For instance," said Mr Fotheringay, greatly encouraged. "Here would be a miracle. That lamp, in the natural course of nature, couldn't burn like that upsy-down, could it, Beamish?"

"*You* say it couldn't," said Beamish.

"And you?" said Fotheringay. "You don't mean to say—eh?"

"No," said Beamish reluctantly. "No, it couldn't."

"Very well," said Mr Fotheringay. "Then here comes someone, as it might be me, along here, and stands as it might be here, and says to the lamp, as I might do, collecting all my will—'Turn upsy-down without breaking, and go on burning steady,' and ——Hullo!"

It was enough to make anyone say "Hullo!" The impossible, incredible, was visible to them all. The lamp hung inverted in the air, burning quietly with its flame pointing down. It was as solid, as indisputable as ever a lamp was, the prosaic common lamp of the Long Dragon bar.

Mr Fotheringay stood with an extended forefinger and the knitted brows of one anticipating a catastrophic smash. The cyclist, who was sitting next the lamp, ducked and jumped across the bar. Everybody jumped, more or less. Miss Maybridge turned and screamed. For nearly three seconds the lamp remained still. A faint cry of mental distress came from Mr Fotheringay. "I can't keep it up," he said, "any longer." He staggered back, and the inverted lamp suddenly flared, fell against the corner of the bar, bounced aside, smashed upon the floor, and went out.

It was lucky it had a metal receiver, or the whole place would have been in a blaze. Mr Cox was the first to speak, and his

The Man Who Could Work Miracles

remark, shorn of needless excrescences, was to the effect that Fotheringay was a fool. Fotheringay was beyond disputing even so fundamental a proposition as that! He was astonished beyond measure at the thing that had occurred. The subsequent conversation threw absolutely no light on the matter so far as Fotheringay was concerned; the general opinion not only followed Mr Cox very closely but very vehemently. Everyone accused Fotheringay of a silly trick, and presented him to himself as a foolish destroyer of comfort and security. His mind was in a tornado of perplexity, he was himself inclined to agree with them, and he made a remarkably ineffectual opposition to the proposal of his departure.

He went home flushed and heated, coat-collar crumpled, eyes smarting and ears red. He watched each of the ten street lamps nervously as he passed it. It was only when he found himself alone in his little bedroom in Church Row that he was able to grapple seriously with his memories of the occurrence, and ask, "What on earth happened?"

He had removed his coat and boots, and was sitting on the bed with his hands in his pockets repeating the text of his defence for the seventeenth time, "*I* didn't want the confounded thing to upset," when it occurred to him that at the precise moment he had said the commanding words he had inadvertently willed the thing he said, and that when he had seen the lamp in the air he had felt that it depended on him to maintain it there without being clear how this was to be done. He had not a particularly complex mind, or he might have stuck for a time at that "inadvertently willed", embracing, as it does, the abstrusest problems of voluntary action; but as it was, the idea came to him with a quite acceptable haziness. And from that, following, as I must admit, no clear logical path, he came to the test of experiment.

He pointed resolutely to his candle and collected his mind, though he felt he did a foolish thing. "Be raised up," he said. But in a second that feeling vanished. The candle was raised, hung in the air one giddy moment, and as Mr Fotheringay gasped, fell with a smash on his toilet-table, leaving him in darkness save for the expiring glow of its wick.

The Man Who Could Work Miracles

For a time Mr Fotheringay sat in the darkness, perfectly still. "It did happen, after all," he said. "And 'ow I'm to explain it I *don't* know." He sighed heavily, and began feeling in his pockets for a match. He could find none, and he rose and groped about the toilet-table. "I wish I had a match," he said. He resorted to his coat, and there were none there, and then it dawned upon him that miracles were possible even with matches. He extended a hand and scowled at it in the dark. "Let there be a match in that hand," he said. He felt some light object fall across his palm, and his fingers closed upon a match.

After several ineffectual attempts to light this, he discovered it was a safety-match. He threw it down, and then it occurred to him that he might have willed it lit. He did, and perceived it burning in the midst of his toilet-table mat. He caught it up hastily, and it went out. His perception of possibilities enlarged, and he felt for and replaced the candle in its candlestick. "Here! *you* be lit," said Mr Fotheringay, and forthwith the candle was flaring, and he saw a little black hole in the toilet-cover with a wisp of smoke rising from it. For a time he stared from this to the little flame and back, and then looked up and met his own gaze in the looking-glass. By this help he communed with himself in silence for a time.

"How about miracles now?" said Mr Fotheringay at last, addressing his reflection.

The subsequent meditations of Mr Fotheringay were of a severe but confused description. So far as he could see, it was a case of pure willing with him. The nature of his first experiences disinclined him for any further experiments except of the most cautious type. But he lifted a sheet of paper, and turned a glass of water pink and then green, and he created a snail, which he miraculously annihilated, and got himself a miraculous new toothbrush. Somewhere in the small hours he had reached the fact that his will-power must be of a particularly rare and pungent quality, a fact of which he had certainly had inklings before, but no certain assurance. The scare and perplexity of his first discovery was now qualified by pride in this evidence of singularity and by vague intimations of advantage. He became aware that the church clock was striking one, and as it did not occur to him that his daily duties at Gomshott's might be miraculously dispensed with, he resumed undressing, in order to get to bed without further delay. As he struggled to get his shirt over his head, he was struck with a brilliant idea. "Let me be in bed," he said, and found himself so. "Undressed," he stipulated; and, finding the sheets cold, added hastily, "and in my nightshirt—no, in a nice soft woollen nightshirt. Ah!" he said with immense enjoyment. "And now let me be comfortably asleep . . ."

He awoke at his usual hour and was pensive all through breakfast-time, wondering whether his overnight experience might not be a particularly vivid dream. At length his mind turned again to cautious experiments. For instance, he had three eggs for breakfast; two his landlady had supplied, good, but shoppy, and one was a delicious fresh goose-egg, laid, cooked, and served by his extraordinary will. He hurried off to Gomshott's in a state of profound but carefully concealed excitement, and only remembered the shell of the third egg when his landlady spoke of it that night. All day he could do no work because of this astonishing new self-knowledge, but this caused him no inconvenience, because he made up for it miraculously in his last ten minutes.

As the day wore on his state of mind passed from wonder to elation, albeit the circumstances of his dismissal from the Long Dragon were still disagreeable to recall, and a garbled account of the matter that had reached his colleagues led to some badinage. It was evident he must be careful how he lifted frangible articles, but in other ways his gift promised more and more as he turned it over in his mind. He intended among other things to increase his personal property by unostentatious acts of creation. He called into existence a pair of very splendid diamond studs, and hastily annihilated them again as young Gomshott came across the counting-house to his desk. He was afraid young Gomshott might wonder how he had come by them. He saw quite clearly the gift required caution and watchfulness in its exercise, but so far as he could judge the difficulties attending its mastery would

The Man Who Could Work Miracles

be no greater than those he had already faced in the study of cycling. It was that analogy, perhaps, quite as much as the feeling that he would be unwelcome in the Long Dragon, that drove him out after supper into the lane beyond the gas-works, to rehearse a few miracles in private.

There was possibly a certain want of originality in his attempts, for apart from his will-power Mr Fotheringay was not a very exceptional man. The miracle of Moses' rod came to his mind, but the night was dark and unfavourable to the proper control of large miraculous snakes. Then he recollected the story of "Tannhäuser" that he had read in the back of the Philharmonic programme. That seemed to him singularly attractive and harmless. He stuck his walking-stick—a very nice Poona-Penang lawyer—into the turf that edged the footpath, and commanded the dry wood to blossom. The air was immediately full of the scent of roses, and by means of a match he saw for himself that this beautiful miracle was indeed accomplished. His satisfaction was ended by advancing footsteps. Afraid of a premature discovery of his powers, he addressed the blossoming stick hastily: "Go back." What he meant was "Change back"; but of course he was confused. The stick receded at a considerable velocity, and incontinently came a cry of anger and a bad word from the approaching person. "Who are you throwing brambles at, you fool?" cried a voice. "That got me on the shin."

"I'm sorry, old chap," said Mr Fotheringay, and then realizing the awkward nature of the explanation, caught nervously at his moustache. He saw Winch, one of the three Immering constables, advancing.

"What d'yer mean by it?" asked the constable. "Hullo! It's you, is it? The gent that broke the lamp at the Long Dragon!"

"I don't mean anything by it," said Mr Fotheringay. "Nothing at all."

"What d'yer do it for then?"

"Oh, bother!" said Mr Fotheringay.

"Bother indeed! D'yer know that stick hurt? What d'yer do it for, eh?"

For the moment Mr Fotheringay could not think what he had

done it for. His silence seemed to irritate Mr Winch. "You've been assaulting the police, young man, this time. That's what *you* done."

"Look here, Mr Winch," said Mr Fotheringay, annoyed and confused. "I'm very sorry. The fact is——"

"Well?"

He could think of no way but the truth. "I was working a miracle." He tried to speak in an off-hand way, but try as he would he couldn't.

"Working a——! 'Ere, don't you talk rot. Working a miracle, indeed! Miracle! Well, that's down-right funny! Why, you's the chap that don't believe in miracles. . . . Fact is, this is another of your silly conjuring tricks—that's what this is. Now, I tell you——"

But Mr Fotheringay never heard what Mr Winch was going to tell him. He realized he had given himself away, flung his valuable secret to all the winds of heaven. A violent gust of irritation swept him to action. He turned on the constable swiftly and fiercely. "Here," he said, "I've had enough of this, I have! I'll show you a silly conjuring trick, I will! Go to Hades! Go, now!"

He was alone!

Mr Fotheringay performed no more miracles that night, nor did he trouble to see what had become of his flowering stick. He returned to the town, scared and very quiet, and went to his bedroom. "Lord!" he said, "it's a powerful gift—an extremely powerful gift. I didn't hardly mean as much as that. Not really. . . . I wonder what Hades is like!"

He sat on the bed taking off his boots. Struck by a happy thought he transferred the constable to San Francisco, and without any more interference with normal causation went soberly to bed. In the night he dreamt of the anger of Winch.

The next day Mr Fotheringay heard two interesting items of news. Someone had planted a most beautiful climbing rose against the elder Mr Gomshott's private house in the Lullaborough Road, and the river as far as Rawling's Mill was to be dragged for Constable Winch.

The Man Who Could Work Miracles

Mr Fotheringay was abstracted and thoughtful all that day, and performed no miracles except certain provisions for Winch, and the miracle of completing his day's work with punctual perfection in spite of all the bee-swarm of thoughts that hummed through his mind. And the extraordinary abstraction and meekness of his manner was remarked by several people, and made a matter for jesting. For the most part he was thinking of Winch.

On Sunday evening he went to chapel, and oddly enough, Mr Maydig, who took a certain interest in occult matters, preached about "things that are not lawful". Mr Fotheringay was not a regular chapel goer, but the system of assertive scepticism, to which I have already alluded, was now very much shaken. The tenor of the sermon threw an entirely new light on these novel gifts, and he suddenly decided to consult Mr Maydig immediately after the service. So soon as that was determined, he found himself wondering why he had not done so before.

Mr Maydig, a lean, excitable man with quite remarkably long wrists and neck, was gratified at a request for a private conversation from a young man whose carelessness in religious matters was a subject for general remark in the town. After a few necessary delays, he conducted him to the study of the Manse, which was contiguous to the chapel, seated him comfortably, and, standing in front of a cheerful fire—his legs threw a Rhodian arch of shadow on the opposite wall—requested Mr Fotheringay to state his business.

At first Mr Fotheringay was a little abashed, and found some difficulty in opening the matter. "You will scarcely believe me, Mr Maydig, I am afraid"—and so forth for some time. He tried a question at last, and asked Mr Maydig his opinion of miracles.

Mr Maydig was still saying "Well" in an extremely judicial tone, when Mr Fotheringay interrupted again: "You don't believe, I suppose, that some common sort of person—like myself, for instance—as it might be sitting here now, might have some sort of twist inside him that made him able to do things by his will."

"It's possible," said Mr Maydig. "Something of the sort, perhaps, is possible."

"If I might make free with something here, I think I might show you by a sort of experiment," said Mr Fotheringay. "Now, take that tobacco-jar on the table, for instance. What I want to know is whether what I am going to do with it is a miracle or not. Just half a minute, Mr Maydig, please."

He knitted his brows, pointed to the tobacco-jar and said: "Be a bowl of vi'lets."

The tobacco-jar did as it was ordered.

Mr Maydig started violently at the change, and stood looking from the thaumaturgist to the bowl of flowers. He said nothing. Presently he ventured to lean over the table and smell the violets; they were fresh-picked and very fine ones. Then he stared at Mr Fotheringay again.

"How did you do that?" he asked.

Mr Fotheringay pulled his moustache. "Just told it—and there you are. Is that a miracle, or is it black art, or what is it? And what do you think's the matter with me? That's what I want to ask."

"It's a most extraordinary occurrence."

"And this day last week I knew no more that I could do things like that than you did. It came quite sudden. It's something odd about my will, I suppose, and that's as far as I can see."

"Is *that*—the only thing? Could you do other things besides that?"

"Lord, yes!" said Mr Fotheringay. "Just anything." He thought, and suddenly recalled a conjuring entertainment he had seen. "Here!" He pointed. "Change into a bowl of fish—no, not that—change into a glass bowl full of water with goldfish swimming in it. That's better. You see that, Mr Maydig?"

"It's astonishing. It's incredible. You are either a most extraordinary . . . But no——"

"I could change it into anything," said Mr Fotheringay. "Just anything. Here! be a pigeon, will you?"

In another moment a blue pigeon was fluttering round the room and making Mr Maydig duck every time it came near him. "Stop there, will you," said Mr Fotheringay; and the pigeon hung motionless in the air. "I could change it back to a

The Man Who Could Work Miracles

bowl of flowers," he said, and after replacing the pigeon on the table worked that miracle. "I expect you will want your pipe in a bit," he said, and restored the tobacco-jar.

Mr Maydig had followed all these later changes in a sort of ejaculatory silence. He stared at Mr Fotheringay and, in a very gingerly manner, picked up the tobacco-jar, examined it, replaced it on the table. "*Well!*" was the only expression of his feelings.

"Now, after that it's easier to explain what I came about," said Mr Fotheringay; and proceeded to a lengthy and involved narrative of his strange experience, beginning with the affair of the lamp in the Long Dragon and complicated by persistent allusions to Winch. As he went on, the transient pride Mr Maydig's consternation had caused passed away; he became the very ordinary Mr Fotheringay of everyday again. Mr Maydig listened intently, the tobacco-jar in his hand, and his bearing changed also with the course of the narrative. Presently, while Mr Fotheringay was dealing with the miracle of the third egg, the minister interrupted with a fluttering extended hand——

"It is possible," he said. "It is credible. It is amazing, of course, but it reconciles a number of difficulties. The power to work miracles is a gift—a peculiar quality like genius or second sight—hitherto it has come very rarely and to exceptional people. But in this case . . . I have always wondered at the miracles of Mahomet, and at Yogis' miracles, and the miracles of Madame Blavatsky. But, of course! Yes, it is simply a gift! It carries out so beautifully the arguments of that great thinker"—Mr Maydig's voice sank—"his Grace the Duke of Argyll. Here we plumb some profounder law—deeper than the ordinary laws of nature. Yes—yes. Go on. Go on!"

Mr Fotheringay proceeded to tell of his misadventure with Winch, and Mr Maydig, no longer overawed or scared, began to jerk his limbs about and interject astonishment. "It's this what troubled me most," proceeded Mr Fotheringay; "it's this I'm most mijitly in want of advice for; of course he's at San Francisco—wherever San Francisco may be—but of course it's awkward for both of us, as you'll see, Mr Maydig. I don't see how he can understand what has happened, and I dare say he's scared and exasperated something tremendous, and trying to get at me. I dare say he keeps on starting off to come here. I send him back, by a miracle, every few hours, when I think of it. And of course, that's a thing he won't be able to understand, and it's bound to annoy him; and, of course, if he takes a ticket every time it will cost him a lot of money. I done the best I could for him, but of course it's difficult for him to put himself in my place. I thought afterwards that his clothes might have got scorched, you know—if Hades is all it's supposed to be—before I shifted him. In that case I suppose they'd have locked him up in San Francisco. Of course I willed him a new suit of clothes on him directly I thought of it. But, you see, I'm already in a deuce of a tangle——"

Mr Maydig looked serious. "I see you are in a tangle. Yes, it's a difficult position. How you are to end it . . ." He became diffuse and inconclusive.

"However, we'll leave Winch for a little and discuss the larger question. I don't think this is a case of the black art or anything of the sort. I don't think there is any taint of criminality about it at all, Mr Fotheringay—none whatever, unless you are suppressing material facts. No, it's miracles—pure miracles—miracles, if I may say so, of the very highest class."

He began to pace the hearthrug and gesticulate, while Mr Fotheringay sat with his arm on the table and his head on his arm, looking worried. "I don't see how I'm to manage about Winch," he said.

"A gift of working miracles—apparently a very powerful gift," said Mr Maydig, "will find a way about Winch—never fear. My dear Sir, you are a most important man—a man of the most astonishing possibilities. As evidence, for example! And in other ways, the things you may do . . ."

"Yes, *I've* thought of a thing or two," said Mr Fotheringay. "But—some of the things came a bit twisty. You saw that fish at first? Wrong sort of bowl and wrong sort of fish. And I thought I'd ask someone."

"A proper course," said Mr Maydig, "a very proper course—

The Man Who Could Work Miracles

altogether the proper course." He stopped and looked at Mr Fotheringay. "It's practically an unlimited gift. Let us test your powers, for instance. It they really *are* . . . If they really are all they seem to be."

And so, incredible as it may seem, in the study of the little house behind the Congregational Chapel, on the evening of Sunday, 10th November 1896, Mr Fotheringay, egged on and inspired by Mr Maydig, began to work miracles. The reader's attention is specially and definitely called to the date. He will object, probably has already objected, that certain points in this story are improbable, that if any things of the sort already described had indeed occurred, they would have been in all the papers a year ago. The details immediately following he will find particularly hard to accept, because among other things they involve the conclusion that he or she, the reader in question, must have been killed in a violent and unprecedented manner more than a year ago. Now a miracle is nothing if not improbable, and as a matter of fact the reader *was* killed in a violent and unprecedented manner a year ago. In the subsequent course of this story that will become perfectly clear and credible, as every right-minded and reasonable reader will admit. But this is not the place for the end of the story, being but little beyond the hither side of the middle. And at first the miracles worked by Mr Fotheringay were timid little miracles—little things with the cups and parlour fitments, as feeble as the miracles of Theosophists, and, feeble as they were, they were received with awe by his collaborator. He would have preferred to settle the Winch business out of hand, but Mr Maydig would not let him. But after they had worked a dozen of these domestic trivialities, their sense of power grew, their imagination began to show signs of stimulation, and their ambition enlarged. Their first larger enterprise was due to hunger and the negligence of Mrs Minchin, Mr Maydig's housekeeper. The meal to which the minister conducted Mr Fotheringay was certainly ill-laid and uninviting as refreshment for two industrious miracle-workers; but they were seated, and Mr Maydig was descanting in sorrow rather than in anger upon his housekeeper's shortcomings, before it occurred to Mr

Fotheringay that an opportunity lay before him. "Don't you think, Mr Maydig," he said, "if it isn't a liberty, I——"

"My dear Mr Fotheringay! Of course! No—I didn't think." Mr Fotheringay waved his hand. "What shall we have?" he said, in a large, inclusive spirit, and, at Mr Maydig's order, revised the supper very thoroughly. "As for me," he said, eyeing Mr Maydig's selection, "I am always particularly fond of a tankard of stout and a nice Welsh rarebit, and I'll order that. I ain't much given to Burgundy," and forthwith stout and Welsh rarebit promptly appeared at his command. They sat long at their supper, talking like equals, as Mr Fotheringay presently perceived with a glow of surprise and gratification, of all the miracles they would presently do. "And, by and by, Mr Maydig," said Mr Fotheringay, "I might perhaps be able to help you—in a domestic way."

"Don't quite follow," said Mr Maydig, pouring out a glass of miraculous old Burgundy.

Mr Fotheringay helped himself to a second Welsh rarebit out of vacancy, and took a mouthful. "I was thinking," he said, "I might be able (*chum chum*) to work (*chum chum*) a miracle with Mrs Minchin (*chum chum*)—make her a better woman."

Mr Maydig put down the glass and looked doubtful. "She's —— She strongly objects to interference, you know, Mr Fotheringay. And—as a matter of fact—it's well past eleven and she's probably in bed and asleep. Do you think, on the whole——"

Mr Fotheringay considered these objections. "I don't see that it shouldn't be done in her sleep."

For a time Mr Maydig opposed the idea, and then he yielded. Mr Fotheringay issued his orders, and a little less at their ease, perhaps, the two gentlemen proceeded with their repast. Mr Maydig was enlarging on the changes he might expect in his housekeeper next day, with an optimism that seemed even to Mr Fotheringay's supper senses a little forced and hectic, when a series of confused noises from upstairs began. Their eyes exchanged interrogations, and Mr Maydig left the room hastily. Mr Fotheringay heard him calling up to his housekeeper and then his footsteps going softly up to her.

The Man Who Could Work Miracles

In a minute or so the minister returned, his step light, his face radiant. "Wonderful!" he said, "and touching! Most touching!" He began pacing the hearthrug. "A repentance—a most touching repentance—through the crack of the door. Poor woman! A most wonderful change! She had got up. She must have got up at once. She had got up out of her sleep to smash a private bottle of brandy in her box. And to confess it too...! But this gives us—it opens—a most amazing vista of possibilities. If we can work this miraculous change in *her*..."

"The thing's unlimited seemingly," said Mr Fotheringay. "And about Mr Winch——"

"Altogether unlimited." And from the hearthrug Mr Maydig, waving the Winch difficulty aside, unfolded a series of wonderful proposals—proposals he invented as he went along.

Now what those proposals were does not concern the essentials of this story. Suffice it that they were designed in a spirit of infinite benevolence, the sort of benevolence that used to be called post-prandial. Suffice it, too, that the problem of Winch remained unsolved. Nor is it necessary to describe how far that series got to its fulfilment. There were astonishing changes. The small hours found Mr Maydig and Mr Fotheringay careering across the chilly market-square under the still moon, in a sort of ecstasy of thaumaturgy. Mr Maydig all flap and gesture, Mr Fotheringay short and bristling, and no longer abashed at his greatness. They had reformed every drunkard in the Parliamentary division, changed all the beer and alcohol to water (Mr Maydig had overruled Mr Fotheringay on this point), they had, further, greatly improved the railway communication of the place, drained Flinders' swamp, improved the soil of One Tree Hill, and cured the Vicar's wart. And they were going to see what could be done with the injured pier at South Bridge. "The place," gasped Mr Maydig, "won't be the same place tomorrow! How surprised and thankful everyone will be!" And just at that moment the church clock struck three.

"I say," said Mr Fotheringay, "that's three o'clock! I must be getting back. I've got to be at business by eight. And besides, Mrs Wimms——"

"We're only beginning," said Mr Maydig, full of the sweetness of unlimited power. "We're only beginning. Think of all the good we're doing. When people wake——"
"But——" said Mr Fotheringay.
Mr Maydig gripped his arm suddenly. His eyes were bright and wild. "My dear chap," he said, "there's no hurry. Look"— he pointed to the moon at the zenith—"Joshua!"
"Joshua?" said Mr Fotheringay.
"Joshua," said Mr Maydig. "Why not? Stop it."
Mr Fotheringay looked at the moon.
"That's a bit tall," he said after a pause.
"Why not?" said Mr Maydig. "Of course it doesn't stop. You stop the rotation of the earth, you know. Time stops. It isn't as if we were doing harm."
"H'm!" said Mr Fotheringay. "Well," he sighed. "I'll try. Here——"
He buttoned up his jacket and addressed himself to the habitable globe, with as good an assumption of confidence as lay in his power. "Jest stop rotating, will you," said Mr Fotheringay.
Incontinently he was flying head over heels through the air at the rate of dozens of miles a minute. In spite of the innumerable circles he was describing per second, he thought; for thought is wonderful—sometimes as sluggish as flowing pitch, sometimes as instantaneous as light. He thought in a second, and willed. "Let me come down safe and sound. Whatever else happens, let me down safe and sound."
He willed it only just in time, for his clothes, heated by his rapid flight through the air, were already beginning to singe. He came down with a forcible but by no means injurious bump in what appeared to be a mound of fresh-turned earth. A large mass of metal and masonry, extraordinarily like the clock-tower in the middle of the market-square, hit the earth near him, ricochetted over him, and flew into stonework, bricks, and masonry, like a bursting bomb. A hurtling cow hit one of the larger blocks and smashed like an egg. There was a crash that made all the most violent crashes of his past life seem like the sound of falling dust, and this was followed by a descending

series of lesser crashes. A vast wind roared throughout earth and heaven, so that he could scarcely lift his head to look. For a while he was too breathless and astonished even to see where he was or what had happened. And his first movement was to feel his head and reassure himself that his streaming hair was still his own.

"Lord!" gasped Mr Fotheringay, scarce able to speak for the gale. "I've had a squeak! What's gone wrong? Storms and thunder. And only a minute ago a fine night. It's Maydig set me on to this sort of thing. *What* a wind! If I go on fooling in this way I'm bound to have a thundering accident . . . !

"Where's Maydig?"

"What a confounded mess everything's in!"

He looked about him so far as his flapping jacket would permit. The appearance of things was really extremely strange. "The sky's all right anyhow," said Mr Fotheringay. "And that's about all that is all right. And even there it looks like a terrific gale coming up. But there's the moon overhead. Just as it was just now. Bright as midday. But as for the rest—— Where's the village? Where's—where's anything? And what on earth set this wind a-blowing? I *didn't* order no wind."

Mr Fotheringay struggled to get to his feet in vain, and after one failure, remained on all fours, holding on. He surveyed the moonlit world to leeward, with the tails of his jacket streaming over his head. "There's something seriously wrong," said Mr Fotheringay. "And what it is—goodness knows."

Far and wide nothing was visible in the white glare through the haze of dust that drove before a screaming gale but tumbled masses of earth and heaps of inchoate ruins, no trees, no houses, no familiar shapes, only a wilderness of disorder vanishing at last into the darkness beneath the whirling columns and streamers, the lightnings and thunderings of a swiftly rising storm. Near him in the livid glare was something that might once have been an elm-tree, a smashed mass of splinters, shivered from boughs to base, and further a twisted mass of iron girders—only too evidently the viaduct—rose out of the piled confusion.

You see, when Mr Fotheringay had arrested the rotation of the solid globe, he had made no stipulation concerning the trifling movables upon its surface. And the earth spins so fast that the surface at its equator is travelling at rather more than a thousand miles an hour, and in these latitudes at more than half that pace. So that the village, and Mr Maydig, and Mr Fotheringay, and everybody and everything had been jerked violently forward at about nine miles per second—that is to say, much more violently than if they had been fired out of a cannon. And every human being, every living creature, every house, and every tree—all the world as we know it—had been so jerked and smashed and utterly destroyed. That was all.

These things Mr Fotheringay did not, of course, fully appreciate. But he perceived that his miracle had miscarried, and with that a great disgust of miracles came upon him. He was in darkness now, for the clouds had swept together and blotted out his momentary glimpse of the moon, and the air was full of fitful struggling tortured wraiths of hail. A great roaring of wind and waters filled earth and sky, and, peering under his hand through the dust and sleet to windward, he saw by the play of the lightnings a vast wall of water pouring towards him.

"Maydig!" screamed Mr Fotheringay's feeble voice amid the elemental uproar. "Here!—Maydig!"

"Stop!" cried Mr Fotheringay to the advancing water. "Oh, for goodness' sake stop!"

"Just a moment," said Mr Fotheringay to the lightnings and thunder. "Stop jest a moment while I collect my thoughts. . . . And now what shall I do?" he said. "What *shall* I do? Lord! I wish Maydig was about."

"I know," said Mr Fotheringay. "And for goodness' sake let's have it right *this time*."

He remained on all fours, leaning against the wind, very intent to have everything right.

"Ah!" he said. "Let nothing what I'm going to order happen until I say 'Off!' . . . Lord! I wish I'd thought of that before!"

He lifted his little voice against the whirlwind, shouting louder and louder in the vain desire to hear himself speak. "Now then!—here goes! Mind about that what I said just now. In the first place, when all I've got to say is done, let me lose my miraculous power, let my will become just like anybody else's will, and all these dangerous miracles be stopped. I don't like them. I'd rather I didn't work 'em. Ever so much. That's the first thing. And the second is—let me be back just before the miracles begin; let everything be just as it was before that blessed lamp turned up. It's a big job, but it's the last. Have you got it? No more miracles, everything as it was—me back in the Long Dragon just before I drank my half-pint. That's it! Yes."

He dug his fingers into the mould, closed his eyes, and said "Off!"

Everything became perfectly still. He perceived that he was standing erect.

"So *you* say," said a voice.

He opened his eyes. He was in the bar of the Long Dragon, arguing about miracles with Toddy Beamish. He had a vague sense of some great thing forgotten that instantaneously passed. You see, except for the loss of his miraculous powers, everything was back as it had been; his mind and memory therefore were now just as they had been at the time when this story began. So that he knew absolutely nothing of all that is told here, knows nothing of all that is told here to this day. And among other things, of course, he still did not believe in miracles.

"I tell you that miracles, properly speaking, can't possibly happen," he said, "whatever you like to hold. And I'm prepared to prove it up to the hilt."

"That's what *you* think," said Toddy Beamish, and "Prove it if you can."

"Looky here, Mr Beamish," said Mr Fotheringay. "Let us clearly understand what a miracle is. It's something contrariwise to the course of nature done by power of Will . . ."

The April Witch

RAY BRADBURY

Into the air, over the valleys, under the stars, above a river, a pond, a road, flew Cecy. Invisible as new spring winds, fresh as the breath of clover rising from twilight fields, she flew. She soared in doves as soft as white ermine, stopped in trees and lived in blossoms, showering away in petals when the breeze blew. She perched in a lime-green frog, cool as mint by a shining pool. She trotted in a brambly dog and barked to hear echoes from the sides of distant barns. She lived in new April grasses, in sweet clear liquids rising from the musky earth.

It's spring, thought Cecy. I'll be in every living thing in the world tonight.

Now she inhabited neat crickets on the tar-pool roads, now prickled in dew on an iron gate. Hers was an adaptably quick mind flowing unseen upon Illinois winds on this one evening of her life when she was just seventeen.

"I want to be in love," she said.

She had said it at supper. And her parents had widened their eyes and stiffened back in their chairs. "Patience," had been their advice. "Remember, you're remarkable. Our whole family is odd and remarkable. We can't mix or marry with ordinary folk. We'd lose our magical powers if we did. You wouldn't want to lose you ability to 'travel' by magic, would you? Then be careful. Be careful!"

But in her high bedroom, Cecy had touched perfume to her throat and stretched out, trembling and apprehensive, on her four-poster, as a moon the colour of milk rose over Illinois country, turning rivers to cream and roads to platinum.

"Yes," she sighed. "I'm one of an odd family. We sleep days and fly nights like black kites on the wind. If we want, we can sleep in moles through the winter, in the warm earth. I can live in anything at all—a pebble, a crocus, or a praying mantis. I can leave my plain, bony body behind and send my mind far out for adventure. Now!"

The wind whipped her away over fields and meadows.

She saw the warm spring lights of cottages and farms glowing with twilight colours.

If I can't be in love, myself, because I'm plain and odd, then I'll be in love through someone else, she thought.

Outside a farmhouse in the spring night a dark-haired girl, no more than nineteen, drew up water from a deep stone well. She was singing.

Cecy fell—a green leaf—into the well. She lay in the tender moss of the well, gazing up through dark coolness. Now she quickened in a fluttering, invisible amoeba. Now in a water droplet! At last, within a cold cup, she felt herself lifted to the girl's warm lips. There was a soft night sound of drinking.

Cecy looked out from the girl's eyes.

She entered into the dark head and gazed from the shining eyes at the hands pulling the rough rope. She listened through the shell ears to this girl's world. She smelled a particular universe through these delicate nostrils, felt this special heart beating, beating. Felt this strange tongue move with singing.

Does she know I'm here? thought Cecy.

The girl gasped. She stared into the night meadows.

"Who's there?"

No answer.

"Only the wind," whispered Cecy.

"Only the wind." The girl laughed at herself, but shivered.

It was a good body, this girl's body. It held bones of finest slender ivory hidden and roundly fleshed. This brain was like a pink tea rose, hung in darkness, and there was cider-wine in this mouth. The lips lay firm on the white, white teeth and the

The April Witch

brows arched neatly at the world, and the hair blew soft and fine on her milky neck. The pores knit small and close. The nose tilted at the moon and the cheeks glowed like small fires. The body drifted with feather-balances from one motion to another and seemed always singing to itself. Being in this body, this head, was like basking in a hearth fire, living in the purr of a sleeping cat, stirring in warm creek waters that flowed by night to the sea.

I'll like it here, thought Cecy.

"What?" asked the girl, as if she'd heard a voice.

"What's your name?" asked Cecy carefully.

"Ann Leary." The girl twitched. "Now why should I say *that* out loud?"

"Ann, Ann," whispered Cecy. "Ann, you're going to be in love."

As if to answer this, a great roar sprang from the road, a clatter and a ring of wheels on gravel. A tall man drove up in a rig, holding the reins high with his monstrous arms, his smile glowing across the yard.

"Ann!"

"Is that you, Tom?"

"Who else?" Leaping from the rig, he tied the reins to the fence.

"I'm not speaking to you!" Ann whirled, the bucket in her hands slopping.

"No!" cried Cecy.

Ann froze. She looked at the hills and the first spring stars. She stared at the man named Tom. Cecy made her drop the bucket.

"Look what you've done!"

Tom ran up.

"Look what you *made* me do!"

He wiped her shoes with a kerchief, laughing.

"Get away!" She kicked at his hands, but he laughed again, and gazing down on him from miles away, Cecy saw the turn of his head, the size of his skull, the flare of his nose, the shine of his eye, the girth of his shoulder, and the hard strength of his hands

The April Witch

doing this delicate thing with the handkerchief. Peering down from the secret attic of this lovely head, Cecy yanked a hidden copper ventriloquist's wire and the pretty mouth popped wide: "Thank you!"

"Oh, so you *have* manners?" The smell of leather on his hands, the smell of the horse rose from his clothes into the tender nostrils, and Cecy, far, far away over night meadows and flowered fields, stirred as with some dream in her bed.

"Not for you, no!" said Ann.

"Hush, speak gently," said Cecy. She moved Ann's fingers out toward Tom's head. Ann snatched them back.

"I've gone mad!"

"You have." He nodded, smiling but bewildered. "Were you going to touch me then?"

"I don't know. Oh, go away!" Her cheeks glowed with pink charcoals.

"Why don't you run? I'm not stopping you." Tom got up. "Have you changed your mind? Will you go to the dance with me tonight? It's special. Tell you why later."

"No," said Ann.

"Yes!" cried Cecy. "I've never danced. I want to dance. I've never worn a long gown, all rustly. I want that. I want to dance all night. I've never known what it's like to be in a woman, dancing; Father and Mother would never permit it. Dogs, cats, locusts, leaves, everything else in the world at one time or another I've known, but never a woman in the spring, never on a night like this. Oh, please—we *must* go to that dance!"

She spread her thought like the fingers of a hand within a new glove.

"Yes," said Ann Leary, "I'll go. I don't know why, but I'll go to the dance with you tonight, Tom."

"Now inside, quick!" cried Cecy. "You must wash, tell your folks, get your gown ready, out with the iron, into your room!"

"Mother," said Ann, "I've changed my mind!"

The rig was galloping off down the pike, the rooms of the farmhouse jumped to life, water was boiling for a bath, the coal stove was heating an iron to press the gown, the mother was rushing about with a fringe of hairpins in her mouth. "What's come over you, Ann? You don't like Tom!"

"That's true." Ann stopped amidst the great fever.

But it's spring! thought Cecy.

"It's spring," said Ann.

And it's a fine night for dancing, thought Cecy.

". . . for dancing," murmured Ann Leary.

Then she was in the tub and the soap creaming on her white seal shoulders, small nests of soap beneath her arms, and the flesh of her warm breasts moving in her hands and Cecy moving the mouth, making the smile, keeping the actions going. There must be no pause, no hesitation, or the entire pantomime might fall in ruins! Ann Leary must be kept moving, doing, acting, wash here, soap there, now out! Rub with a towel! Now perfume and powder!

"You!" Ann caught herself in the mirror, all whiteness and pinkness like lilies and carnations. "*Who* are you tonight?"

"I'm a girl, seventeen." Cecy gazed from her violet eyes. "You can't see me. Do you know I'm here?"

Ann Leary shook her head. "I've rented my body to an April witch, for sure."

"*Close*, very close!" laughed Cecy. "Now, on with your dressing."

The luxury of feeling good clothes move over an ample body! And then the halloo outside.

"Ann, Tom's back!"

"Tell him to wait." Ann sat down suddenly. "Tell him I'm not going to that dance."

"What?" said her mother, in the door.

Cecy snapped back into attention. It had been a fatal relaxing, a fatal moment of leaving Ann's body for only an instant. She had heard the distant sound of horses' hoofs and the rig rambling through moonlit spring country. For a second she thought, I'll go find Tom and sit in his head and see what it's like to be in a man of twenty-two on a night like this. And so she had started

The April Witch

quickly across a heather field, but now, like a bird to a cage, flew back and rustled and beat about in Ann Leary's head.

"Ann!"

"Tell him to go away!"

"Ann!" Cecy settled down and spread her thoughts. But Ann had the bit in her mouth now. "No, no, I hate him!"

I shouldn't have left—even for a moment. Cecy poured her mind into the hands of the young girl, into the heart, into the head, softly, softly. *Stand up,* she thought.

Ann stood.

Put on your coat!

Ann put on her coat.

Now, march!

No! thought Ann Leary.

March!

"Ann," said her mother, "don't keep Tom waiting another minute. You get on out there now and no nonsense. What's come over you?"

"Nothing, Mother. Good night. We'll be home late."

Ann and Cecy ran together into the spring evening.

A room full of softly dancing pigeons ruffling their quiet, trailing feathers, a room full of peacocks, a room full of rainbow eyes and lights. And in the centre of it, around, around, around, danced Ann Leary.

"Oh, it *is* a fine evening," said Cecy.

"Oh, it's a fine evening," said Ann.

"You're odd," said Tom.

The music whirled them in dimness, in rivers of song; they floated, they bobbed, they sank down, they arose for air, they gasped, they clutched each other like drowning people and whirled on again, in fan motions, in whispers and sighs, to "Beautiful Ohio."

Cecy hummed. Ann's lips parted and the music came out.

"Yes, I'm odd," said Cecy.

"You're not the same," said Tom.

"No, not tonight."

The April Witch

"You're not the Ann Leary I knew."

"No, not at all, at all," whispered Cecy, miles and miles away. "No, not at all," said the moved lips.

"I've the funniest feeling," said Tom.

"About what?"

"About you." He held her back and danced her and looked into her glowing face, watching for something. "Your eyes," he said, "I can't figure it."

"Do you see *me*?" asked Cecy.

"Part of you's here, Ann, and part of you's not." Tom turned her carefully, his face uneasy.

"Yes."

"Why did you come with me?"

"I didn't want to come," said Ann.

"Why, then?"

"Something made me."

"What?"

"I don't know." Ann's voice was faintly hysterical.

"Now, now, hush, hush," whispered Cecy. "Hush, that's it. Around, around."

They whispered and rustled and rose and fell away in the dark room, with the music moving and turning them.

"But you *did* come to the dance," said Tom.

"I did," said Cecy.

"Here." And he danced her lightly out an open door and walked her quietly away from the hall and the music and the people.

They climbed up and sat together in the rig.

"Ann," he said, taking her hands, trembling. "Ann." But the way he said the name it was as if it wasn't her name. He kept glancing into her pale face, and now her eyes were open again. "I used to love you, you know that," he said.

"I know."

"But you've always been fickle and I didn't want to be hurt."

"It's just as well, we're very young," said Ann.

"No, I mean to say, I'm sorry," said Cecy.

"What *do* you mean?" Tom dropped her hands and stiffened.

The April Witch

The night was warm and the smell of the earth shimmered up all about them where they sat, and the fresh trees breathed one leaf against another in a shaking and rustling.

"I don't know," said Ann.

"Oh, but *I* know," said Cecy. "You're tall and you're the finest-looking man in all the world. This is a good evening; this is an evening I'll always remember, being with you." She put out the alien cold hand to find his reluctant hand again and bring it back, and warm it and hold it very tight.

"But," said Tom, blinking, "tonight you're here, you're there. One minute one way, the next minute another. I wanted to take you to the dance tonight for old times' sake. I meant nothing by it when I first asked you. And then, when we were standing at the well, I knew something had changed, really changed, about you. You were different. There was something new and soft, something . . ." He groped for a word. "I don't know, I can't say. The way you looked. Something about your voice. And I know I'm in love with you again."

"No," said Cecy. "With me, with *me*."

"And I'm afraid of being in love with you," he said. "You'll hurt me again."

"I might," said Ann.

No, no, I'd love you with all my heart! thought Cecy. Ann, say it to him, say it for me. Say you'd love him with all your heart.

Ann said nothing.

Tom moved quietly closer and put his hand up to hold her chin. "I'm going away. I've got a job a hundred miles from here. Will you miss me?"

"Yes," said Ann and Cecy.

"May I kiss you good-bye, then?"

"Yes," said Cecy before anyone else could speak.

He placed his lips to the strange mouth. He kissed the strange mouth and he was trembling.

Ann sat like a white statue.

"Ann!" said Cecy. "Move your arms, *hold* him!"

She sat like a carved wooden doll in the moonlight.

Again he kissed her lips.

"I do love you," whispered Cecy. "I'm here, it's me you saw in her eyes, it's me, and I love you if she never will."

He moved away and seemed like a man who had run a long distance. He sat beside her. "I don't know what's happening. For a moment there..."

"Yes?" asked Cecy.

"For a moment I thought——" He put his hands to his eyes. "Never mind. Shall I take you home now?"

"Please," said Ann Leary.

He clucked to the horse, snapped the reins tiredly, and drove the rig away. They rode in the rustle and slap and motion of the moonlit rig in the still early, only eleven o'clock spring night, with the shining meadows and sweet fields of clover gliding by.

And Cecy, looking at the fields and meadows, thought, It would be worth it, it would be worth everything to be with him from this night on. And she heard her parents' voices again, faintly, "Be careful. You wouldn't want to lose your magical powers, would you—married to a mere mortal? Be careful. You wouldn't want that."

Yes, yes, thought Cecy, even that I'd give up, here and now, if he would have me. I wouldn't need to roam the spring nights then, I wouldn't need to live in birds and dogs and cats and foxes, I'd need only to be with him. Only him. Only him.

The road passed under, whispering.

"Tom," said Ann at last.

"What?" He stared coldly at the road, the horse, the trees, the sky, the stars.

"If you're ever, in years to come, at any time, in Green Town, Illinois, a few miles from here, will you do me a favour?"

"Perhaps."

"Will you do me the favour of stopping and seeing a friend of mine?" Ann Leary said this haltingly, awkwardly.

"Why?"

"She's a good friend. I've told her of you. I'll give you her address. Just a moment." When the rig stopped at her farm she drew forth a pencil and paper from her small purse and wrote

The April Witch

in the moonlight, pressing the paper to her knee. "There it is. Can you read it?"

He glanced at the paper and nodded bewilderedly.

"Cecy Elliott, 12 Willow Street, Green Town, Illinois," he said.

"Will you visit her some day?" asked Ann.

"Some day," he said.

"Promise?"

"What has this to do with us?" he cried savagely. "What do I want with names and papers?" He crumpled the paper into a tight ball and shoved it in his coat.

"Oh, please promise!" begged Cecy.

". . . promise . . ." said Ann.

"All right, all right, now let me be!" he shouted.

I'm tired, thought Cecy. I can't stay. I have to go home. I'm weakening. I've only the power to stay a few hours out like this in the night, travelling, travelling. But before I go . . .

". . . before I go," said Ann.

She kissed Tom on the lips.

"This is *me* kissing you," said Cecy.

Tom held her off and looked at Ann Leary and looked deep, deep inside. He said nothing, but his face began to relax slowly, very slowly, and the lines vanished away, and his mouth softened from its hardness, and he looked deep again into the moonlit face held here before him.

Then he put her off the rig and without so much as a good night was driving swiftly down the road.

Cecy let go.

Ann Leary, crying out, released from prison, it seemed, raced up the moonlit path to her house and slammed the door.

Cecy lingered for only a little while. In the eyes of a cricket she saw the spring night world. In the eyes of a frog she sat for a lonely moment by a pool. In the eyes of a night bird she looked down from a tall, moon-haunted elm and saw the light go out in two farmhouses, one here, one a mile away. She thought of herself and her family, and her strange power, and the fact that no one in the family could every marry any one of the people in this vast world out here beyond the hills.

"Tom?" Her weakening mind flew in a night bird under the trees and over deep fields of wild mustard. "Have you still got the paper, Tom? Will you come by some day, some year, some time, to see me? Will you know me then? Will you look in my face and remember then where it was you saw me last and know that you love me as I love you, with all my heart for all time?"

She paused in the cool night air, a million miles from towns and people, above farms and continents and rivers and hills. "Tom?" Softly.

Tom was asleep. It was deep night; his clothes were hung on chairs or folded neatly over the end of the bed. And in one silent, carefully upflung hand upon the white pillow, by his head, was a small piece of paper with writing on it. Slowly, slowly, a fraction of an inch at a time, his fingers closed down upon and held it tightly. And he did not even stir or notice when a blackbird, faintly, wondrously, beat softly for a moment against the clear moon crystals of the windowpane, then, fluttering quietly, stopped and flew away toward the east, over the sleeping earth.

Strange Fish

LEON GARFIELD

The signpost's battered finger pointed towards the sea as if it was accusing it of something disagreeable. A man and youth, breathing heavily from the effort of walking over rough ground, stared at it in silence.

"What do you say?" asked the man at length. The youth squinted up. He was about fifteen, sturdy and with humorous eyes already well-crinkled from sun and sea. "One mile to somewhere, Pa," he said. "All that's left is Saint; but Saint what, the Lord knows. It's gone with the weather."

The man grunted and clapped his great roughened hand about his son's shoulder as if congratulating him on his scholarship. Then they trudged on through the cold November sunshine to the village that had lost its name. It lay in the crook of a narrow bay—a quiet huddle of stone cottages with an old church standing a little way apart as if it had taken offence, perhaps on account of the forgotten saint. Indeed, the air of reproach seemed to hang pretty heavily over the whole village and even over the bay where the bright sea sighed and dragged as if it longed to take itself off elsewhere. There was only one boat on the beach and no nets to be seen; but this was not surprising as the weather was fair. The father and son halted again and stared out to sea for a glimpse of fishermen; but the lowering sun was bright on the water and no amount of eye-shading or squinting could distinguish anything for certain so they continued down the rough path that dropped away between tufted hillocks that here and there rose shoulder high. Suddenly the youth clutched his face and gave a cry of anger and pain.

"What is it, Sammy? Fly?" "Stone, Pa. Someone threw a stone." He scrambled up the bank with his father following and, crouching in the long grass some five yards off, saw the first signs of life from the quiet village. Three children, supernaturally ragged and dirty. They were about five years old, one boy and two girls; but which of them had thrown the stone was impossible to say. They all looked as savage and hostile as each other.

"Where's your pa?" asked Sam, rubbing his cheek and scowling threateningly. The boy stood up and pointed towards the church. "And yours?" he asked the girls, who looked to be no relation. They glanced at their companion and climbed to their feet. They too pointed towards the church.

"It ain't Sunday, is it, Sammy?" asked his father, who'd lost count of the days during their journey across country. Sam turned to answer that to the best of his belief it was a Tuesday, when the three venomous children took advantage of the distraction and fled. They had not uttered a single word, either to Sam and his father, or to each other. They might have been malignant spirits who'd vanished into the air.

None the less the man and youth turned their steps towards the church, though with no great hopes. God-fearing though the village might have been, Tuesday afternoon was an unnatural time to be in church.

Sure enough, the church was deserted. Empty pews gazed at the empty altar, and a roughly made ship's model that hung in the doorway cast its shadow across the aisle, where it swayed and foundered among the shadows of the pew backs.

Puzzled and angry, they went outside again resolved to knock up the nearest cottage, holy Tuesday or no, when Sam pointed to the churchyard that lay beyond the church's western wall. Aged stones leaned among the tall grass, peering and peeping as if striving to read each other's inscriptions. But past this tumbled crumbling part was another, very neat and green. It looked almost like a great gown laid out to dry and fixed with pegs and stone.

Strange Fish

Curiously the father and son walked towards it; for it was an odd, almost uncanny sight ... the graves being so neatly laid as if a small regiment had perished on parade and been buried where they'd stood.

"What do they say, Sammy?" muttered his father. "You know I come without me spectacles."

Sam nodded. Though his father had a pair of spectacles which he'd found in the cabin of a wreck; and though he often wore them of an evening by the fire, they were more of a personal ornament then anything else as he was quite unable to read. He never admitted this weakness to his wife or son (though they knew it perfectly well), not because he was ashamed but because he was the head of the house and it was against nature for a woman or a boy to be more proficient than he. So when there was any reading to be done, his spectacles were more useful in their absence than on his nose, where they only served to hide the marvellous brightness of his eyes.

"Jacob Tulliver," read Sam from the nearest stone. "Taken November seven, 1749. Rest in Peace."

"Only a year in his grave," murmured Sam's father. "And the grass as thick as a cushion."

"John Blazey," continued Sam, from the next stone. "Taken November seven, 1749. Rest in Peace." He frowned, then moved on. "Ezra Till. Taken November seven, 1749. Rest in Peace."

"What? Three of 'em on the same day? Sure you read 'em right, lad?"

"Read 'em yourself, Pa," said Sam mockingly, "if you don't trust me scholarship."

"You know I ain't got me spectacles. Just you go on and remember I'm watching."

So Sam went on and read the names on all the graves—of which there were three and forty—and every man who lay beneath had been taken on that same day of that same year. It was as if the Angel of Death had decided to kill three and forty birds with one stone to save himself the trouble of calling on the village again.

Strange Fish

A chill crept over the boy as he stared at the quiet grass and the quiet stones. "Must have been a storm or something," he whispered.

"Or something," repeated his father.

"Plague, maybe?"

"What plague takes only menfolk—and all on the same day?"

"Storm, then, Pa."

"And what storm to reach out and hook 'em all together?"

"Let's find the inn, Pa, and ask the landlord."

His father nodded—then tightened his lips. "No wild spending, mind."

"Food and drink, Pa. Nothing more."

"Food I hold with; but not wine."

"They say Our Lord wasn't against wine, Pa—"

"He was the Son of God. You're the son of Job Wilkins. Ale and water for you, lad; and leave the wine be."

They left the churchyard and walked through the narrow street that twisted among the cottages with many a sharp angle and hiding place for shadows. Sometimes women's faces peered out as they passed; but they looked no more welcoming than had the three fierce children. Being Cornish, they were as sharp and hard as the rocks of their dangerous coast.

At last Job and his son reached the inn, which was the cottage furthest off from the church and had a post outside with a swinging sign of a ship executed as poorly as had been the model in the church. Plainly the villagers had no time for anything but their livelihood from the sea. The father and son pushed open the door and entered directly into the tiny parlour. Ignoring the landlord and his solitary customer, Job made straight for the list of prices that hung in a frame behind the door. "Read me what it says, lad."

"We ain't robbers, stranger," grinned the landlord, not so much to Job as to his scowling customer; "Parson here'll see you ain't done down."

The landlord was a short, red-faced man with a remarkably merry expression, like a nutcracker carved out of a very hard wood and coloured and varnished to a high gloss. The parson, on the other hand, was still in a state of nature, so to speak, having a pale, unseasoned complexion with no shine at all save at the tip of his nose which was faintly red as if colouring had been begun and then abandoned as a waste.

"No fish?" said Job, when his son came to the last item on the list which was mutton chops.

"No fish," confirmed the landlord, nodding his varnished head.

"What becomes of it when it's brought in?"

"Never is, stranger. Never is brought in."

"Then what do your menfolks do hereabouts?"

"What menfolk, stranger? Have you seen any, maybe?"

"Ain't they out in their boats on this fine day?"

"Yes indeed," said the parson suddenly coming out of his glass of brandy and setting it down so sharply that the landlord started. "They're out in their boats all right. Every last one of them. But their boats are long and narrow, each with a lid screwed down tight. And the sea they sail is churchyard earth, with a breaker above of cold grey stone. This is a village of widows, my friends; this is a village that has been damned."

The parson took up his brandy again, seemed to wash his nose in it, then drank it down. "They went to hell together, November seven, 1749."

"Heaven, stranger. Take my word on it," interposed the cheerful landlord, "they went in a state of grace; but parson here's fond of his drop of fire and brimstone as he is of his brandy."

"This is a damned village. Even the sea hates it now," went on the parson, a holy fire in his faded eyes.

Job shrugged his shoulders and then, in answer to the landlord's inquiry, explained that he and his son were fishermen from the north; but the fish had shifted from their waters so they'd travelled overland in the hopes of finding a better livelihood in the south. The landlord listened with interest and declared that fish had always been plentiful just beyond the bay; and, further, that a widow of his acquaintance owned a capable craft that she'd be willing to rent or sell, if the price proved right.

"Don't listen to him, friends," warned the parson grimly. "Better to starve elsewhere than go out from this accursed spot into this accursed sea. At night you can hear it, beating on the shore and cursing it for all eternity."

"What for?" asked Sam.

"Murder, friend. Foul and hateful murder. When the landlord said fish are plentiful hereabouts, he spoke the truth. No one ever caught them. The sea had a richer harvest. Ships. This was a village of wreckers, my friends."

There was silence in the little parlour. The landlord had gone to fetch water and ale and the fire danced and spat in the hearth as if in defence of his good name.

"Vessel after vessel they brought onto the rocks with lanterns swung from the headland. And whenever it happened that some poor wretch gained the shore, frantic with relief and thanking God for his escape, they'd murder him as if he'd been no more than a twisting fish. If he wore rings, they'd hack off his fingers before they threw him back into the sea..."

The parson stopped as the landlord returned with his unchanging smile. "Now, now," he said, setting the jugs of ale and water before Job and his son, "I don't hold with a churchman speaking against the dead. None of us is perfect and our departed friends may have had their faults. But they went like martyrs and it's certain they went to heaven together. Whatever they might have done in the past, was washed away on that night last year. Judge for yourselves, strangers," he went on, prodding the fire with his bright boot as if bidding it hold its peace while he talked of the dead. "Judge for yourselves, and then say honestly whether them three and forty in the graveyard was redeemed or went to roast in hell.

"There was maybe a dozen of us in the parlour that evening. Jacob Tulliver, God rest him, was sitting right where you are, lad." Hastily, Sam shifted along the bench, and the landlord nodded approvingly, as if he respected Sam's courtesy to a ghost.

"Some of us was playing dice, and there was dominoes on the table in a long, spotted cross. There was no talk of going up on the headland that night, as the weather was calm and fair ...

even as it's been today. So what came to pass was a real act of God, sent to test 'em all. And they came through in glory!"

Here the landlord stared blandly at the parson as if daring him to contradict; but the reverend gentleman contented himself with a holy sneer, so the landlord went on with his calling up of the churchyard sleepers on that fair calm evening of November seven.

Such was his voice and the heated air of the little parlour, together with the weariness of Job and his son, that the dead villagers seemed very real; and as he turned from corner to corner, remembering what they'd said and done, how they'd laughed and bickered and talked over grim old times, Sam could have sworn he felt them jostle him away from the fire . . .

"It had been pretty late; the sun had been down some while and there'd fallen on the parlour one of those queer silences that seem to come at twenty past or twenty to the hour. Some say it's on account of an angel flying overhead. Indeed, Ezra Till made that very observation; so Jacob Tulliver, with a great greasy grin said he'd nip outside and wave to the high flying gentleman. He got up and, being a big man, knocked over a glass on his way.

"He was outside for maybe half a minute," went on the landlord, staring at the door with a smile that was not so much varnished as frozen, "when he came back. Burst in with a great commotion. 'A ship, a ship!' he shouted. 'There's a big ship on the rocks! It's done for, I think!'

"We all rushed out and I remember half the dominoes went flying into the fire. Sure enough, Jacob was right. There was a real monster of a vessel at the end of the bay. She was very high in the poop, like them Spanish or Dutch craft, and she seemed to be hooked for'ard on the rocks; for her stern kept coming round. She was under full sail so it must just have happened . . . though what dozy helmsman could have brought her here out of a calm sea was a mystery.

"Then we heard a shouting far off—a shouting for help; and then the great booming thump as her timbers kept striking on stone. We stood watching for I don't know how long, maybe five minutes, maybe more. The women had come out and the children too, for the night was that clear we could almost make out her name. It was the Santa something . . . but it looked like the sea and the weather had washed out the rest. Then the wind freshened and a parcel of stars was doused. A shadow, like a great hand, fell across the ship and the thumping came quicker and fairly rattled her on the rocks.

" 'She's holed!' shouted Ezra, who'd been watching through his glass. 'For the love of Jesus! Take a squint, Jacob! I'm going out to her, before all's lost!'

"He gave the glass to Tulliver and I can still see the big fellow's face as the look on it changed as he squinted through it. His greasy grin turned to real passion and pity as if he'd seen dear creatures perishing. 'I'm with you, Ezra!' he muttered. 'Even if the wind blows straight from hell! Let's go afore it's too late!' Then he and Ezra went down for their boat and all the rest followed after.

"So they went out to that holed ship on the rocks and the wind blew like an iron fist and fair hammered the sea in the bay. But it never stopped them and on they went, hopping over the waves till they was lost from sight in the dark and spray and a ragbag of mist the wind had blown in."

The landlord paused and shivered as if the sight was still before his eyes. "It weren't till next morning that they came back; and then it was one by one. They came floating, drifting on the tide . . . face down, face up . . . one or two with not much face at all. Pieces of their boats came too—but no more than would have made a rowboat for a child. They'd been smashed on the rocks and drowned—every last one of them. They'd given their lives for that there vessel that cried for help."

The landlord paused again and stared into the fire that gleamed on his bright cheeks. "Judge for yourselves, strangers, whether they wasn't redeemed by their last acts?"

Before Job and his son could answer, the parson spoke quietly. "That was no ordinary ship on the rocks, friends. Neither stitch nor spar of it was ever found; nor did any bodies come ashore save our own three and forty."

Strange Fish

"It must have got off the rocks and sailed away," said the landlord. "Tides and currents have done queerer things."

"It was holed. It couldn't have stayed afloat five minutes in the sea," said the parson; but the landlord shrugged his stout shoulders and said that whatever became of it was of no consequence. Till and Tulliver had seen something so piteous through the glass that all evil had left them in compassion for it. Thus they perished in a state of grace—

"They went to hell; and it was the devil who fetched them."

"Then why did they go so eagerly?"

"Who knows what Till and Tulliver saw through their glass?"

"Then give 'em the benefit, parson."

Thus they argued and pleaded the case for the souls of the three and forty—the parson prosecuting and the landlord defending—as if it rested with the two strangers whether the accused were liberated to heaven or condemned to burn in hell. Little by little the light faded from the sky and still they argued, for none knew what had been seen through the glass that had made three and forty murdering wreckers strike out into the storm and stay in it till the sea cast them back, cold and dead.

"Judge for yourselves, strangers," repeated the landlord at length, the smile gone from his face and leaving only the shine behind, "for it's a year ago tonight that they went, and I'm a-thinking they'll be up before the Bench for sentence." He paused and peered from parson to strangers and then to the fire. A silence fell over the parlour in which the ticking of the mantel clock grew loud. It looked like a small coffin with a white face staring out. The time was twenty after eight. "An angel's flying overhead," murmured Sam; when of a sudden, there came another sound . . . a dull booming . . .

All looked to each other in bewilderment; then Job got to his feet and made for the door, upsetting a glass as he did so. A moment later he was back. His heavy face was frowning in alarm. "A ship," he muttered. "There's a ship out in the bay. She's caught on the rocks!"

She was a large vessel, built high in the poop, more Spanish than Dutch, with much gilding that glinted in the starlight. She was under full sail and the huge canvases leaped and cracked at the yards. The dull booming came as her stern kept swinging round and hammering the underwater rocks, for she was caught under her prow . . .

"It's the same ship!" whispered the parson, grey with terror.

"No!" cried the landlord, polishing his forehead with his sleeve as if he felt the varnish cracking. "It's like, I grant, but it ain't the same vessel. It can't be!"

"Well, whatever it is, we'd best get out to it," said Job abruptly.

"The same . . . the same . . ." breathed the parson as a dark shadow brushed across the weird ship at the mouth of the bay.

"You said there was a boat," said Job to the landlord. "Quick, man, let's go before it's too late!"

But there was no crew for the boat save widows, protested the landlord. And the parson supported him, making it as plain as need be that they'd not abandon the inn and the church to go and rescue phantoms from the coming storm.

For the storm was now approaching rapidly. The stars had been put out and the wind had increased so that the distant booming of the ship striking the rock grew more frequent. Faint cries also came in on the wind, and then a sharper, wilder sound.

"She's holed," muttered Job. "Did you hear the timbers go, Sammy?"

"You and me, Pa," said Sam with a grin at his father that spoke of a fondness and humour that was fathoms deep. "We're crew enough!"

The boat was high on the shingle and the widow who owned it came out of her cottage and shook her fist and shrieked into the wind when she saw her property being heaved down to the water by the parson, the landlord and the two bulky strangers. The fierce air tore at her hair and gown till she looked like some thin, wing-stretched bird of ill-omen. Then she caught a glimpse of the huge vessel beating on the rocks. She screamed and covered her face with her hands.

Strange Fish

"There's nought of this world about yonder ship, friends!" cried the parson, backing away.

"All the more reason for a parson to come with us!" urged Sam, as the boat began to pull away.

"Save your breath for your oar, Sammy," grunted Job.

"Right, Pa."

"Keep her steady, Sammy. Go easy."

"I'm easy, Pa. It's you what's puffing."

"Civil tongue, Sammy, or I'll fetch you one with this oar."

"No offence, Pa."

"None taken, Sammy; but watch it."

Thus father and son, pulling through the dangerous sea, bickered and mocked and provoked each other with a briskness under which lay a deep affection and an unbounded confidence in each other's strength and skill. The little boat rode the great waves with marvellous certainty; and from time to time, Job and Sam, in the midst of some peculiarly sharp exchange, would glance at one another and smile most knowingly . . .

They could only see a short way ahead, for the spray sent up when the bows struck the chests of the waves, hung like grey and silver curtains, screening the recesses of the night. Their chief guide was the dreadful booming of the distressed vessel which now beat in the darkness like the gigantic heart of the sea itself.

"Give a shout, Sammy!"

"Ahoy, there! Stand by for Wilkins and Son!"

"A shout, Sammy, not a squeak. Ain't your voice broke yet?"

"Too much water in me ale, Pa. Ahoy, there!"

"There she is, Sammy! What a monster!"

Vague and enormous, the stricken vessel loomed out of the turbulent darkness. Water rushed down the rattling sails in cataracts and poured from the shrouds and yards. She rocked and swung with a mighty uproar like some tremendous carved beast caught in a merciless trap. There was a great hole in her side where a rock had stove her in; but nowhere could Job and Sam see any living souls.

"What's her name, Sammy? Left me spectacles behind."

The boy lifted his drenched head and peered at the gilded poop.

"Santa—Santa—Can't make out any more . . ."

Then his blood turned chilly as he added, "It's gone with the weather, Pa, like on the signpost."

"Ahoy, there!" shouted Job. "Come out and be saved! We ain't here for our health!"

"Pa! Pa! Look in the hole! For the love of Jesus, look!"

"Don't blaspheme, Sammy, lad, or—" Then Job saw what Sam had seen, and his jaw fell open, letting in the sea. The hole was amidships and almost on the water line. It yawned like a ragged mouth, and several chests which had slipped their moorings, slid back and forth within it like dim, broken teeth. One of them had been smashed and out of it there ran a stream of golden coins, that dribbled into the reedy sea.

"Set up for life, Pa!" shouted Sam, and pulled on his oar till their boat swung round to approach the leaking gold.

Then, suddenly, there came a faint cry from the darkness to their left. The father and son, poised to go in and collect their fortunes, turned and stared. Briefly they glimpsed a spar, leaping and dipping in the water. A hand was waving.

"Here we go, Sammy." The boat swung as Wilkins and Son, with one accord, made for the spar. As they did so, the sea drew back from the path they might have taken and revealed a row of rocks with edges like knives. They would have been ripped in two.

They reached the spar. Four men were clinging to it. Their faces were white as bone. "Care for a trip?" grinned Sam, and reached out to heave them aboard. They were bitterly cold. Their eyes were open but seemed sightless, for an oily film lay across them. Their mouths were gaping, but no words or even breath seemed to issue from them. They were like dead men, and each had his ring finger chopped off below the knuckle. They flopped into the bottom of the boat and lay there while father and son shuddered in bewilderment. But they said nothing to each other of what they thought of their uncanny catch—any more than they'd exchanged words about the danger of the sea.

These were private matters and not for the ears of the wind. Instead, they shrugged their shoulders and pulled about and made towards the cargo of gold.

"Quick! Quick! Afore it's all gone!"

"What was that, Pa?"

"Never spoke, Sammy. Wash your ears out."

The boy frowned. The voice he'd heard had been hoarse, urgent and near at hand. "Pull away, Ezra!" The boy trembled violently, and all but let go of his oar.

"There's ghosts aboard, Pa!"

Job looked sideways at his son. "Then bid 'em lend a hand, Sammy—or fetch 'em one with your oar!"

A second chest aboard the wrecked vessel had cracked open and a river of guineas came dancing out; but again there was heard a faint cry for help from the darkly churning sea.

"Here we go again, Sammy!"

The boy nodded and struggled with his oar. It had become heavier, as if other hands than his were pulling to keep the boat towards the running gold, and away from the cry in the sea. But Sam prevailed and the boat dipped and lifted and swung about till it came alongside a length of planking to which clung three more white-faced men. They also lacked ring fingers and had filmed, sightless eyes. Not knowing to which world they belonged, Job and his son heaved them aboard to join the others who lay, watchful and still at the bottom of the boat.

And again as they'd turned, the sea had drawn back to reveal the murderous rocks that would have sunk them. Then the waves swept high and concealed the danger.

"Third time lucky, Pa."

The gold was pouring out of the queer vessel's side like life's blood. In a few seconds Wilkins and Son could have gathered enough to have been aldermen and respected. As they heaved away, Sam's oar seemed light as a feather—as if other hands than his were helping . . . and the wrecked ship towered in the night.

The wind was lessening, the sea lost its sharp edges and rolled in thick, smooth folds. A mist was coming in, dense and grey.

Strange Fish

Already the masts and sails were eaten up in the vapours and the high gilding of the poop was partly nibbled away.

"Make haste, Sammy—"

But Job's words were interrupted by a weird chorus of cries—like an anthem of despair.

"Yonder, Sammy, yonder!"

The boy stared hard to where his father pointed . . . and shuddered to the depths of his soul. As the sea rolled dark and oily under the heavy folds of mist, he saw what seemed to be a vast coverlet of men, women and children rising and falling in a weird, slow dance. Hundreds and hundreds of them, with bone-white faces gleaming like bubbles on the wave.

"God in heaven, Pa!"

"That's as maybe, Sammy; but we're down below. Let's do what we can, boy!"

So once again they turned from fortune, and once again Sam shut his ears to the hoarse voices that pleaded, "The gold! The gold!"

"Women and children, Sammy!" panted Job as they nosed among the floating crowd. Then Wilkins and Son began to fill the little boat till it seemed that they must all sink under the weight. They dragged and heaved and piled them in—and Sam saw, with nightmarish terror, that there was not a whole hand anywhere among them. Fingers were gone, even from children.

At last they were stacked so thick and high that there was scarce room to row, when Sam heard a soft scream almost in his ear. "Jacob Tulliver! They've come for us! There's the child I killed last week! And there's the mother that cried so afore you knocked her on the head! Look—look! All of them!"

"Pa!" howled Sam, feeling the unnatural chill of their cargo pressing against his legs, his back and his neck. "They're all ghosts! They're the ghosts of them the wreckers murdered!"

"That's as maybe, Sammy," answered Job, pale of face and stern of eye. "But ghosts or otherwise, we ain't got room for any gold now. It's back to the shore, lad!"

They turned and began to row through the all engulfing mists towards where Job's unfailing instinct told him the shore lay.

Strange Fish

As they moved blindly across the foggy sea, Sam heard distinct shrieks and howls and the splitting of timber on rock as the phantoms of the three and forty wreckers foundered again, even as they'd foundered a year ago that night, under the tempting stream of gold.

"Looks like the parson was right, Pa!" panted Sam. "Looks like they went to hell like he said!"

"Like as you said before, Sammy," grunted Job, "God's in His heaven; and like I said, we're down below. Where that three and forty went is none of your business or mine. Don't go poking your nose in, boy; just keep rowing."

The fog was now so dense that Job and Sam were almost hidden from each other, and their uncanny cargo, stirring, sighing and muttering, was no longer seen. Presently the motion of the boat was arrested and the keel whispered on sand. They had reached the shore.

"Ahoy, there!" shouted Job, for the air was thick as wool. There came an answering shout and at length the landlord, the parson and the bony widow came stumbling out of the nothingness to stare incredulously at the returned strangers.

"Never thought to see you back!" was the landlord's greeting, as he heaved to bring the boat clear of the sea.

"What was it, friends? What was that terrible ship, and what was it those damned souls saw that drew them out to destruction? For they were damned, weren't they?"

"Can't say, parson," answered Job, shaking the sea off his arms and out of his thick grey hair. "Left me spectacles behind." He stared severely at Sam whose mouth had opened as if to confirm the parson's words.

"The mist's lifting," said the landlord, turning his gleaming face out to sea. "Comes and goes in these parts with marvellous speed."

The little group on the shore stared as the air grew thin and clean again. The great ship had vanished; neither spar nor stitch of canvas remained to be seen. Uneasily Sam looked into their boat. He sighed. The fearful catch for which they'd turned from fortune and risked their lives had shrunk. In place of the ghostly murdered dead lay a heap of faintly shining mackerel whose filmy eyes stared back at him.

"It was a phantom ship!" ranted the parson, his eyes burning with brandy and holy fire. "And they all went to hell with it! This place is accursed."

"There was souls in the sea," murmured Job softly, "and maybe they was phantoms too. And maybe your three and forty went out to fetch 'em in. Ain't it possible?"

"Pa!" cried Sam, who'd good cause to know otherwise. "They—" He got no further, for Job Wilkins clipped him smartly round the ear.

"Speak when you're spoke with, Sammy boy!"

"So—so they might have been redeemed?" whispered the landlord, polishing his forehead as if he meant to exhibit it.

"As like as maybe," nodded Job, eyeing the heap of mackerel. "At all events, the sea hereabouts is mighty rich, I'd say; and with your permission, ma'am" (to the widow), "Sam and me'll come back with Mrs Wilkins and be happy to take a lease on your vessel—if the price is right."

"You're lying my friends," said the parson when they were back in the inn and drying off before the fire. "I know you saw what really happened that night a year ago. Come, admit it. Say they were damned and this placed is accursed."

But Job did not seem to hear him. He'd gone to the little window and gazed out towards the church. There was a splinter of moon and under it the village slept in silver dreams; while the three and forty graves in the churchyard seemed to have broken ranks . . . as if their long parade had finished and they might lie easy.

"This here's a pretty village," murmured Job to Sam. "What call have the dead to curse it, so long as we don't curse them? Rest easy, gents. If you wasn't redeemed last year, it's as like as maybe you are now. Eh. Sammy?"

"Right, Pa."

The Riddle

WALTER DE LA MARE

So these seven children, Ann and Matilda, James, William and Henry, Harriet and Dorothea, came to live with their grandmother. The house in which their grandmother had lived since her childhood was built in the time of the Georges. It was not a pretty house, but roomy, substantial, and square; and a great cedar tree outstretched its branches almost to the windows.

When the children were come out of the cab (five sitting inside and two beside the driver), they were shown into their grandmother's presence. They stood in a little black group before the old lady, seated in her bow-window. And she asked them each their names, and repeated each name in her kind, quavering voice. Then to one she gave a work-box, to William a jack-knife, to Dorothea a painted ball; to each a present according to age. And she kissed all her grand-children to the youngest.

"My dears," she said, "I wish to see all of you bright and gay in my house. I am an old woman, so that I cannot romp with you; but Ann must look to you, and Mrs Fenn, too. And every morning and every evening you must all come in to see your granny; and bring me smiling faces, that call back to my mind my own son Harry. But all the rest of the day, when school is done, you shall do just as you please, my dears. And there is only one thing, just one, I would have you remember. In the large spare bedroom that looks out on the slate roof there stands in the corner an old oak chest; aye, older than I, my dears, a great deal older; older than my grandmother. Play anywhere else in the house, but not there." She spoke kindly to them all, smiling

The Riddle

at them; but she was very old, and her eyes seemed to see nothing of this world.

And the seven children, though at first they were gloomy and strange, soon began to be happy and at home in the great house. There was much to interest and to amuse them there; all was new to them. Twice every day, morning and evening, they came in to see their grandmother, who every day seemed more feeble; and she spoke pleasantly to them of her mother, and her childhood, but never forgetting to visit her store of sugar-plums. And so the weeks passed by . . .

It was evening twilight when Henry went upstairs from the nursery by himself to look at the oak chest. He pressed his fingers into the carved fruit and flowers, and spoke to the dark-smiling heads at the corners; and then, with a glance over his shoulder, he opened the lid and looked in. But the chest concealed no treasure, neither gold nor baubles, nor was there anything to alarm the eye. The chest was empty, except that it was lined with silk of old-rose seeming darker in the dusk, and smelling sweet of potpourri. And while Henry was looking in, he heard the softened laughter and the clinking of the cups downstairs in the nursery; and out at the window he saw the day darkening. These things brought strangely to his memory his mother who in her glimmering white dress used to read to him in the dusk; and he climbed into the chest; and the lid closed gently down over him.

When the other six children were tired with their playing, they filed into their grandmother's room for her good-night and her sugar-plums. She looked out between the candles at them as if she were uncertain of something in her thoughts. The next day Ann told her grandmother that Henry was not anywhere to be found.

"Dearie me, child. Then he must be gone away for a time," said the old lady. She paused. "But remember, all of you, do not meddle with the oak chest."

But Matilda could not forget her brother Henry, finding no pleasure in playing without him. So she would loiter in the house thinking where he might be. And she carried her wooden doll in her bare arms, singing under her breath all she could

The Riddle

make up about it. And when one bright morning she peeped in on the chest, so sweet-scented and secret it seemed that she took her doll with her into it—just as Henry himself had done.

So Ann, and James, and William, Harriet and Dorothea were left at home to play together. "Some day maybe they will come back to you, my dears," said their grandmother, "or maybe you will go to them. Heed my warning as best you may."

Now Harriet and William were friends together, pretending to be sweethearts; while James and Dorothea liked wild games of hunting, and fishing and battles.

On a silent afternoon in October, Harriet and William were talking softly together, looking out over the slate roof at the green fields, and they heard the squeak and frisking of a mouse behind them in the room. They went together and searched for the small, dark hole from whence it had come out. But finding no hole, they began to finger the carving of the chest, and to give names to the dark-smiling heads, just as Henry had done. "I know! let's pretend you are Sleeping Beauty, Harriet," said William, "and I'll be the Prince that squeezes through the thorns and comes in." Harriet looked gently and strangely at her brother but she got into the box and lay down, pretending to be fast asleep, and on tiptoe William leaned over, and seeing how big was the chest, he stepped in to kiss the Sleeping Beauty and to wake her from her quiet sleep. Slowly the carved lid turned on its noiseless hinges. And only the clatter of James and Dorothea came in sometimes to recall Ann from her book.

But their old grandmother was very feeble, and her sight dim, and her hearing extremely difficult.

Snow was falling through the still air upon the roof; and Dorothea was a fish in the oak chest, and James stood over the hole in the ice, brandishing a walking-stick for a harpoon, pretending to be an Esquimau. Dorothea's face was red, and her wild eyes sparkled through her tousled hair. And James had a crooked scratch upon his cheek. "You must struggle, Dorothea, and then I shall swim back and drag you out. Be quick now!" He shouted with laughter as he was drawn into the open chest. And the lid closed softly and gently down as before.

The Riddle

Ann, left to herself, was too old to care overmuch for sugar-plums, but she would go solitary to bid her grandmother goodnight; and the old lady looked wistfully at her over her spectacles. "Well, my dear," she said with trembling head; and she squeezed Ann's fingers between her own knuckled finger and thumb. "What lonely old people we two are, to be sure!" Ann kissed her grandmother's soft, loose cheek. She left the old lady sitting in her easy chair, her hands upon her knees, and her head turned sidelong towards her.

When Ann was gone to bed she used to sit reading her book by candlelight. She drew up her knees under the sheets, resting her book upon them. Her story was about fairies and gnomes, and the gently-flowing moonlight of the narrative seemed to illumine the white pages, and she could hear in fancy fairy voices, so silent was the great many-roomed house, and so mellifluent were the words of the story. Presently she put out her candle, and, with a confused babel of voices close to her ear, and faint swift pictures before her eyes, she fell asleep.

And in the dead of night she rose out of her bed in dream, and with eyes wide open yet seeing nothing of reality, moved silently through the vacant house. Past the room where her grandmother was snoring in brief, heavy slumber, she stepped lightly and surely, and down the wide staircase. And Vega the far-shining stood over against the window above the slate roof. Ann walked into the strange room beneath as if she were being guided by the hand towards the oak chest. There, just as if she were dreaming it was her bed, she laid herself down in the old rose silk, in the fragrant place. But it was so dark in the room that the movement of the lid was indistinguishable.

Through the long day, the grandmother sat in her bow-window. Her lips were pursed, and she looked with dim, inquisitive scrutiny upon the street where people passed to and fro, and vehicles rolled by. At evening she climbed the stair and stood in the doorway of the large spare bedroom. The ascent had shortened her breath. Her magnifying spectacles rested upon her nose. Leaning her hand on the doorpost she peered in towards the glimmering square of window in the quiet gloom. But she could not see far, because her sight was dim and the light of day feeble. Nor could she detect the faint fragrance as of autumnal leaves. But in her mind was a tangled skein of memories—laughter and tears, and children long ago become old-fashioned, and the advent of friends, and last farewells. And gossiping fitfully, inarticulately, with herself, the old lady went down again to her window-seat.

The Tube that Stuck

CLAIRE CRESWELL

Suddenly the silver tube train stuck in the tunnel.

Two minutes they waited.

The dark furry pipes that squirled outside the window had stopped squirling.

Five minutes.

A newspaper cracked like a floorboard.

Ten minutes.

In the front coach the six people began to come out of their own lives and secretly, under their eyelids, as if they weren't at all frightened, they looked at each other.

Twenty minutes.

Was it getting hotter?

The businessman, still reading the pink *Financial Times*, ran his finger round under his collar.

The African student sweated and thought how much he hated the stifling London heat. It was the dry heat of buildings. At home there was always a soft wet breeze from the sea . . .

The old man, who was on his way home from busking in Baker Street, curled his hand round his flute for company.

The lady from the country thought of brown bracken glowing in the drizzle.

The little Jamaican girl wriggled in her seat.

And they all tried not to think of the weight of earth above them.

"We'll have to get out and walk! D'you think we'll have to get out and walk along the track, then?"

The Tube that Stuck

It was the boy with glasses. He'd spoken. In a London tube! But you could feel the relief throb through everybody.

"Oh, I doubt if that will be necessary," said the lady from the country, briskly dismissing the boy's opinion.

"They'll turn off the current," said the boy, whose name was Peter. "That's what they always do when anything goes wrong."

And his hand in his pocket curled round his penknife-corkscrew-bottle-opener-horseshoe-stone-remover-torch.

"No," burst out Shirley, the little Jamaican girl. "My Dad, he works on the Tube, and they don't turn off the current for just anything, my Dad says."

Shirley couldn't bear sitting down any more, got up, jumped up to touch the straps that people hold on to when they're standing, squirmed herself round the shiny silver pole, swung on the cross-bar.

Peter watched her, wanted to join her, but decided that life at the moment was too serious for moving about. His penknife was warm in his hand.

"How long have we been here now?" asked the country lady, not wanting the silence to bulldoze back.

The businessman stirred, looked at his watch—one of those gold watches where the face joins the neck as smooth as a snake's muscles.

"Thirty-two minutes," he said, his lined and chubby face blushing at the strangeness of speaking in the Tube.

"I was once stuck in the Tube for three-quarters of an hour," came the stereo voice of the African, Ibrahim Mbano.

"Really?" said the businessman, and his voice sounded like a radio that needs new batteries.

Silence.

Silence swelled till it was as big as a bear and pushed them away from each other.

How long was it now? How hot was it now? How long was it now? Should they break a window?

Fear, like a silver box with whistling chill teeth, clamped down on them.

The Tube that Stuck

But then the old man took his flute from the torn lining of his coat and put it to his lips.

"PU—u—u—u—U."

It was as if the sky was inside their stifling Tube.

The flute sang what they all longed for.

Maybe it was a ghost that could escape through the packed earth above them.

"Don't—you're using up our air," said the businessman. "This is ridiculous," he said, acting the executive, putting an edge on to every word to sound impressive: "This is ridiculous. Where's the driver?"

And he rattled on the communicating door between the coach and driver.

It was locked.

"Hullo there—! Driver, I say!" he shouted, prawn-pink with embarrassment.

There was no answer.

"What about the communication cord?"

"What about the communication cord?" said Ibrahim and Peter together, and Peter jumped up and pulled it.

He was hot and afraid, and now walking on the tracks didn't seem as much fun as it had.

Nothing. Nothing happened.

"But there must be other passengers," said the country lady. "We must get in touch."

"We must be decisive," said the businessman, and he strode down the coach to the other end, looked through to the next coach.

"What is it?" asked Ibrahim, when the businessman had stood there too long in silence.

"No one there."

"Perhaps in the coach after next," said Ibrahim, and he stood up.

Shirley and Peter looked at each other, ran towards the door to the next coach: "We'll go!"

"Stop, children," said the country lady.

Shirley and Peter waited.

The country lady looked at the businessman.

The Tube that Stuck

"What do *you* think, Mr—er—?" she said.

"Hartley-Crumley. Nigel Hartley-Crumley. Don't usually travel by Tube. Trouble with the old Jensen." He was having a sparking-plug replaced for £22.

"And you, madam. I don't think we've been introduced—er—?"

"Binns. Heather Binns. Mrs, of course," she smirked, patting her hair.

"And—er?" asked Hartley-Crumley, after a pause.

"Ibrahim Mbano. Reading Geology at London University."

"Don't know any of that science stuff myself," guffawed Mr Hartley-Crumley, sure of himself.

They shook hands. Perhaps touching another human's flesh helped their fear.

But the old man with the flute sat silent, gazing out of the black window at his own face.

"Well, now, the driver must be there, mustn't he?" said Mr Hartley-Crumley. "Come now, he must be there."

They shouted and banged on the blue door between the coach and the driver's cabin.

Silence.

And under their talk and action fear crept back again like cold after you have been warm.

"Isn't there an axe on these trains, or something?"

AXE. A word as dangerous as ice. AXE.

"Don't you think we should try and get in touch with the other passengers first? I mean, breaking things down with an *axe* ... and there may be a guard at the other end."

Mrs Binns was terrified at the thought of anything smooth and neat being hacked and ripped. She hid the kitchen knives every night before she went to bed.

"Maybe it's an automatic train. Maybe there's no driver."

"They have to have someone on them, don't they? Er—little girl, didn't your father work on the Tube?"

"Shirley. Yes, but my Dad says on this line they don't have ghost trains, my Dad says."

"GHOST TRAINS?"

The Tube that Stuck

They all looked at her in horror.

"Ghost trains have no drivers."

"Very well. First we try to contact the other passengers. Second, if that fails, we break down the door to the driver's cabin. Agreed?"

Mr Hartley-Crumley looked at them as if they were a board-meeting, and they nodded.

"Now—" he was beginning again, but the children, who were bulging with the unused energy of fear, had run to the end door, opened it, tackled the door of the next coach and were through it before Mr Hartley-Crumley's board-meeting thoughts had begun to take their solid mahogany shapes.

"Children! Stop! You mustn't—"called Mrs Heather Binns after them and her voice squeaked with fear and fury.

"It's *dangerous*—" she edged at Mr Hartley-Crumley and Ibrahim.

But by the time the men had started opening the doors and shouting and walking through, the children had run through to the next coach, and the grown-ups gave up.

Shirley and Peter, alone in the empty coach, looked at each other.

"Now," said Peter. "Now we can get on with it, without those grown-ups."

Peter walked and Shirley bounded noisily through the empty coach, as if their noise would drive away fear. Anyway, there were sure to be people in the next coach.

But there weren't.

Well, there were sure to be people in the middle of the train. The middle of the train was always crowded.

But they scrambled through door after door and nothing met them but empty coach after empty coach, brightly lit, with screwed up papers on the grubby slats of the floor, and bright strained advertisements for a never-never world shouting silently at them from the walls.

"We must be near the end now," said Peter, whispering.

Shirley shrugged her shoulders as if she wasn't in the least terrified.

The Tube that Stuck

And they reached the end. The dead end. In the last coach the door between the coach and the guard's cabin was not locked. They opened it.

But it was empty. Just the dirty window looking on the black stillness where the rails gleamed, and the poky guard's cabin with worn paint and well-used controls.

No other trains waiting with them in the tunnel. No other people.

They looked at each other and turned to go back.

In the first carriage Mr Hartley-Crumley was standing as straight as concrete with one of Ibrahim's shoes in his hand.

"No axe!" he barked. "Modern Britain! Hnf!"

"Right. Now, Ibrahim, old chap. You and I'll do this bit. We're the strong men around here."

But at the second blow the thin blue door fell apart, and there was the driver's cabin.

Empty.

A beat of silence.

A beat of silence.

"But—I thought you said—"

"But there must have been a driver . . ."

And they remembered leaving the last station, Baker Street. It seemed a thousand years ago, now. But they remembered there had been lots of people pushing about on the platform, pushing in and out of the next coach to theirs, shouting, running, strap-hanging, coughing, laughing.

And there had been a driver. They'd heard him shout to the station sweeper.

Something must have happened.

Something more than a Tube train getting stuck in a tunnel in the everyday world.

In the trap of the silent steel box they held their fear. Aching.

But Mr Hartley-Crumley was blowing up:

"Must *do* something. Now really, you people, we must *do* something!"

"I cannot think of anything logical that we can do," said Ibrahim.

The Tube that Stuck

"DON'T ANSWER BACK, YOU—!" bombed Mr Hartley-Crumley.

"You, boy," he said to Peter. "You and I will get out and walk."

"But where to?" asked Peter; because, although he was bursting to move and do something, another part of him said there was no sense in it. He looked at Ibrahim.

Ibrahim braced himself as if Mr Hartley-Crumley was going to hit him, but said, "I am sorry, Mr Hartley-Crumley, but if there are no people on the train, there will be no station."

"NONSENSE. Peter, come with me."

And he rattled the stubbornly closed outside doors of the silver train, shouted "DAMN!", banged against them angrily, his volcanic cheeks rattling too.

Then he grabbed the shoe and crashed the glass. Zink! How easily glass gives in! And then crash and slabs slow motion away smooth as icing. He pointed his fat leg through the gap, waved it.

"I'll go first, sir," said Peter, furious with himself for saying "sir". But he wouldn't admit to himself that his muscles were jumping like eels to be free of the Tube.

FREE.

And Peter was alone in the black drop, between train and tunnel, the black drop you've dreamt a flash of times that you're caught in and slipped down in the suction as the train moves, and crunch.

But he drew a breath through his dizziness, and felt better. He looked up at the high train lighted cosily and could still see the fat blue leg waving, shiny, like an insect.

"I'll go, then," he shouted, and avoided looking at Shirley who was leaning past Mr Hartley-Crumley.

"Don't be silly! Peter! Come back! *I'll come!*" and he saw them grab her to stop her.

The tunnel was just wide enough for him to squeeze along. As long as the train didn't move. And he stared at the train, stared at it with all the power of his eyes as he balanced against its untrustworthy stillness, willing it, willing it, not to move.

The Tube that Stuck

And he was past it.

Gasp of blackness. But his penknife lay warm and heavy in his hand in his pocket. He took it out carefully as if it had been a mouse, groped with its blade edges, careful not to break his nails, and found the torch switch. Its timid light slit the black fear, and the rails caught it and shone solid.

All he had to do now was walk along the rails the way they had come, and he'd get there. Back to the real-life station.

But the current. Which was the rail that carried the current?

Was it the big dark rail at the side, or the shiniest one in the middle?

Nightmare. Often he had had nightmares about sliding along that middle rail. You had to keep both feet on at once, like a hopping bird, they said, that's why birds don't get electrocuted. But if you take only one foot off you earth yourself and—

But how much of that was the truth?

He couldn't risk it. So he stumbled along the side by the dark and dangerous pipes.

Stumbled. Walked. Stumbled. Walked.

Surely if he went back the way the train had come it would be all right. Surely if you go back and start again things can come right?

He tripped.

Hagh! Gasp of a chasm of fright he was coming back from at the thought of falling. He grabbed—and it could not have been a live pipe he grabbed, or he would have been dead.

Horribly, with a jumping lurch, his whole body began to shake. Not just tremble gently, but shudder all over like hiccups of flesh, shudder so much with fear he couldn't even see.

But when it passed and he could see again, there were the lines still, glimmering cold as planet-tracks in eternal darkness.

And, hagh, just a minute, shouldn't they be straight?

There hadn't been a bend here. Not a sharp right-angle bend like that.

He shuddered. Looked back. Tried to work out the distance.

Yes. There should have been one sharp bend, but not two.

Must have been wrong. Hold on to your mind. Hold on to

The Tube that Stuck

words that were thoughts in your mind. Keep on. Walk a little further. You're so nervous, silly, you've made the distance jump.

But when the glimmering tracks began to slope sharply downwards he knew he hadn't been wrong.

Something had changed.

And before he could bear to think about it, he turned and stumble-ran back to the train.

God, make the train still be there.

Gap of spaces of time in his mind while he stumbled—and turned the corner.

Empty.

Empty rails.

But when he dared to look up again he saw that the train *was* there.

Tears jumped in him with delight, and he saw Shirley and the others at the back window, staring out for him with human care, and now they were pulling him in.

And as soon as he was sitting on a friendly scratchy London Transport seat, the train went "Hf—f-f-f" as if the brakes were let off, and the engine went "nick-nick-nick-nick", and the train began to move.

They got up and stood in the broken cabin, Shirley and Peter and Ibrahim, while the train clickered and clankered along the dark arch of the tunnel.

Nothing but darkness and the rails gleaming.

"Eh."

It was the old man with the flute. He was standing up now, his torn coat tied round the waist with flex, with a three-point plug still dangling from it.

"Eh."

He gestured towards the side window where he had been sitting.

"Eh."

The others looked out of the window. But they could see nothing. Just blackness.

"I can't see anything," said Mr Hartley-Crumley, timid now.

The Tube that Stuck

Then Ibrahim said something but his voice wouldn't come. It was a whisper:

"No . . . pipes."

Silence.

"There are no pipes running along the walls."

The flute-man nodded, his rain-red cheeks shaking.

In front of the train the rails still gleamed—but what was happening to the tunnel?

It was changing from the dirty bolted-down London arch into something rougher.

And the tunnel was slanting gently but definitely downwards.

"I don't like it. I don't like it," whispered Mr Hartley-Crumley, and he cringed against the worn paintwork of the cabin.

"Stop it! Stop the train!" shouted Mrs Binns in a high voice. "Shirley! You know about them. At least you *said* you did!"

But though Shirley gingerly touched and then yanked at the controls, nothing happened.

The train went on.

What would happen to them?

And again they felt the cold silver-white box of fear clutch round them.

And then: "Look!" shouted Shirley, in spite of the lurch of fear in her. "Oh, look!"

Gleam. Glance.

Shimmering out among the rosy sandstone rock was a sheet of something that shone like a waterfall, like the Northern Lights.

"Beau-tiful," whispered Shirley, and, for a moment, in a rest from fear, the dazzle in Peter's eyes agreed.

And at the same moment they felt the train slow down, felt it snicker-clinker along the suddenly more level tunnel.

"Quartz," said Ibrahim. "That means we are among the igneous rocks that are deep below the London clay. We are deep."

A beat of quiet after the roar of plunge and clatter. The train was almost still, almost level.

"It's hot," whispered Mrs Binns. "I can't bear the heat."

The Tube that Stuck

And as she said these words—grrrrrrrrnch—the train plunged down again, fast, in a roar of heated air.

Hotter. Mr Hartley-Crumley now sat in a crumpled heap on one of the scratchy Tube-train seats, not looking out. Mrs Binns sat opposite him, clutching her basket, unable to take her eyes off the tunnel outside the window, her eyes so wide that you could see the white round the blue.

But Ibrahim, the flute-man, and the children all stood in the cabin, gazing in wonder at the rocks.

And the more they looked, the slower the train went.

The rocks, as if they were showing off, now started zigzagging violently up and down along the sides of the tunnel.

"You see?" said Ibrahim, as proudly as if he had made them. "Once, long ago, long long ago, they crumpled up under enormous force. Like this—" he crumpled up a tissue—then wiped his face with it. "It *is* getting hot," he added. "We must be going very deep. It gets one degree hotter every seventy feet you go down."

And fear bubbled up in them again as he said it, and the train speeded up and plunged further. They watched the tunnel still slanting down and down and down. They felt the heat stand round them.

"What is going to become of us?" wavered Mrs Binns.

But Mr Hartley-Crumley couldn't bring himself to speak.

"What's that ahead?" said Peter suddenly. "Shiny—and black."

"Coal?" said Shirley.

And again they forgot their fear and looked, and the train slowed down, quietened, clunkered slowly past the blackness.

Even in the train you could smell the mustard sneezy coal smell.

"What—look, Peter. Like a tree in the coal!" breathed Shirley, whispering with excitement. "Like our own Jamaica tree, man!"

"What's that, then?" cried Peter, shaking Ibrahim out of his heat exhaustion. And the train hovered by the curves of the tree that was marked into the shimmering coal in every detail of bark scale and leaf edge.

The Tube that Stuck

"Once upon a time," he said, smiling slowly at them," in this very spot where we are now, there was a jungle. Hot. Where the real full sun drew up mists and you could see them together."

"I know," said Shirley.

"In those days the ferns grew as big as houses, here where the weather and the houses are so grey."

(But I like it soft and grey, thought Peter.)

"Now one day this jungle tree, it had lived long enough in the sun and rain. And it died and fell in the swamp, and mud settled on it, and more mud, and dust, and time. For ten years, a hundred years, a thousand years, a million years—three hundred million years."

They took in the time.

"For three hundred million years this tree got squashed by weight. Flattened like a coin you put on the rail and a train goes over it. Changed to coal, but still there."

The children stared at the tiny edges of leaf cut in the blackness.

And then, lurching up inside Shirley, at the sight of the fern like at home, blooming and brimming hot all round her, was her love of home.

Only once or twice a year does a wish as strong as that come up in an immigrant in a chilling strange country. Most of the time home-sickness simmers along, but once or twice a year it gets triggered off by something—a smell, a song, a film—into a touch.

And now, strong enough, maybe, to burst up through the cold white steel shell of the train and escape to the air, came her wish for home. Into her stuck the nubs of the coal fern, and she remembered the soft dull underside of a fern, the bumps, the curl, and the stiff shoe-shine green of the top. She smelt the fish drying under the shade in the village, and the kerosene and flowers. "Shirley, you sleepin'?" called her mamma.

"Shirley? You dreaming?"

It was Peter, and they were in the Tube, caught under the earth.

But the train still went very slowly along the level, and the children and Ibrahim wondered if the worst was past.

But "This is unendurable! We must *do* something!" came Mr Hartley-Crumley's voice, as he revived in the lull.

He doesn't change, thought Ibrahim. For a moment we'd forgotten the fear, but now we're back in it. Fear.

And as he thought it—

"We're going faster!" said Shirley, afraid.

"Put the brake on," said Peter, and they both grabbed it.

But the tunnel plunged steeper and steeper, and the train got faster and faster.

The train swung like a tree in the wind, whipped backwards and forwards against the sides of the rails at breakneck speed.

Ibrahim, in the driver's seat, clung to the window ledge, staring ahead. The flute-man had tumbled back on to the floor of the coach, clinging on to the base of a seat, while Mr Hartley-Crumley and Mrs Binns crouched in their seats, terrified.

And, as the train hurtled, they could all feel heat well up in them and blast through them.

It was more than heat. It was beyond what any of them had felt on the hottest day in the world upstairs where there is air, air and movement.

How much deeper?

In Peter's mind scraps of stuff he'd been told at school and not really bothered with ran about.

What happened at the middle of the earth?

It was so hot the rocks melted, he was sure of that. Rocks, the most solid thing you could find. Melted.

How far before they got down through this thin pie-crust on the top of the melted rocks? He knew the crust of the earth was very thin; as thin maybe as the ice on a puddle that you put your boot through.

Peter crouched afraid, thinking how carefully he would tread on the grass and road if ever he got to the top again.

And how he would see a bird sing, loose in the air.

Ten miles. That was it. That was how thin the crust was in a lot of places. Not much more than the height of Everest, and that was seven miles. Only as far as home to his auntie in Watford.

The Tube that Stuck

Hot. Hot. And the packed packed packed earth pressed on them.

And now they could hear a roaring above the noise of the train.

What was it? The molten rock below? Or fear in their own ears?

"How hot will it get?" shouted Peter.

"Impossible!" shouted Ibrahim. "We must be dead now! The pressures. The heat—well over boiling. Impossible. Scientifically impossible," he muttered to himself.

Ibrahim had been calm up till now because he had trusted in his knowledge of geology, trusted in the belief that if you work things out according to the facts, there is a solution.

"It's impossible that we should be here. It's impossible that we should go any further."

His thoughts went stiff in the trap of his head.

His thoughts packed.

Their thoughts packed.

And now they could feel under their brains, and now each one of them knew what the enchantment was.

They knew, all of them, that the train was going to be crushed into a fossil like the tree in the coal. It was going to be a long silver worm in a rock squashed by hundreds of millions of years—unless—and they all knew this too—unless they could find enough inside them to fountain up out of the Tube, to squirt up through the silver shell of the train.

Hot.

Their thoughts crushed smaller.

Chunkier.

Mr Hartley-Crumley: his shell was the great balloon of self-importance that he'd puffed up round his life. And phut—like something hitting your tummy when you want to pee—it collapsed on him pht, in wrinkles with the wet stuff oozing out.

Mrs Binns: her Tube train shell was made of the wire where she held herself off from the mud of life. And it crushed, collapsed in the mud.

Ibrahim: his shell of Tube train was passing exams and passing

The Tube that Stuck

exams and passing exams to get up to the place of safety. Safe. The soft rich juice in the middle he didn't have time to bother about till later. And here, in the fear in the centre of the earth, some of it spurted up. But not enough to set them free.

Shirley: her tree had bloomed full of juice up through her hard shell that a black girl has to build in cruel London. But her tree had not been able to stop the Tube for long.

Peter: he had stopped trying to run away, remembered the smell of his mother cooking (she smelt like cabbage), and his sore throat from racing model cars, and fury at his small brother who wanted to crash them. But this spurted up a little way above the Tube, and then died down.

Hotter and deep crucsh—gr—sh—g.

Crsh—skrrr—eeek—grg.

Hartley-Crumley: sun—hgh! mother sun crunched.

Binns: creeeeek. I didn't mean—

Ibrahim: rockstrucmother.

Peter: vrrrmmmmmum. Mum!

Shirley: Mammasun.

"PU—u—u—u—U—u."

The only sound was the air booming through their train as the old man, crouched on the racketing floor, played his flute.

"Pu—u—prp—a—u."

The flute sang what they all longed for.

BOOM-CRASH—lightning and thunder—a cloudburst of sound.

They were in music. And their train, the little silver Tube train, was the flute.

The windows were open to the sky, and the air like mountain water clattered through.

"Pu—u—U?"

Like a forest the music answered, and their solo flew through it like a bird. Stretched like a Golden Gate Bridge all over the blackness, balancing on it. You could feel sound in you like your heart beating blood to the tip of your finger.

"Pu—u—U—u—prrrp."

Ibrahim heard it search like a honeybird through the forest.

"Prp—pu—a—pu—prrrp."

The Tube that Stuck

To Shirley the sound turned wet with runs and trickles in the complicated reggae wave.

"Prp—pu—pu—U? U—PUUUUUUU."

Then Ibrahim saw that of course they *couldn't* be hurtling through the earth at such a depth. They would be dead. It was illogical.

So he looked out again at the tunnel and saw that the pipes had not disappeared, but only curved down where the engineers were trying to avoid a seepage.

And he stood up, as the others round him began to roll themselves together, and saw that there were people in the next coach, joggling on the straps and shouting to each other in the noise as the train, after its long wait, started again.

And the driver coughed as he sat unseen behind the bland blue partition.

Mr Hartley-Crumley looked at his watch.

"That's the first time it's taken an hour and a half from Baker Street to Regents Park," he said. "That was a long sit!"

But he said it shakily.

And when, a few months later, Peter saw a fossil in a museum that was a long worm with curious square edges and regular holes and even sections, he told himself that metal can't turn into a fossil. But he wondered what happened to trains that were not lucky enough to have a magic flute.

The Bottle Imp

R. L. STEVENSON

There was a man of the island of Hawaii, whom I shall call Keawe; for the truth is, he still lives, and his name must be kept secret; but the place of his birth was not far from Honaunau, where the bones of Keawe the Great lie hidden in a cave. This man was poor, brave, and active; he could read and write like a schoolmaster; he was a first-rate mariner besides, sailed for some time in the island steamers, and steered a whale-boat on the Hamakua coast. At length it came in Keawe's mind to have a sight of the great world and foreign cities, and he shipped on a vessel bound to San Francisco.

This is a fine town, with a fine harbour, and rich people uncountable; and, in particular, there is one hill which is covered with palaces. Upon this hill Keawe was one day taking a walk, with his pocket full of money, viewing the great houses upon either hand with pleasure. "What fine houses there are!" he was thinking, "and how happy must these people be who dwell in them, and take no care for the morrow!" The thought was in his mind when he came abreast of a house that was smaller than some others, but all finished and beautiful like a toy; the steps of that house shone like silver, and the borders of the garden bloomed like garlands, and the windows were bright like diamonds; and Keawe stopped and wondered at the excellence of all he saw. So stopping, he was aware of a man that looked forth upon him through a window, so clear that Keawe could see him as you see a fish in a pool upon the reef. The man was

The Bottle Imp

elderly, with a bald head and a black beard; and his face was heavy with sorrow, and he bitterly sighed. And the truth of it is, that as Keawe looked in upon the man, and the man looked out upon Keawe, each envied the other.

All of a sudden the man smiled and nodded, and beckoned Keawe to enter, and met him at the door of the house.

"This is a fine house of mine," said the man, and bitterly sighed. "Would you not care to view the chambers?"

So he led Keawe all over it, from the cellar to the roof, and there was nothing there that was not perfect of its kind, and Keawe was astonished.

"Truly," said Keawe, "this is a beautiful house; if I lived in the like of it, I should be laughing all day long. How comes it, then, that you should be sighing?"

"There is no reason," said the man, "why you should not have a house in all points similar to this, and finer, if you wish. You have some money, I suppose?"

"I have fifty dollars," said Keawe; "but a house like this will cost more than fifty dollars."

The man made a computation. "I am sorry you have no more," said he, "for it may raise you trouble in the future; but it shall be yours at fifty dollars."

"The house?" asked Keawe.

"No, not the house," replied the man; "but the bottle. For I must tell you, although I appear to you so rich and fortunate, all my fortune, and this house itself and its garden, came out of a bottle not much bigger than a pint. This is it."

And he opened a lockfast place, and took out a round-bellied bottle with a long neck; the glass of it was white like milk, with changing rainbow colours in the grain. Within-sides something obscurely moved, like a shadow and a fire.

"This is the bottle," said the man; and, when Keawe laughed, "You do not believe me?" he added. "Try, then, for yourself. See if you can break it."

So Keawe took the bottle up and dashed it on the floor till he was weary; but it jumped on the floor like a child's ball, and was not injured.

"This is a strange thing," said Keawe. "For by the touch of it, as well as by the look, the bottle should be of glass."

"Of glass it is," replied the man, sighing more heavily than ever; "but the glass of it was tempered in the flames of hell. An imp lives in it, and that is the shadow we behold there moving; or, so I suppose. If any man buy this bottle the imp is at his command; all that he desires—love, fame, money, houses like this house, aye, or a city like this city—all are his at the word uttered. Napoleon had this bottle, and by it he grew to be the king of the world; but he sold it at the last and fell. Captain Cook had this bottle, and by it he found his way to so many islands; but he too sold it, and was slain upon Hawaii. For, once it is sold, the power goes and the protection; and unless a man remain content with what he has, ill will befall him."

"And yet you talk of selling it yourself?" Keawe said.

"I have all I wish, and I am growing elderly," replied the man. "There is one thing the imp cannot do—he cannot prolong life; and it would not be fair to conceal from you there is a drawback to the bottle; for if a man die before he sells it, he must burn in hell for ever."

"To be sure, that is a drawback and no mistake," cried Keawe. "I would not meddle with the thing. I can do without a house, thank God; but there is one thing I could not be doing with one particle, and that is to be damned."

"Dear me, you must not run away with things," returned the man. "All you have to do is to use the power of the imp in moderation, and then sell it to someone else, as I do to you, and finish your life in comfort."

"Well, I observe two things," said Keawe. "All the time you keep sighing like a maid in love—that is one; and for the other, you sell this bottle very cheap."

"I have told you already why I sigh," said the man. "It is because I fear my health is breaking up; and, as you said yourself, to die and go to the devil is a pity for any one. As for why I sell so cheap, I must explain to you there is a peculiarity about the bottle. Long ago, when the devil brought it first upon earth, it was extremely expensive, and was sold first of all to Prester

John for many millions of dollars; but it cannot be sold at all, unless sold at a loss. If you sell it for as much as you paid for it, back it comes to you again like a homing pigeon. It follows that the price has kept falling in these centuries, and the bottle is now remarkably cheap. I bought it myself from one of my great neighbours on this hill, and the price I paid was only ninety dollars. I could sell it for as high as eighty-nine dollars and ninety-nine cents, but not a penny dearer, or back the thing must come to me. Now, about this there are two bothers. First, when you offer a bottle so singular for eighty-odd dollars, people suppose you to be jesting. And second—but there is no hurry about that—and I need not go into it. Only remember it must be coined money that you sell it for."

"How am I to know that this is all true?" asked Keawe.

"Some of it you can try at once," replied the man. "Give me your fifty dollars, take the bottle, and wish your fifty dollars back into your pocket. If that does not happen, I pledge you my honour I will cry off the bargain and restore your money."

"You are not deceiving me?" said Keawe.

The man bound himself with a great oath.

"Well, I will risk that much," said Keawe, "for that can do no harm," and he paid over his money to the man, and the man handed him the bottle.

"Imp of the bottle," said Keawe, "I want my fifty dollars back." And sure enough, he had scarce said the word before his pocket was as heavy as ever.

"To be sure this is a wonderful bottle," said Keawe.

"And now good-morning to you, my fine fellow, and the devil go with you for me," said the man.

"Hold on," said Keawe, "I don't want any more of this fun. Here, take your bottle back."

"You have bought it for less than I paid for it," replied the man, rubbing his hands. "It is yours now; and, for my part, I am only concerned to see the back of you." And with that he rang for his Chinese servant, and had Keawe shown out of the house.

Now, when Keawe was in the street, with the bottle under his arm, he began to think. "If all is true about this bottle, I may

The Bottle Imp

have made a losing bargain," thinks he. "But perhaps the man was only fooling me." The first thing he did was to count his money; the sum was exact—forty-nine dollars, American money, and one Chili piece. "That looks like the truth," said Keawe. "Now I will try another part."

The streets in that part of the city were as clean as a ship's decks, and though it was noon, there were no passengers. Keawe set the bottle in the gutter and walked away. Twice he looked back, and there was the milky, round-bellied bottle where he left it. A third time he looked back and turned a corner; but he had scarce done so, when something knocked upon his elbow, and behold! it was the long neck sticking up; and as for the round belly, it was jammed into the pocket of his pilot-coat.

"And that looks like the truth," said Keawe.

The next thing he did was to buy a corkscrew in a shop, and go apart into a secret place in the fields. And there he tried to draw the cork, but as often as he put the screw in, out it came again, and the cork was as whole as ever.

"This is some new sort of cork," said Keawe, and all at once he began to shake and sweat, for he was afraid of that bottle.

On his way back to the port-side he saw a shop where a man sold shells and clubs from the wild islands, old heathen deities, old coined money, pictures from China and Japan, and all manner of things that sailors bring in their sea-chests. And here he had an idea. So he went in and offered the bottle for a hundred dollars. The man of the shop laughed at him at first, and offered him five; but, indeed, it was a curious bottle, such glass was never blown in any human glass-works, so prettily the colours shone under the milky white, and so strangely the shadow hovered in the midst; so, after he had disputed a while after the manner of his kind, the shopman gave Keawe sixty silver dollars for the thing and set it on a shelf in the midst of his window.

"Now," said Keawe, "I have sold that for sixty which I bought for fifty—or, to say truth, a little less, because one of my dollars was from Chili. Now I shall know the truth upon another point."

So he went back on board his ship, and when he opened his

chest, there was the bottle, which had come more quickly than himself. Now Keawe had a mate on board whose name was Lopaka.

"What ails you," said Lopaka, "that you stare in your chest?"

They were alone in the ship's forecastle, and Keawe bound him to secrecy, and told all.

"This is a very strange affair," said Lopaka; "and I fear you will be in trouble about this bottle. But there is one point very clear—that you are sure of the trouble, and you had better have the profit in the bargain. Make up your mind what you want with it; give the order, and if it is done as you desire, I will buy the bottle myself; for I have an idea of my own to get a schooner, and go trading through the islands."

"That is not my idea," said Keawe; "but to have a beautiful house and garden on the Kona coast, where I was born, the sun shining in at the door, flowers in the garden, glass in the windows, pictures on the walls, and toys and fine carpets on the tables, for all the world like the house I was in this day—only a storey higher, and with balconies all about like the king's palace; and to live there without care and make merry with my friends and relatives."

"Well," said Lopaka, "let us carry it back with us to Hawaii; and if all comes true as you suppose, I will buy the bottle, as I said, and ask a schooner."

Upon that they were agreed, and it was not long before the ship returned to Honolulu, carrying Keawe and Lopaka, and the bottle. They were scarce come ashore when they met a friend upon the beach, who began at once to condole with Keawe.

"I do not know what I am to be condoled about," said Keawe.

"Is it possible you have not heard," said the friend, "your uncle—that good old man—is dead, and your cousin—that beautiful boy—was drowned at sea?"

Keawe was filled with sorrow, and, beginning to weep and to lament, he forgot about the bottle. But Lopaka was thinking to himself, and presently, when Keawe's grief was a little abated, "I have been thinking," said Lopaka, "had not your uncle lands in Hawaii, in the district of Kaü?"

The Bottle Imp

"No," said Keawe, "not in Kaü: they are on the mountain-side—a little be-south Hookena."

"These lands will now be yours?" asked Lopaka.

"And so they will," says Keawe, and began again to lament for his relatives.

"No," said Lopaka, "do not lament at present. I have a thought in my mind. How if this should be the doing of the bottle? For here is the place ready for your house."

"If this be so," cried Keawe, "it is a very ill way to serve me by killing my relatives. But it may be, indeed; for it was in just such a station that I saw the house with my mind's eye."

"The house, however, is not yet built," said Lopaka.

"No, nor like to be!" said Keawe; "for though my uncle has some coffee and ava and bananas, it will not be more than will keep me in comfort; and the rest of that land is the black lava."

"Let us go to the lawyer," said Lopaka; "I have still this idea in my mind."

Now, when they came to the lawyer's, it appeared Keawe's uncle had grown monstrous rich in the last days, and there was a fund of money.

"And here is the money for the house!" cried Lopaka.

"If you are thinking of a new house," said the lawyer, "here is the card of a new architect of whom they tell me great things."

"Better and better!" cried Lopaka. "Here is all made plain for us. Let us continue to obey orders."

So they went to the architect, and he had drawings of houses on his table.

"You want something out of the way," said the architect. "How do you like this?" and he handed a drawing to Keawe.

Now, when Keawe set eyes on the drawing, he cried out aloud for it was the picture of his thought exactly drawn.

"I am in for this house," thought he. "Little as I like the way it comes to me, I am in for it now, and I may as well take the good along with the evil."

So he told the architect all that he wished, and how he would have that house furnished, and about the pictures on the walls and the knick-knacks on the tables; and he asked the man plainly for how much he would undertake the whole affair.

The architect put many questions, and took his pen and made a computation; and when he had done he named the very sum that Keawe had inherited.

Lopaka and Keawe looked at one another and nodded.

"It is quite clear," thought Keawe, "that I am to have this house, whether or no. It comes from the devil, and I fear I will get little good by that; and of one thing I am sure, I will make no more wishes as long as I have this bottle. But with the house I am saddled, and I may as well take the good along with the evil."

So he made his terms with the architect, and they signed a paper; and Keawe and Lopaka took ship again and sailed to Australia; for it was concluded between them they should not interfere at all, but leave the architect and the bottle imp to build and to adorn the house at their own pleasure.

The voyage was a good voyage, only all the time Keawe was holding in his breath, for he had sworn he would utter no more wishes, and take no more favours from the devil. The time was up when they got back. The architect told them that the house was ready, and Keawe and Lopaka took a passage in the *Hall*, and went down Kona way to view the house, and see if all had been done fitly according to the thought that was in Keawe's mind.

Now, the house stood on the mountain-side, visible to ships. Above, the forest ran up into the clouds of rain: below, the black lava fell in cliffs, where the kings of old lay buried. A garden bloomed about the house with every hue of flowers; and there was an orchard of papaia on the one hand and an orchard of bread-fruit on the other, and right in front, towards the sea, a ship's mast had been rigged up and bore a flag. As for the house, it was three storeys high, with great chambers and broad balconies on each. The windows were of glass, so excellent that it was as clear as water and as bright as day. All manner of furniture adorned the chambers. Pictures hung upon the wall in golden frames—pictures of ships, and men fighting, and

The Bottle Imp

of the most beautiful women, and of singular places; nowhere in the world are there pictures of so bright a colour as those Keawe found hanging in his house. As for the knick-knacks, they were extraordinarily fine: chiming clocks and musical boxes, little men with nodding heads, books filled with pictures, weapons of price from all quarters of the world, and the most elegant puzzles to entertain the leisure of a solitary man. And as no one would care to live in such chambers, only to walk through and view them, the balconies were made so broad that a whole town might have lived upon them in delight; and Keawe knew not which to prefer, whether the back porch, where you got the land breeze and looked upon the orchards and the flowers, or the front balcony, where you could drink the wind of the sea, and look down the steep wall of the mountain and see the *Hall* going by once a week or so between Hookena and the hills of Pele, or the schooners plying up the coast for wood and ava and bananas.

When they had viewed all, Keawe and Lopaka sat on the porch.

"Well," asked Lopaka, "is it all as you designed?"

"Words cannot utter it," said Keawe. "It is better than I dreamed, and I am sick with satisfaction."

"There is but one thing to consider," said Lopaka; "all this may be quite natural, and the bottle imp have nothing whatever to say to it. If I were to buy the bottle, and got no schooner after all, I should have put my hand in the fire for nothing. I gave you my word, I know; but yet I think you would not grudge me one more proof."

"I have sworn I would take no more favours," said Keawe. "I have gone already deep enough."

"This is no favour I am thinking of," replied Lopaka. "It is only to see the imp himself. There is nothing to be gained by that, and so nothing to be ashamed of, and yet, if I once saw him, I should be sure of the whole matter. So indulge me so far, and let me see the imp; and, after that, here is the money in my hand, and I will buy it."

"There is only one thing I am afraid of," said Keawe. "The

The Bottle Imp

imp may be very ugly to view, and if you once set eyes upon him you might be very undesirous of the bottle."

"I am a man of my word," said Lopaka. "And here is the money betwixt us."

"Very well," replied Keawe, "I have a curiosity myself. So come, let us have one look at you, Mr Imp."

Now as soon as that was said, the imp looked out of the bottle and in again, swift as a lizard; and there saw Keawe and Lopaka turned to stone. The night had quite come, before either found a thought to say or voice to say it with; and then Lopaka pushed the money over and took the bottle.

"I am a man of my word," said he, "and had need to be so, or I would not touch this bottle with my foot. Well, I shall get my schooner and a dollar or two for my pocket; and then I will be rid of this devil as fast as I can. For to tell you the plain truth, the look of him has cast me down."

"Lopaka," said Keawe, "do not you think any worse of me than you can help; I know it is night, and the roads bad, and the pass by the tombs an ill place to go by so late, but I declare since I have seen that little face, I cannot eat or sleep or pray till it is gone from me. I will give you a lantern, and a basket to put the bottle in, and any picture or fine thing in all my house that takes your fancy; and be gone at once, and go sleep at Hookena with Nahinu."

"Keawe," said Lopaka, "many a man would take this ill; above all, when I am doing you a turn so friendly, as to keep my word and buy the bottle; and for that matter, the night and the dark, and the way by the tombs, must be all tenfold more dangerous to a man with such a sin upon his conscience and such a bottle under his arm. But for my part, I am so extremely terrified myself, I have not the heart to blame you. Here I go, then; and I pray God you may be happy in your house, and I fortunate with my schooner, and both get to heaven in the end in spite of the devil and his bottle."

So Lopaka went down the mountain; and Keawe stood in his front balcony, and listened to the clink of the horses' shoes, and watched the lantern go shining down the path, and along the cliff of caves where the old dead are buried; and all the time he trembled and clasped his hands, and prayed for his friend, and gave glory to God that he himself was escaped out of that trouble.

But the next day came very brightly, and that new house of his was so delightful to behold that he forgot his terrors. One day followed another, and Keawe dwelt there in perpetual joy. He had his place on the back porch; it was there he ate and lived, and read the stories in the Honolulu newspapers; but when any one came by they would go in and view the chambers and the pictures. And the fame of the house went far and wide; it was called *Ka-Hale Nui*—the Great House—in all Kona; and sometimes the Bright House, for Keawe kept a Chinaman, who was all day dusting and furbishing; and the glass, and the gilt, and the fine stuffs, and the pictures, shone as bright as the morning. As for Keawe himself, he could not walk in the chambers without singing, his heart was so enlarged; and when ships sailed by upon the sea, he would fly his colours on the mast.

So time went by, until one day Keawe went upon a visit as far as Kailua to certain of his friends. There he was well feasted; and left as soon as he could the next morning, and rode hard, for he was impatient to behold his beautiful house; and, besides, the night then coming on was the night in which the dead old days go abroad in the sides of Kona; and having already meddled with the devil, he was the more chary of meeting with the dead. A little beyond Honaunau, looking far ahead, he was aware of a woman bathing in the edges of the sea; and she seemed a well-grown girl, but he thought no more of it. Then he saw her white shift flutter as she put it on, and then her red holoku; and by the time he came abreast of her she was done with her toilet, and had come up from the sea, and stood by the trackside in her red holoku, and she was all freshened with the bath, and her eyes shone and were kind. Now Keawe no sooner beheld her than he drew rein.

"I thought I knew every one in this country," said he. "How comes it that I do not know you?"

"I am Kokua, daughter of Kiano," said the girl, "and I have just returned from Oahu. Who are you?"

The Bottle Imp

"I will tell you who I am in a little," said Keawe, dismounting from his horse, "but not now. For I have a thought in my mind and if you knew who I was, you might have heard of me, and would not give me a true answer. But tell me, first of all, one thing: are you married?"

At this Kokua laughed out aloud. "It is you who ask questions," she said. "Are you married yourself?"

"Indeed, Kokua, I am not," replied Keawe, "and never thought to be until this hour. But here is the plain truth. I have met you here at the roadside, and I saw your eyes, which are like the stars, and my heart went to you as swift as a bird. And so now, if you want none of me, say so and I will go on to my own place; but if you think me no worse than any other young man, say so, too, and I will turn aside to your father's for the night, and tomorrow I will talk with the good man."

Kokua said never a word, but she looked at the sea and laughed.

"Kokua," said Keawe, "if you say nothing, I will take that for the good answer; so let us be stepping to your father's door."

She went on ahead of him, still without speech; only sometimes she glanced back and glanced away again, and she kept the strings of her hat in her mouth.

Now, when they had come to the door, Kiano came out on his veranda, and cried out and welcomed Keawe by name. At that the girl looked over, for the fame of the great house had come to her ears; and, to be sure, it was a great temptation. All that evening, they were very merry together; and the girl was as bold as brass under the eyes of her parents, and made a mark of Keawe, for she had a quick wit. The next day he had a word with Kiano, and found the girl alone.

"Kokua," said he, "you made a mark of me all the evening; and it is still time to bid me go. I would not tell you who I was, because I have so fine a house, and I feared you would think too much of that house and too little of the man that loves you. Now you know all, and if you wish to have seen the last of me, say so at once."

"No," said Kokua, but this time she did not laugh, nor did Keawe ask for more.

This was the wooing of Keawe; things had gone quickly; but so an arrow goes, and the ball of a rifle swifter still, and yet both may strike the target. Things had gone fast, but they had gone far also, and the thought of Keawe rang in the maiden's head; she heard his voice in the breach of the surf upon the lava, and for this young man that she had seen but twice she would have left father and mother and her native islands. As for Keawe himself, his horse flew up the path of the mountain under the cliff of tombs, and the sound of the hoofs, and the sound of Keawe singing to himself for pleasure, echoed in the caverns of the dead. He came to the Bright House, and still he was singing. He sat and ate in the broad balcony, and the Chinaman wondered at his master, to hear how he sang between the mouthfuls. The sun went down into the sea, and the night came; and Keawe walked the balconies by lamplight, high on the mountains, and the voice of his singing started men on ships.

"Here am I now upon my high place," he said to himself. "Life may be no better; this is the mountain top; and all shelves about me towards the worse. For the first time I will light up the chambers, and bathe in my fine bath with the hot water and the cold, and sleep above in the bed of my bridal chamber."

So the Chinaman had word, and he must rise from sleep and light the furnaces; and as he walked below, beside the boilers, he heard his master singing and rejoicing above him in the lighted chambers. When the water began to be hot the Chinaman cried to his master: and Keawe went into the bathroom; and the Chinaman heard him sing as he filled the marble basin; and heard him sing, and the singing broken, as he undressed; until of a sudden, the song ceased. The Chinaman listened, and listened; he called up the house to Keawe to ask if all were well, and Keawe answered him "Yes", and bade him go to bed; but there was no more singing in the Bright House; and all night long the Chinaman heard his master's feet go round and round the balconies without repose.

Now, the truth of it was this: as Keawe undressed for his

The Bottle Imp

bath, he spied upon his flesh a patch like a patch of lichen on a rock, and it was then that he stopped singing. For he knew the likeness of that patch, and knew that he was fallen in the Chinese Evil.*

Now, it is a sad thing for any man to fall into this sickness. And it would be a sad thing for any one to leave a house so beautiful and so commodious; and depart from all his friends to the north coast of Molokai, between the mighty cliff and the sea-breakers. But what was that to the case of the man Keawe, he who had met his love but yesterday and won her but that morning, and now saw all his hopes break, in a moment, like a piece of glass?

A while he sat upon the edge of the bath, then sprang, with a cry, and ran outside; and to and fro, to and fro, along the balcony, like one despairing.

"Very willingly could I leave Hawaii, the home of my fathers," Keawe was thinking. "Very lightly could I leave my house, the high-placed, the many-windowed, here upon the mountains. Very bravely could I go to Molokai, to Kalaupapa by the cliffs, to live with the smitten and to sleep there, far from my fathers. But what wrong have I done, what sin lies upon my soul, that I should have encountered Kokua coming cool from the sea-water in the evening? Kokua, the soul-ensnarer! Kokua, the light of my life! Her may I never wed, her may I look upon no longer, her may I no more handle with my loving hand; and it is for this, it is for you, O Kokua! that I pour my lamentations!"

Now you are to observe what sort of a man Keawe was, for he might have dwelt there in the Bright House for years, and no one been the wiser of his sickness; but he reckoned nothing of that, if he must lose Kokua. And again he might have wed Kokua even as he was; and so many would have done, because they have the souls of pigs; but Keawe loved the maiden manfully, and he would do her no hurt and bring her in no danger.

A little beyond the midst of the night, there came in his mind the recollection of that bottle. He went round to the back

* Leprosy.

porch, and called to memory the day when the devil had looked forth; and at the thought ice ran in his veins.

"A dreadful thing is the bottle," thought Keawe, "and dreadful is the imp, and it is a dreadful thing to risk the flames of hell. But what other hope have I to cure my sickness or to wed Kokua! What!" he thought, "would I beard the devil once, only to get me a house, and not face him again to win Kokua?"

Thereupon he called to mind it was the next day the *Hall* went by on her return to Honolulu. "There must I go first," he thought, "and see Lopaka. For the best hope that I have now is to find that same bottle I was so pleased to be rid of."

Never a wink could he sleep; the food stuck in his throat; but he sent a letter to Kiano, and about the time when the steamer would be coming, rode down beside the cliff of the tombs. It rained; his horse went heavily; he looked up at the black mouths of the caves, and he envied the dead that slept there and were done with trouble; and called to mind how he had galloped by the day before, and was astonished. So he came down to Hookena, and there was all the country gathered for the steamer as usual. In the shed before the store they sat and jested and passed the news; but there was no matter of speech in Keawe's bosom, and he sat in their midst and looked without on the rain falling on the houses, and the surf beating among the rocks, and the sighs arose in his throat.

"Keawe of the Bright House is out of spirits," said one to another. Indeed, and so he was, and little wonder.

Then the *Hall* came, and the whale-boat carried him on board. The after-part of the ship was full of Haoles*—who had been to visit the volcano, as their custom is; and the midst was crowned with Kanakas, and the forepart with wild bulls from Hilo and horses from Kaü; but Keawe sat apart from all in his sorrow, and watched for the house of Kiano. There it sat low upon the shore in the black rocks, and shaded by the cocoa-palms, and there by the door was a red holoku, no greater than a fly, and going to and fro with a fly's busyness. "Ah, queen of my heart," he cried, "I'll venture my dear soul to win you!"

* Whites.

Soon after darkness fell and the cabins were lit up, and the Haoles sat and played at the cards and drank whisky as their custom is; but Keawe walked the deck all night; and all the next day, as they steamed under the lee of Maui or of Molokai, he was still pacing to and fro like a wild animal in a menagerie.

Towards evening they passed Diamond Head, and came to the pier of Honolulu. Keawe stepped out among the crowd and began to ask for Lopaka. It seemed he had become the owner of a schooner—none better in the islands—and was gone upon an adventure as far as Pola-Pola or Kahiki; so there was no help to be looked for from Lopaka. Keawe called to mind a friend of his, a lawyer in the town (I must not tell his name), and inquired of him. They said he was grown suddenly rich, and had a fine new house upon Waikiki shore; and this put a thought in Keawe's head, and he called a hack and drove to the lawyer's house.

The house was all brand new, and the trees in the garden no greater than walking-sticks, and the lawyer, when he came, had the air of a man well pleased.

"What can I do to serve you?" said the lawyer.

"You are a friend of Lopaka's," replied Keawe, "and Lopaka purchased from me a certain piece of goods that I thought you might enable me to trace."

The lawyer's face became very dark. "I do not profess to misunderstand you, Mr Keawe," said he, "though this is an ugly business to be stirring in. You may be sure I know nothing, but yet I have a guess, and if you would apply in a certain quarter I think you might have news."

And he named the name of a man, which, again, I had better not repeat. So it was for days, and Keawe went from one to another, finding everywhere new clothes and carriages, and fine new houses, and men everywhere in great contentment, although, to be sure, when he hinted at his business their faces would cloud over.

"No doubt I am upon the track," thought Keawe. "These new clothes and carriages are all the gifts of the little imp, and these glad faces are the faces of men who have taken their profit and

The Bottle Imp

got rid of the accursed thing in safety. When I see pale cheeks and hear sighing, I shall know that I am near the bottle."

So it befell at last he was recommended to a Haole in Beritania Street. When he came to the door, about the hour of the evening meal, there were the usual marks of the new house, and the young garden, and the electric light shining in the windows; but when the owner came, a shock of hope and fear ran through Keawe; for here was a young man, white as a corpse, and black about the eyes, the hair shedding from his head, and such a look in his countenance as a man may have when he is waiting for the gallows.

"Here it is, to be sure," thought Keawe, and so with this man he noways veiled his errand. "I am come to buy the bottle," said he.

At the word, the young Haole of Beritania Street reeled against the wall.

"The bottle!" he gasped. "To buy the bottle!" Then he seemed to choke, and seizing Keawe by the arm, carried him into a room and poured out wine in two glasses.

"Here is my respects," said Keawe, who had been much about with Haoles in his time. "Yes," he added, "I am come to buy the bottle. What is the price by now?"

At that word the young man let his glass slip through his fingers, and looked upon Keawe like a ghost.

"The price," says he; "the price! You do not know the price?"

"It is for that I am asking you," returned Keawe. "But why are you so much concerned? Is there anything wrong about the price?"

"It has dropped a great deal in value since your time, Mr Keawe," said the young man, stammering.

"Well, well, I shall have the less to pay for it," says Keawe. "How much did it cost you?"

The young man was as white as a sheet. "Two cents," said he.

"What!" cried Keawe, "two cents? Why, then, you can only sell it for one. And he who buys it——" The words died upon Keawe's tongue; he who bought it could never sell it again, the bottle and the bottle imp must abide with him until he died, and when he died must carry him to the red end of hell."

The young man of Beritania Street fell upon his knees. "For God's sake, buy it!" he cried. "You can have all my fortune in the bargain. I was mad when I bought it at that price. I had embezzled money at my store; I was lost else; I must have gone to jail."

"Poor creature," said Keawe, "you would risk your soul upon so desperate an adventure, and to avoid the proper punishment of your own disgrace; and you think I could hesitate with love in front of me. Give me the bottle, and the change which I make sure you have all ready. Here is a five-cent piece."

It was as Keawe supposed; the young man had the change ready in a drawer; the bottle changed hands, and Keawe's fingers were no sooner clasped upon the stalk than he had breathed his wish to be a clean man. And sure enough, when he got home to his room, and stripped himself before a glass, his flesh was whole like an infant's. And here was the strange thing; he had no sooner seen this miracle than his mind was changed within him, and he cared naught for the Chinese Evil, and little enough for Kokua; and had but the one thought, that here he was bound to the bottle imp for time and for eternity, and had no better hope but to be a cinder for ever in the flames of hell. Away ahead of him he saw them blaze with his mind's eye, and his soul shrank, and darkness fell upon the light.

When Keawe came to himself a little, he was aware it was the night when the band played at the hotel. Thither he went, because he feared to be alone; and there, among happy faces, walked to and fro, and heard the tunes go up and down, and saw Berger beat the measure, and all the while he heard the flames crackle and saw the red fire burning in the bottomless pit. Of a sudden the band played *Hiki-ao-ao*; that was a song that he had sung with Kokua, and at the strain courage returned to him.

"It is done now," he thought, "and once more let me take the good along with the evil."

So it befell that he returned to Hawaii by the first steamer, and as soon as it could be managed he was wedded to Kokua, and carried her up the mountain-side to the Bright House.

Now it was so with these two, that when they were together Keawe's heart was stilled; but as soon as he was alone he fell into a brooding horror, and heard the flames crackle, and saw the red fire burn in the bottomless pit. The girl, indeed, had come to him wholly; her heart leaped in her side at sight of him, her hand clung to his; and she was so fashioned, from the hair upon her head to the nails upon her toes, that none could see her without joy. She was pleasant in her nature. She had the good word always. Full of song she was, and went to and fro in the Bright House, the brightest thing in its three storeys, carolling like the birds. And Keawe beheld and heard her with delight, and then must shrink upon one side, and weep and groan to think upon the price that he had paid for her; and then he must dry his eyes and wash his face, and go and sit with her on the broad balconies, joining in her songs, and, with a sick spirit, answering her smiles.

There came a day when her feet began to be heavy and her songs more rare; and now it was not Keawe only that would weep apart, but each would sunder from the other and sit in opposite balconies with the whole width of the Bright House betwixt. Keawe was so sunk in his despair he scarce observed the change, and was only glad he had more hours to sit alone and brood upon his destiny, and was not so frequently condemned to pull a smiling face on a sick heart. But one day, coming softly through the house, he heard the sound of a child sobbing, and there was Kokua rolling her face upon the balcony floor, and weeping like the lost.

"You do well to weep in this house, Kokua," he said. "And yet I would give the head off my body that you (at least) might have been happy."

"Happy!" she cried. "Keawe, when you lived alone in your Bright House you were the word of the island for a happy man; laughter and song were in your mouth, and your face was as bright as the sunrise. Then you wedded poor Kokua; and the good God knows what is amiss in her—but from that day you

The Bottle Imp

have not smiled. Oh!" she cried, "what ails me? I thought I was pretty, and I knew I loved him. What ails me, that I throw this cloud upon my husband?"

"Poor Kokua," said Keawe. He sat down by her side, and sought to take her hand; but that she plucked away. "Poor Kokua," he said again. "My poor child—my pretty. And I had thought all this while to spare you! Well, you shall know all. Then, at least, you will pity poor Keawe; then you will understand how much he loved you in the past—that he dared hell for your possession—and how much he loves you still (the poor condemned one), that he can yet call up a smile when he beholds you."

With that he told her all, even from the beginning.

"You have done this for me?" she cried. "Ah, well, then what do I care!" and she clasped and wept upon him.

"Ah, child!" said Keawe, "and yet, when I consider of the fire of hell, I care a good deal!"

"Never tell me," said she, "no man can be lost because he loved Kokua, and no other fault. I tell you, Keawe, I shall save you with these hands, or perish in your company. What! you loved me and gave your soul, and you think I will not die to save you in return?"

"Ah, my dear, you might die a hundred times: and what difference would that make?" he cried, "except to leave me lonely till the time comes for my damnation?"

"You know nothing," said she. "I was educated in a school in Honolulu; I am no common girl. And I tell you I shall save my lover. What is this you say about a cent? But all the world is not American. In England they have a piece they call a farthing, which is about half a cent. Ah! sorrow!" she cried, "that makes it scarcely better, for the buyer must be lost, and we shall find none so brave as my Keawe! But then, there is France; they have a small coin there which they call a centime, and these go five to the cent, or thereabout. We could not do better. Come, Keawe, let us go to the French islands; let us go to Tahiti, as fast as ships can bear us. There we have four centimes, three centimes, two centimes, one centime; four possible sales to come and go

The Bottle Imp

on; and two of us to push the bargain. Come, my Keawe! kiss me, and banish care. Kokua will defend you."

"Gift of God!" he cried. "I cannot think that God will punish me for desiring aught so good. Be it as you will, then, take me where you please; I put my life and my salvation in your hands."

Early the next day Kokua went about her preparations. She took Keawe's chest that he went with sailoring; and first she put the bottle in a corner, and then packed it with the richest of their clothes and the bravest of the knick-knacks in the house. "For," said she, "we must seem to be rich folks, or who would believe in the bottle?" All the time of her preparation she was as gay as a bird; only when she looked upon Keawe the tears would spring in her eye, and she must run and kiss him. As for Keawe a weight was off his soul; now that he had his secret shared, and some hope in front of him, he seemed like a new man; his feet went lightly on the earth, and his breath was good to him again. Yet was terror still at his elbow; and ever and again, as the wind blows out a taper, hope died in him, and he saw the flame toss and the red fire burn in hell.

It was given out in the country they were gone pleasuring in the States, which was thought a strange thing, and yet not so strange as the truth, if any could have guessed it. So they went to Honolulu in the *Hall*, and thence in the *Umatilla* to San Francisco with a crowd of Haoles, and at San Francisco took their passage by the mail brigantine, the *Tropic Bird*, for Papeete, the chief place of the French in the south islands. Thither they came, after a pleasant voyage, on a fair day of the Trade Wind, and saw the reef with the surf breaking and Motuiti with its palms, and the schooner riding withinside, and the white houses of the town low down along the shore among green trees, and overhead the mountains and the clouds of Tahiti, the wise island.

It was judged the most wise to hire a house, which they did accordingly, opposite the British Consul's, to make a great parade of money, and themselves conspicuous with carriages and horses. This it was very easy to do so long as they had the bottle in their possession; for Kokua was more bold than Keawe, and,

The Bottle Imp

whenever she had a mind, called on the imp for twenty or a hundred dollars. At this rate they soon grew to be remarked in the town; and the strangers from Hawaii, their riding and their driving, the fine holokus, and the rich lace of Kokua, became the matter of much talk.

They got on well after the first with the Tahitian language, which is indeed like to the Hawaiian, with a change of certain letters; and as soon as they had any freedom of speech, began to push the bottle. You are to consider it was not an easy subject to introduce; it is not easy to persuade people you are in earnest, when you offer to sell them for four centimes the spring of health and riches inexhaustible. It was necessary, besides, to explain the dangers of the bottle; and either people disbelieved the whole thing and laughed, or they thought the more of the darker part, became overcast with gravity, and drew away from Keawe and Kokua, as from persons who had dealings with the devil. So far from gaining ground, these two began to find they were avoided in the town; the children ran away from them screaming, a thing intolerable to Kokua; Catholics crossed themselves as they went by; and all persons began with one accord to disengage themselves from their advances.

Depression fell upon their spirits. They would sit at night in their new house, after a day's weariness, and not exchange one word, or the silence would be broken by Kokua bursting suddenly into sobs. Sometimes they would pray together; sometimes they would have the bottle out upon the floor, and sit all evening watching how the shadow hovered in the midst. At such times they would be afraid to go to rest. It was long ere slumber came to them, and, if either dozed off, it would be to wake and find the other silently weeping in the dark, or, perhaps, to wake alone, the other having fled from the house and the neighbourhood of that bottle, to pace under the bananas in the little garden, or to wander on the beach by moonlight.

One night it was so when Kokua awoke. Keawe was gone. She felt in the bed and his place was cold. Then fear fell upon her, and she sat up in bed. A little moonshine filtered through the shutters. The room was bright, and she could spy the bottle on the floor. Outside it blew high, the great trees of the avenue cried aloud, and the fallen leaves rattled in the veranda. In the midst of this Kokua was aware of another sound; whether of a beast or of a man she could scarce tell, but it was as sad as death, and cut her to the soul. Softly she arose, set the door ajar, and looked forth into the moonlit yard. There, under the bananas, lay Keawe, his mouth in the dust, and as he lay he moaned.

It was Kokua's first thought to run forward and console him; her second potently withheld her. Keawe had borne himself before his wife like a brave man; it became her little in the hour of weakness to intrude upon his shame. With the thought she drew back into the house.

"Heaven," she thought, "how careless have I been—how weak! It is he, not I, that stands in this eternal peril; it was he, not I, that took the curse upon his soul. It is for my sake, and for the love of a creature of so little worth and such poor help, that he now beholds so close to him the flames of hell—aye, and smells the smoke of it, lying without there in the wind and moonlight. Am I so dull of spirit that never till now have I surmised my duty, or have I seen it before and turned aside? But now, at least, I take up my soul in both the hands of my affection; now I say farewell to the white steps of heaven and the waiting faces of my friends. A love for a love, and let mine be equalled with Keawe's! A soul for a soul, and be it mine to perish!"

She was a deft woman with her hands, and was soon apparelled. She took in her hands the change—the precious centimes they kept ever at their side; for this coin is little used, and they had made provision at a government office. When she was forth in the avenue clouds came on the wind, and the moon was blackened. The town slept, and she knew not whither to turn till she heard one coughing in the shadow of the trees.

"Old man," said Kokua, "what do you here abroad in the cold night?"

The old man could scarce express himself for coughing, but he made out that he was old and poor, and a stranger in the sland.

"Will you do me a service?" said Kokua. "As one stranger to

The Bottle Imp

another, and as an old man to a young woman, will you help a daughter of Hawaii?"

"Ah," said the old man. "So you are the witch from the Eight Islands, and even my old soul you seek to entangle. But I have heard of you, and defy your wickedness."

"Sit down here," said Kokua, "and let me tell you a tale." And she told him the story of Keawe from the beginning to the end.

"And now," said she, "I am his wife, whom he bought with his soul's welfare. And what should I do? If I went to him myself and offered to buy it, he will refuse. But if you go, he will sell it eagerly; I will await you here; you will buy it for four centimes, and I will buy it again for three. And the Lord strengthen a poor girl!"

"If you meant falsely," said the old man, "I think God would strike you dead."

"He would!" cried Kokua. "Be sure He would. I could not be so treacherous; God would not suffer it."

"Give me the four centimes and await me here," said the old man.

Now, when Kokua stood alone in the street, her spirit died. The wind roared in the trees, and it seemed to her the rushing of the flames of hell; the shadows towered in the light of the street lamp, and they seemed to her the snatching hands of evil ones. If she had had the strength, she must have run away, and if she had had the breath, she must have screamed aloud; but, in truth, she could do neither, and stood and trembled in the avenue, like an affrighted child.

Then she saw the old man returning, and he had the bottle in his hand.

"I have done your bidding," said he. "I left your husband weeping like a child; tonight he will sleep easy." And he held the bottle forth.

"Before you give it me," Kokua panted, "take the good with the evil—ask to be delivered from your cough."

"I am an old man," replied the other, "and too near the gate of the grave to take a favour from the devil. But what is this? Why do you not take the bottle? Do you hesitate?"

"Not hesitate!" cried Kokua. "I am only weak. Give me a moment. It is my hand resists, my flesh shrinks back from the accursed thing. One moment only!"

The old man looked upon Kokua kindly. "Poor child!" said he, "you fear: your soul misgives you. Well, let me keep it. I am old, and can never more be happy in this world, and as for the next..."

"Give it me!" gasped Kokua. "There is your money. Do you think I am so base as that? Give me the bottle."

"God bless you, child," said the old man.

Kokua concealed the bottle under her holoku, said farewell to the old man, and walked off along the avenue, she cared not whither. For all roads were now the same to her, and led equally to hell. Sometimes she walked and sometimes ran; sometimes she screamed out loud in the night, and sometimes lay by the wayside in the dust and wept. All that she had heard of hell came back to her; she saw the flames blaze, and she smelled the smoke, and her flesh withered on the coals.

Near day she came to her mind again, and returned to the house. It was even as the old man said—Keawe slumbered like a child. Kokua stood and gazed upon his face.

"Now, my husband," said she, "it is your turn to sleep. When you wake it will be your turn to sing and laugh. But for poor Kokua, alas! that meant no evil—for poor Kokua no more sleep, no more singing, no more delight, whether in earth or heaven."

With that she lay down in the bed by his side, and her misery was so extreme that she fell in a deep slumber instantly.

Late in the morning her husband woke her and gave her the good news. It seemed he was silly with delight, for he paid no heed to her distress, ill though she dissembled it. The words stuck in her mouth; it mattered not, Keawe did the speaking. She ate not a bite, but who was to observe it? For Keawe cleared the dish. Kokua saw and heard him, like some strange thing in a dream; there were times when she forgot or doubted, and put her hands to her brow; to know herself doomed and hear her husband's babble, seemed so monstrous.

The Bottle Imp

All the while Keawe was eating and talking, and planning the time of their return, and thanking her for saving him and fondling her, and calling her the true helper after all. He laughed at the old man that was fool enough to buy that bottle.

"A worthy old man he seemed," Keawe said. "But no one can judge by appearances. For why did the old reprobate require the bottle?"

"My husband," said Kokua humbly, "his purpose may have been good."

Keawe laughed like an angry man.

"Fiddle-de-dee!" cried Keawe. "An old rogue, I tell you; and an old ass to boot. For the bottle was hard enough to sell at four centimes; and at three it will be quite impossible. The margin is not broad enough, the thing begins to smell of scorching—brrr!" said he, and shuddered. "It is true I bought it myself at a cent, when I knew not there were smaller coins. I was a fool for my pains; there will never be found another, and whoever has that bottle now will carry it to the pit."

"O my husband!" said Kokua. "Is it not a terrible thing to save oneself by the eternal ruin of another? It seems to me I could not laugh. I would be humbled. I would be filled with melancholy. I would pray for the poor holder."

Then Keawe, because he felt the truth of what she said, grew the more angry. "Heighty-teighty!" cried he. "You may be filled with melancholy if you please. It is not the mind of a good wife. If you thought at all of me, you would sit shamed."

Thereupon he went out, and Kokua was alone.

What chance had she to sell that bottle at two centimes? None, she perceived. And if she had any, here was her husband hurrying her away to a country where there was nothing lower than a cent. And here—on the morrow of her sacrifice—was her husband leaving her and blaming her.

She would not even try to profit by what time she had but sat in the house, and now had the bottle out and viewed it with unutterable fear, and now, with loathing, hid it out of sight.

By-and-by Keawe came back, and would have her take a drive.

The Bottle Imp

"My husband, I am ill," she said. "I am out of heart. Excuse me, I can take no pleasure."

Then was Keawe more wroth than ever. With her, because he thought she was brooding over the case of the old man; and with himself, because he thought she was right and was ashamed to be so happy.

"This is your truth," cried he, "and this your affection! Your husband is just saved from eternal ruin, which he encountered for the love of you—and you can take no pleasure! Kokua, you have a disloyal heart."

He went forth again furious, and wandered in the town all day. He met friends, and drank with them; they hired a carriage and drove into the country, and there drank again. All the time Keawe was ill at ease, because he was taking this pastime while his wife was sad, and because he knew in his heart that she was more right than he; and the knowledge made him drink the deeper.

Now there was an old brutal Haole drinking with him, one that had been a boatswain of a whaler—a runaway, a digger in gold mines, a convict in prisons. He had a low mind and a foul mouth; he loved to drink and to see others drunken; and he pressed the glass upon Keawe. Soon there was no more money in the company.

"Here you!" says the boatswain, "you are rich, you have been always saying. You have a bottle or some foolishness."

"Yes," says Keawe, "I am rich; I will go back and get some money from my wife, who keeps it."

"That's a bad idea, mate," said the boatswain. "Never you trust a petticoat with dollars. They're all as false as water; you keep an eye on her."

Now this word struck in Keawe's mind; for he was muddled with what he had been drinking.

"I should not wonder but she was false, indeed," thought he. "Why else should she be so cast down at my release? But I will show her I am not the man to be fooled. I will catch her in the act."

Accordingly, when they were back in town, Keawe bade

the boatswain wait for him at the corner, by the old calaboose, and went forward up the avenue alone to the door of his house. The night had come again; there was a light within, but never a sound; and Keawe crept about the corner, opened the back door softly, and looked in.

There was Kokua on the floor, the lamp at her side; before her was a milk-white bottle, with a round belly and a long neck; and as she viewed it, Kokua wrung her hands.

A long time Keawe stood and looked in the doorway. At first he was struck stupid; and then fear fell upon him that the bargain had been made amiss, and the bottle had come back to him as it came at San Francisco; and at that his knees were loosened, and the fumes of the wine departed from his head like mists off a river in the morning. And then he had another thought; and it was a strange one, that made his cheeks to burn.

"I must make sure of this," thought he.

So he closed the door, and went softly round the corner again, and then came noisily in, as though he were but now returned. And, lo! by the time he opened the front door no bottle was to be seen; and Kokua sat in a chair and started up like one awakened out of sleep.

"I have been drinking all day and making merry," said Keawe. "I have been with good companions, and now I only came back for money, and return to drink and carouse with them again."

Both his face and voice were as stern as judgement, but Kokua was too troubled to observe.

"You do well to use your own, my husband," said she, and her words trembled.

"Oh, I do well in all things," said Keawe, and he went straight to the chest and took out money. But he looked beside in the corner where they kept the bottle, and there was the bottle there.

At that the chest heaved upon the floor like a sea-billow, and the house spun about him like a wreath of smoke, for he saw she was lost now, and there was no escape. "It is what I feared," he thought. "It is she who has bought it."

And then he came to himself a little and rose up; but the

sweat streamed on his face as thick as the rain and cold as the well-water.

"Kokua," said he, "I said to you today what ill became me. Now I return to house with my jolly companions," and at that he laughed a little quietly. "I will take more pleasure in the cup if you forgive me."

She clasped his knees in a moment, she kissed his knees with flowing tears.

"Oh," she cried, "I ask but a kind word!"

"Let us never one think hardly of the other," said Keawe, and was gone out of the house.

Now, the money that Keawe had taken was only some of that store of centime pieces they had laid in at their arrival. It was very sure he had no mind to be drinking. His wife had given her soul for him, now he must give his for hers; no other thought was in the world with him.

At the corner, by the old calaboose, there was the boatswain waiting.

"My wife has the bottle," said Keawe, "and, unless you help me to recover it, there can be no more money and no more liquor tonight."

"You do not mean to say you are serious about that bottle?" cried the boatswain.

"There is the lamp," said Keawe. "Do I look as if I was jesting?"

"That is so," said the boatswain. "You look as serious as a ghost."

"Well, then," said Keawe, "here are two centimes; you just go to my wife in the house, and offer her these for the bottle, which (if I am not much mistaken) she will give you instantly. Bring it to me here, and I will buy it back from you for one; for that is the law with this bottle, that it still must be sold for a less sum. But whatever you do, never breathe a word to her that you have come from me."

"Mate, I wonder are you making a fool of me?" asked the boatswain.

"It will do you no harm if I am," returned Keawe.

The Bottle Imp

"That is so, mate," said the boatswain.

"And if you doubt me," added Keawe, "you can try. As soon as you are clear of the house, wish to have your pocket full of money, or a bottle of the best rum, or what you please, and you will see the virtue of the thing."

"Very well, Kanaka," says the boatswain. "I will try; but if you are having your fun out of me, I will take my fun out of you with a belaying-pin."

So the whaler-man went off up the avenue; and Keawe stood and waited. It was near the same spot where Kokua had waited the night before; but Keawe was more resolved, and never faltered in his purpose; only his soul was bitter with despair.

It seemed a long time he had to wait before he heard a voice singing in the darkness of the avenue. He knew the voice to be the boatswain's; but it was strange how drunken it appeared upon a sudden.

Next the man himself came stumbling into the light of the lamp. He had the devil's bottle buttoned in his coat; another bottle was in his hand; and even as he came in view he raised it to his mouth and drank.

"You have it," said Keawe. "I see that."

"Hands off!" cried the boatswain, jumping back. "Take a step near me, and I'll smash your mouth. You thought you could make a catspaw of me, did you?"

"What do you mean?" cried Keawe.

"Mean?" cried the boatswain. "This is a pretty good bottle, this is; that's what I mean. How I got it for two centimes I can't make out; but I am sure you shan't have it for one."

"You mean you won't sell?" gasped Keawe.

"No, sir," cried the boatswain. "But I'll give you a drink of the rum, if you like."

"I tell you," said Keawe, "the man who has that bottle goes to hell."

"I reckon I'm going anyway," returned the sailor; "and this bottle's the best thing to go with I've struck yet. No, sir!" he cried again, "this is my bottle now, and you can go and fish for another."

Can this be true?" Keawe cried. "For your own sake, I beseech you, sell it me!"

"I don't value any of your talk," replied the boatswain. "You thought I was flat, now you see I'm not; and there's an end. If you won't have a swallow of the rum, I'll have one myself. Here's your health, and good-night to you!"

So off he went down the avenue towards town, and there goes the bottle out of the story.

But Keawe ran to Kokua light as the wind; and great was their joy that night; and great, since then, has been the peace of all their days in the Bright House.